WHEN THE EARL WAS WICKED

THE COMERFORD COURTESANS
BOOK TWO

JESS MICHAELS

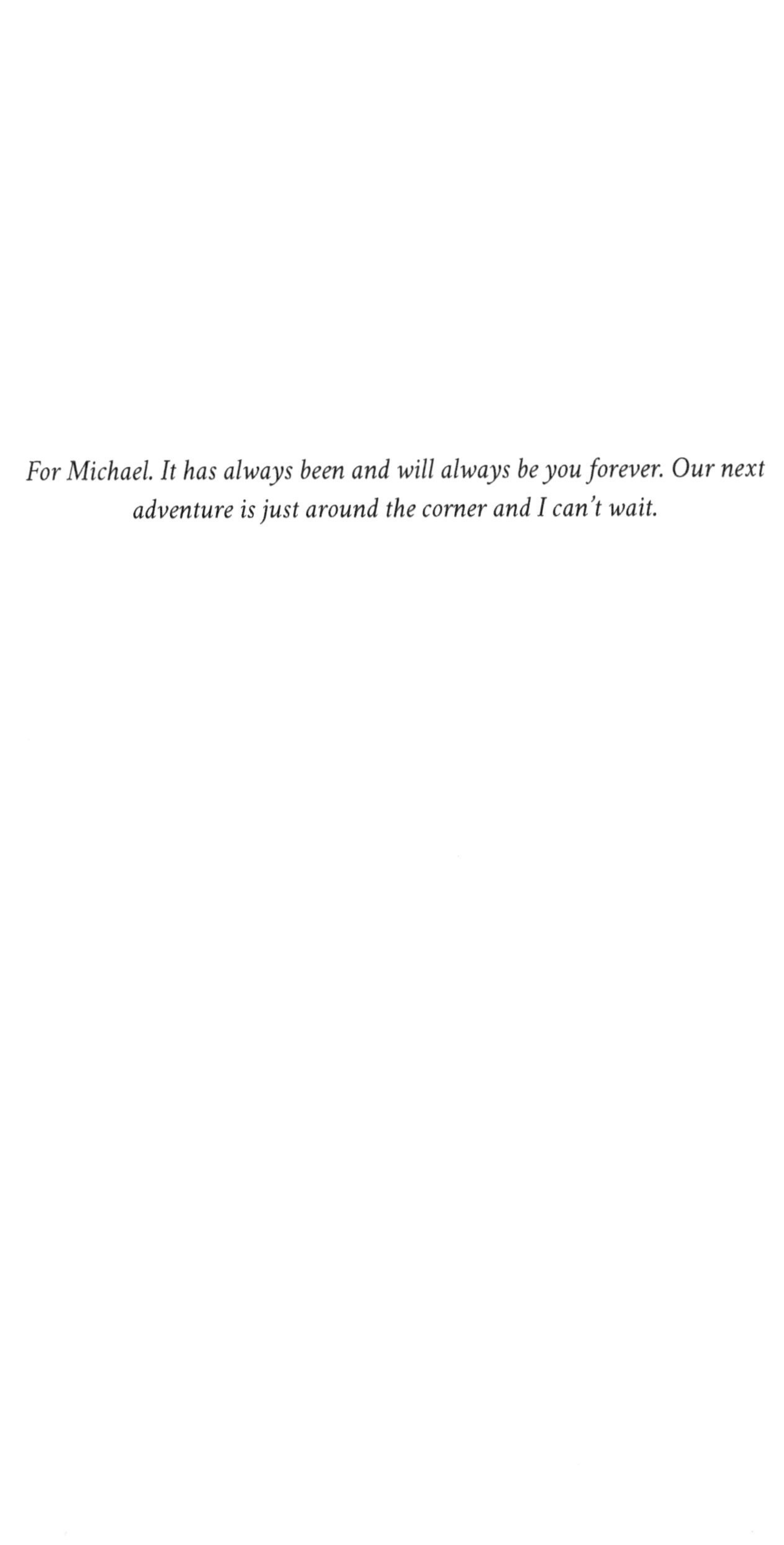

For Michael. It has always been and will always be you forever. Our next adventure is just around the corner and I can't wait.

PROLOGUE

Even after five years as a courtesan, Evelina Comerford didn't take comfort in sparkling balls, the wicked masquerades or the erotic dance of the chase. No, she was, at heart, still a simple woman. And tonight, since her longtime protector, Harold Talbot, the Duke of Southwater, had left her early, she was indulging in equally simple pleasures.

She'd had a decadent chocolate tart, taken a long, hot bath sweetened with orange essence and now she sat tucked into her bed in a flannel nightrail, reading the latest gothic masterpiece she and her sisters had been sharing. And it was not even nine at night. Bliss.

It wasn't that she didn't enjoy it when Harry stayed with her. She'd been with the duke for nearly two years. His mistress, but certainly more than that. He was the love of her life. She told anyone who asked the same and she knew he loved her, even if he rarely said the words. He always handled her gently whether that was when they danced or when they fell into their bed. There was value in that, certainly no one knew that better than herself. She enjoyed his touch, they made love twice weekly at this house and he often stayed and shared breakfast with her. Life was perfectly fine.

Well, perhaps not *fine*. She set her book aside with a little sigh as thoughts troubled her. The same thoughts that had been bothering her for the last few months. Ever since her beloved older sister, Arabella, had nearly been killed after their estranged father had kidnapped her. That awful night Evelina had begged Harry to help, to go with Arabella's now-husband, Silas, to find her.

Harry had refused. There had been no bending him. He didn't wish to be part of a scandal and he had left her behind when she refused to depart with him. That night had shifted something between them, no matter how much she tried to forget it. To wish it away. To pretend it away.

It was a scar on the otherwise smooth history of their affiliation, and it still hurt. Still made her angry even though she tamped both reactions down with all her might and never spoke of them to him or to her sisters. She just had to work harder to overcome those pesky emotions. Harry was, after all, otherwise a good companion and he had made a great deal of promises about her future. Even when he married to make his heirs and spares, he had declared he would continue to offer her a life as his beloved companion, one filled with comfort and his affection. A courtesan didn't walk away from something like that just because a gentleman didn't rush to her aid every time she requested it. To do so would be foolishness.

There was a light knock on her door and she started from her spiraling thoughts. "Yes?"

"I beg your pardon, Miss Comerford," her maid, Deborah, said as she entered the chamber. "There's been a message delivered, from the Duke of Southwater."

Evelina caught her breath as she set her book aside and got up from her comfortable cocoon to receive the note. It wasn't like Harry to reach out after they'd been together for a night, but he had been a little odd that evening. They'd eaten supper and were supposed to go to the opera, but he had cried off. They'd made love and then he'd left her and seemed distracted when he said his goodbyes.

Perhaps something was wrong.

She nodded to Deborah. "I'll ring if the duke intends to return or if I require anything else. Thank you."

Her maid bobbed out a nod and left her. Evelina rushed to the seat before her fire and sank into the comfortable cushion to break the seal on the folded sheets and read whatever was within.

Dear Miss Comerford.

Evelina blinked at the address. Miss Comerford? Harry hadn't addressed her so formally for years. It was always Evelina. Her heart raced and she had to force herself to read the next line as the sense of impending doom filled her.

I cannot express to you my appreciation of our time spent together these last two years. You have been a fine companion. However, these sorts of arrangements always have their end and I'm afraid that is where we have arrived.

Now Evelina couldn't breathe at all as she stared at Harry's even, careful hand and those shocking, hateful words written in it.

The home I have let for you will remain available to you for the next month so that you may take your time in vacating it. And I have arranged for my solicitor to settle you with one thousand pounds, to be delivered in four monthly payments of two-hundred fifty pounds. This should provide for any gap in protector you may encounter, as well as provide you with an investment for your future. Please accept it, along with my thanks for the time we have shared.

Yours Respectfully,

Southwater

Evelina couldn't stop staring at the words swimming before her eyes, blurring in and out as she tried to make sense of them. But she couldn't.

She stood and staggered to her door, pulling her bell with a shaking hand. Deborah reappeared in what could have been only a moment but felt like a lifetime.

"Yes, Miss—" Her servant stopped and her hands lifted to clench at her chest in worry. "Oh, Miss Comerford, you are pale as paper. Please let me help you, I fear you'll fall over."

She caught Evelina's elbow and helped her back to her seat at the fire. Evelina tried to find her breath to speak.

"My—my sisters," she gasped out. "I need you to send for my sisters. Tell them I'm—I'm not ill, but I need them to come to me. Now. Please."

There must have been something in Evelina's face, because her maid didn't ask questions or say anything else, but rushed from the room to do as she was told. Evelina knew Arabella and Julia would come to her side right away, assuming they were each home when her message arrived. Since neither lived very far away, they would likely be with her soon.

So all she could do was wait, reading and re-reading Harry's words, trying to find an explanation in two short paragraphs that ended two years of partnership and, she had believed, affection. But she could find nothing. She folded and unfolded the letter, as if reopening it would change what was to be found inside. She rubbed her eyes in the hopes she would wake from this nightmare. But the letter remained unchanged, as did her shock and horror at its contents.

She was startled when there was a knock on her door again. When she glanced at the clock, she realized nearly an hour had passed since she received this horrid news. She hadn't even reached the door when it flew open and Arabella and Julia rushed in together, faces pale with worry.

"Oh, Evie," Julia said as she tugged Evelina in for a hug. "You look terrible. What is it? What's happened?"

Evelina opened and closed her mouth, trying to find words and coming up mute instead. She extended a shaking hand at last and gave over the letter that had blown up her world and all her future and paced to the window so she wouldn't have to see her sisters' expressions when they read it.

"Poxy bastard!" Arabella gasped out after a few moments had passed.

Evelina did turn then, watched as Arabella threw the letter aside, her blue eyes bright with righteous anger. Her older sister had always been like that. Certain and ready to go to war if she felt someone needed it.

Arabella was coming toward her as Julia bent to retrieve the discarded letter and read it again, her face as pale as Evelina's felt.

"I don't understand," Julia said softly. "Harry loves you. He *loves* you."

Those words pierced Evelina's breaking heart and she bent over just as Arabella reached her. Her sister shored her up as she let out a long, pained wail that echoed in the room.

"How could he love me, have ever loved me, and end things this way?" she sobbed, her breath coming short, tingling pain rushing through her chest and her limbs like claws scraping along every vein and nerve. "How? How could this happen?"

She sank down then onto the settee, Arabella's arms coming around her, Julia rushing to flank her on the opposite side as she sobbed out her confusion and heartbreak and the loss of every dream she had apparently foolishly allowed herself to have.

Every dream that had been ripped away in a few cold words from a man whose heart she had so deeply misjudged.

CHAPTER 1

One Month Later

In the end, Evelina didn't require the time Harry had granted her to move out of the home he'd gifted her. No, that wasn't right. He *hadn't* gifted it to her because a gift couldn't be snatched away like her home and life had been. Every time that thought passed through her mind, Evelina tasted bitterness on her tongue and felt the same rush of pain and humiliation and anger as she had that first night when he'd ended things.

Still, by the time that last day had passed, Evelina had already been comfortably settled in the home Arabella had been *truly* gifted by a protector years and years ago. Her sister and brother-in-law no longer lived there. After their recent marriage, they'd started over in a beautiful new home just half a mile farther into the city, so Evelina had the place to herself.

She had hardly left the confines of her chamber since coming there. She couldn't bear to do so. The idea of wandering around London, pretending all was well? Bumping into friends who would look at her with interest and pity? Potentially even seeing Harry for the first time and finding not love or affection in his stare but... nothingness?

Impossible.

And even if she had been strong enough of character to endure those things, she felt *physically* weak at present. She only wished to sleep and cry and revisit every moment of her relationship with Harry as if she could find the one scrap of time together that had caused the unexpected break.

She had been pacing her chamber with these thoughts and flopped back on the bed at last, resting her forearm across her eyes as she let out a shuddering sigh.

"Why?" she whispered, just as she had been whispering through every moment, every dream, every nightmare.

There was a light knock on her door and she lifted her arm. "Yes?"

When it opened, Julia stepped in. Her younger sister had moved out of Arabella's house at just about the same time that Evelina had moved in. She'd made a match with a new protector and was settling into life as the mistress of...God, what was he? An earl or a viscount or something? He never came around, so it was hard to make a measure of him or even create a memory strong enough to recall any facts about him.

"Julia," she said, and tried to force a smile so her sister wouldn't give her the same worried and pitying look that both her siblings seemed to have permanently ready to flash across their lovely faces.

"Dearest," Julia said, and entered. She crossed to Evelina and sat beside her on the bed, enveloping her in the kind of hug one gave someone with a terrible illness or a broken bone.

Sometimes the situation did feel so dire.

"What are you doing here? I thought you'd be flitting about with your new protector."

"Laurence was busy with his cousin this evening," Julia said with a slightly sour look to her expression. "Alexander Castleton doesn't approve of me, I suppose. Gives me the most irritated looks when he deigns to look at me at all."

"*Castleton!*" Evelina said. "Viscount Laurence Castleton. I couldn't recall his name."

Julia gave her a playful glare. "I hope you'll have a great deal of time to learn it. At any rate, I was free and *longed* to see you. Not just see you, I so want to go out with you."

Evelina let out her breath in a little huff. "Oh, good Lord. Has Arabella sent you here to perform charity work? Did you two draw straws for who would have to beg me to go out and then ferry me around while I looked ghostly and tragic?"

"Of course not, you've been reading too many novels," Julia said, folding her arms. But her sweet sister had never been very good at covering her emotions and it was evident Evelina had struck close to the truth. She rolled her eyes when Evelina arched a brow at her. "We *did* discuss that one of us should approach you with this idea. Arabella thought you'd use Silas as an excuse against her, so I volunteered most enthusiastically."

"Silas as an excuse?" Evelina said. "What does that mean?"

She truly adored Arabella's new husband. He was devilishly handsome, quick to laugh, entirely wicked and also completely devoted to her sister. Plus, he had been nothing but kind to Evelina since the end of her relationship. He'd helped whenever he was needed and treated her with nothing but care. He'd even made her laugh a few times when all she wanted to do was cry. How could one not adore him?

"Oh, Arabella says that anytime she tries to push you, you tell her to go spend time with Silas. You tell her she's a newlywed and ought to still be wearing out every piece of furniture in that big new house of theirs."

Evelina pursed her lips. "Well. I'm correct on that score. She really should be enjoying her marriage, not worrying about her silly sister who should have known better than to trust the promises of a protector."

Julia's expression softened and she covered Evelina's hand. "Oh, Evie. That wasn't your failing, but his. He never should have made those promises if he didn't intend to keep them."

"We don't need to talk about it in circles all over again, everyone must be getting tired of it." Evelina withdrew her hand and got up to pace to the window. "I truly don't wish to go out."

Julia frowned. "Please." She moved to the window, as well and reached up to brush some hair away from Evelina's forehead. "Come on, lovie, it's just you and me, isn't it? I miss spending time with you. I miss laughing with you. Please, won't you come with me and go gaming at Flynn's?"

Evelina shut her eyes with a long sigh. This was the last thing she wanted, but she'd very rarely been able to deny her sweet baby sister. Julia knew exactly how to bat her eyelashes and get what she wanted. And she'd picked the location of her request well, too. Harry hadn't ever liked Flynn's and had only gone there when Evelina dragged him. It was almost impossible that he would be there now.

"Oh, very well," she said with a shake of her head as Julia clapped her hands in delight. "I suppose the longer I stay locked up in my sad little dungeon, the harder it will ever be to return to the world. Might as well face the whispers now and start anew."

Julia squeezed her hands. "We are going to make you look so beautiful that no one will whisper about anything except how glorious you are. Come, I'll ring the bell and we'll pick a gown. I'd say either the blue with the silver roping or that pink thing that makes men drool when they look at your cleavage."

Her sister rushed across the room to ring for Deborah and Evelina found herself laughing, though it sounded rusty, indeed. She didn't want to go out, but perhaps her sister was correct. Perhaps it was what she actually needed.

And it was happening either way. So she might as well make the best of it.

The last six months of the Earl of Blackburn's life had been a living nightmare. Divorce was almost unheard of in any class, but certainly not often in the Upper Ten Thousand. And yet that was what Vaughn was enduring, first in private and now in scandalized and gossiping public. His wife of five years, Florence, had demanded the official divorce and the more he'd uncovered about her behavior behind his back, the more he'd realized this was truly the only way. Those facts didn't reduce the humiliation when he went out in public and all eyes followed him.

Even here in Flynn's gambling hell where everyone was usually doing something worth talking about, he felt them watching *him*, heard *his* name flicker by on the wind. *Wife. Divorce. Affair.*

Vaughn downed his second drink in less than twenty minutes and let the burn of the whisky recenter him. That was the idea, anyway, but it didn't work. His mind kept spinning, kept taking him to dark places. Dark feelings. He hated everything and everyone, including himself. Perhaps mostly himself. What he wanted most was to lock himself away like some beast in a fairytale and never come out again. He was well on the way to that end, given that whenever anyone came close, he found himself growling and snapping.

He never should have come out. And he was preparing to down yet another drink and then head back to his home and its drawn curtains when he saw a woman enter the hell.

Evelina Comerford. Seeing her made the sting in his chest even worse, considering what he now knew about the end of his marriage. But he didn't blame Evelina for that. He'd always liked the pretty courtesan, with her gentle disposition and bright laugh.

As always, she stood out. She was wearing a bright pink frock that was dangerously low cut with paste jewels in a tantalizing trail along the midline. Her dark hair was spun up in soft curls that trailed artfully along her very bare shoulders. But her face...he saw the pain in her face even though she tried to hide it. A pain very like his own.

She was with her younger sister, Julia Comerford, another of the infamous Comerford Courtesans, a group which included Evelina's oldest sister, Arabella. Though, one could hardly call *her* a courtesan anymore. She'd recently married Silas Windham, who Vaughn had known vaguely in school and liked well enough.

Evelina looked around the room for a moment, her lips pursed as if she were troubled. He understood that better than most. Then her gaze caught his and she gave a little smile and a tiny wave. She said something to her sister and then began across the room toward him. He was rather shocked she was doing so when it would only cause more talk, especially given the last twenty-four hours.

But he had no intention to refuse her and stood as she arrived to him, inclining his head slightly. "Miss Comerford," he said.

She gave a rusty laugh. "Oh, my lord, you cannot revert back to Miss Comerford after years of calling me Evelina. Just because I'm no longer with Southwater doesn't mean we aren't friends." She hesitated and there was a flicker of concern that entered her gaze. "Unless it does?"

He shook his head. "Indeed, not. I would be honored to be counted as one of your friends. I think I prefer your friendship at any rate. Far less damaging."

She cocked her head as if she were confused by that statement and then her expression became lined with pity. "We haven't seen each other in some time. I wanted to say how sorry I am, my lord."

He reached out for the drink he'd set on the bar top behind him when she approached and downed what remained in one burning gulp. "As am I for you. How are you coping with all this?"

"Well, it's been a month since Harry and I parted ways." She smiled but it was clearly forced. "And a courtesan must be sensible, mustn't she?"

He wrinkled his brow because it felt like they were holding two separate conversations. "I suppose. But I meant about everything that's come out in the last day or so. It must trouble you, even if you play off the importance of the affiliation."

"I—" She struggled for words for a moment, her brow wrinkling. "I'm not sure I take your meaning, my lord."

He felt the blood spiral away from his cheeks as he realized why there had been a disconnection in their interaction so far. Lord, what had he just done? He cleared his throat. "You—you didn't know. You haven't heard the news."

She was staring at him like a doe who'd been startled by a hunter. Like she was frozen with fear about whatever horror he was about to reveal. "I don't know what you're talking about."

He drew in a sharp breath and that self-loathing he'd been contemplating earlier rushed forward even more powerfully. "My good *friend*, your former lover, the Duke of Southwater has been fucking my wife. For over a year. And now they're no longer hiding it. Apparently when this wretched divorce mess is finally resolved, he intends to marry her, scandal be damned."

Not a fragment of Evelina's expression changed despite the words that burned his own soul. She was now blank and pale, the only revelation that this shocked or horrified her was the slightest flare to her nostrils. Slowly, she stepped back, hands clenched at her sides, and then she whispered one word.

"*Liar.*"

He had hoped she was being pretending her denial that she knew about anything going on. It was apparent now that she wasn't. No matter how she schooled her reaction, his words had hit her like a sword in a battle and he hated himself for being the one who struck her down.

"I'm sorry, Evelina, I truly thought you must have known. The courtesan network…"

She shook her head. "I've been in hiding. And my sisters have been spending much of their time with me lately. Or else they knew but didn't tell me. But no. *No.* You are *wrong*."

"I wish I was."

"No!" she repeated, this time more loudly and now those around them started to stare. She didn't seem to care, not when her cheeks were bright with anger and hurt, her eyes wide with the same. "I don't know why you would say such wretched things, but I don't wish to speak to you anymore. Good night, Lord Blackburn."

She pivoted on her heel and stormed back off through the crowd.

"Fuck," Vaughn said, gripping his empty glass. He glared at the few people near him who were still staring and started across the room himself. However much he'd hated himself ten minutes ago, the feeling was now doubled. All he wanted to do was go home and bury himself in darkness and drink and ledgers so he wouldn't hurt anyone else.

Evelina dragged her sister onto the drive and waved frantically at her driver. The man appeared perplexed as it had hardly been a quarter of an hour since he brought the sisters here, but he started back up to the seat of the carriage regardless, tossing his cigar over the side of the vehicle as he did it.

"What is wrong with you?" Julia asked, pulling her arm free and rubbing it like Evelina had gripped her too hard. "We only just arrived and then you grab me and drag me out to go home. What happened?"

Evelina could hardly breathe and it took a few gasping attempts to formulate words. "Did you know?"

"Did I know what?"

"Don't lie to me!" Evelina ground out. "*Did you know?*"

Julia shook her head and her concern was becoming more and more clear, as well as her confusion. "I promise you, I've no idea what you're talking about."

Evelina tended to believe her. Not only did her sister look truthful, there was the fact that she'd told Julia that she was going to speak to Blackburn upon their arrival. Evelina had to assume that if Julia had known anything about his horrible accusations she would have said something. Surely her sweet sister wouldn't be so cruel. Arabella wouldn't either, but Arabella was also far more likely to know the truth and hide it.

The carriage pulled up to where they stood and she looked up at her driver as Julia got into the vehicle. "Take me to Arabella and Silas's."

"Yes, miss," he said, and she must have appeared quite wild, because he seemed as concerned as Julia. That seemed to be what she inspired now: quiet pity and worry. She ignored the humiliation of that fact and threw herself into the carriage across from Julia.

"*Please*, what is going on?" Julia asked. "I know you didn't want to go out at all tonight, but when you came across that room like the demons of hell themselves were at your heels and dragged me out… you are frightening me."

"Is Harry with Lady Blackburn?"

Julia blinked a few times. "I—what?"

"Countess Blackburn," she repeated. "The earl's wife. They are divorcing, it's all the scandal. Is Harry with her? Has he been fucking her for a *year*?" Her voice elevated on the last word and she struggled for breath to calm herself.

"That cannot be possible," Julia said with a small shake of her head. She looked as shocked as Evelina felt. She wasn't certain whether to be relieved or even more horrified at that fact.

"So you hadn't heard this horrible rumor, you didn't drag me there knowing it?"

Julia caught her hand. "You ask me that, truly? You think that I would bring you to a lion's den without warning you if I'd heard such a dreadful thing?"

"No." Evelina whispered, trying desperately to control her wild emotions so she wouldn't burst into loud tears. "No. I cannot think you would ever be so cruel. You aren't capable of it. But Arabella…"

"Arabella isn't capable of such a thing, either!" Julia burst out.

"Not of cruelty, no. But of trying to protect me by lies of omission? Oh, yes."

"But she wouldn't have sent me to take you out without telling me, at least."

That made sense and it calmed Evelina a little. "No. You're right. Still, I need to ask her. To look her in the face and see that she didn't try to protect me even while she left me open to such a horrible revelation."

The sisters stared at each other a moment and Julia shivered. "Oh, Evie, is it true? Could the duke have done such a thing?"

"It's a *lie!*" she said. "Harry may be many things, I may not understand his motives in ending things with me, but I cannot and I will *not* believe that he would be so cruel as to take his friend's wife in such a public manner. He is not so craven as that."

Julia didn't seem fully convinced, but she asked, "And who told you?"

"Blackburn himself."

"Oh."

Her sister's gaze dropped away and Evelina folded her arms. "Why do you say it like that? Why *oh* like you pity me?"

Julia shifted on the carriage seat. "I-I only wonder what motive the earl would have for lying. The scandal around him is so loud and horrible already that it will likely never be fully forgotten. Why would he add to it?"

Evelina shifted. She didn't want to consider that very rational question overly long. Or think about the true pain and burning rage in Blackburn's startling green eyes when he told her.

"Well..." She tried to find a reason. "As you say, the scandal is complete anyway. Why wouldn't he say something so horrible about the countess, even if just to form some kind of sympathy for himself?"

"But haven't he and Harry known each other since school?" Julia asked. "Why would he be so cruel to his old friend? You knew him a bit before, was that his character?"

"No." There was no hesitation to her answer. As much as she wanted to paint Blackburn with a liar's brush, she couldn't act as though he hadn't always been decent and honorable in any interaction she'd exchanged with him. He'd actually always been her favorite amongst Harry's friends. The one she enjoyed talking to and interacting with most.

But to believe Blackburn to be honest was far more painful than to think she'd simply misjudged him for years.

"Perhaps he's been misled," she said, trying to find some middle ground where they could both be right. "Told this untruth by some third party in order to put a wedge between him and his dearest friend in a time of need. There are some who might find sport in such behavior. The men of the *ton* can be wretched."

"That is certainly true," Julia said softly, and then took Evelina's hand. "One way or another, we'll determine the truth of it. I've been out of the courtesan network loop these past weeks as I've settled in with Laurence, and I know Arabella is still solely focused on Silas and the life they're building, but no one can get to the crux of a rumor faster than our dear sister."

"Yes," Evelina said, and yet she felt dread not anticipation of that fact. A deep fear that Blackburn hadn't been lying. That the very small shreds she had left from her life with Harry were about to be burned at last, disintegrated on a fire of humiliation and lies and pain.

The carriage slowed as it turned into the drive in front of Arabella and Silas's new home. Evelina exited the vehicle without waiting for assistance and hardly looked up at the lovely white brick-faced home with its latticed terraces and brightly painted shutters.

She pushed past Barnaby, Arabella's longtime butler who had gone with her to the new home, and strode down the hallway, Julia at her heels, saying her name, though it sounded like it was all underwater. Far away.

The door to the one of the parlors was partially shut, but there was bright light flowing from it into the hallway and Evelina went to it. She pushed inside and found her sister perched on her new husband's lap, fingers threaded through his thick hair as he looked up at her in pure, unadulterated love and passion.

Evelina flinched and dropped her gaze. Walking in on something sensual was one thing, but intruding upon such connection felt wrong. It also made her chest ache, like she'd lost something, though she didn't know that she'd ever felt such naked affection as what she saw on her sister's face.

The couple glanced toward her and there was no embarrassment on their expressions. Not that there ever could be. Silas and Arabella were like two sparks who had come together in explosive flame. They gave very little care to how others saw them and were known to passionately kiss on the street, race in the parks and cackle at bawdy jokes they whispered to each other no matter the company.

Evelina had never been so happy for her sister, but at that moment she had to shove all her complicated feelings aside as Arabella slowly got up from Silas's lap and tilted her head.

"Evie? And Julia. What in the world are you doing barging into my parlor at eleven at night?"

Silas's gaze flitted over Evelina's face and any softness he'd exhibited toward Arabella fled. "What's wrong?" he asked, coming to his feet, his posture suddenly on guard.

Evelina swallowed. She'd come here to confront Arabella, but now that she was standing before her, she didn't know how to formulate the words. How to demand answers that she didn't truly want. That she didn't think she could bear.

"Is it true?" she asked, and hated how her voice shook and barely carried.

"True?" Arabella repeated with a blank expression. She stepped forward slowly and reached out to take Evelina's hand. "I don't know what you mean, dearest."

"Is it true?" Evelina repeated, this time sharper. "Is Harry with the Countess of Blackburn? Has he been with her since long before we parted? Is he…is he planning to marry her when this nastiness of the divorce is over?"

Arabella caught her breath as Evelina asked every pointed, painful question. She glanced at Silas and their eyes met, and in that moment Evelina had every answer she'd sought. She felt her knees give out a fraction and Silas leapt forward to catch her elbow, steady her.

She yanked away and took a long step back. "You did know!"

Arabella let out a shaky breath. "I-I had heard a few whispers in the last few days. I'd heard he had someone new and that there were hints of a scandal about it all. But—"

"And why didn't you tell me?" Evelina interrupted, fisting her hands at her sides and wishing it made them shake less.

"Because he hurt you," Arabella said. "And I didn't want to hurt you further until I could meet with Simone and get all the information available."

Evelina flinched. Simone was the courtesan who had helped Arabella and both her sisters when they entered into the life years ago. She was a true friend and one of the sharpest people Evelina had ever met. Of course, Arabella would look to her for the truth.

She reached out to steady herself on the nearest chair before she collapsed into it with a thunk. She stared at the fire rather than her sisters and brother-in-law. "Could it be true? That Harry could really be with Lady Blackburn? That he was with her behind my back all the while he told me I was the true love of his life and that he would only marry for duty?" She flinched as she thought of Lord Blackburn's crestfallen expression earlier in the night. "Could it be true that he would do something so horrible to his friend, a man who I never saw be anything but kind and supportive to him?"

Arabella dropped down to her knees before Evelina and cupped her cheeks. They held gazes for a long moment and she could see how much her sister hurt for her. That had always been their way.

Their pains were shared, they protected each other, sometimes to their own detriment.

"I will go to Simone first thing in the morning," Arabella said. "I'll detangle her from the arms of whatever lover she's entertaining at present, and I will find out."

Evelina looked past her sister to the fire again and shook her head. "No. No, I need to find out myself. I need to do this *myself*."

"Evie, that cannot be wise," Arabella whispered. "It could only hurt you more."

Evelina blinked down at her. "Nothing could hurt me more, could it? There must be an end to it at some point."

Her sister's expression softened, but even as Arabella embraced her, as Julia joined their sisterly hug and Silas went to pour her a very strong drink, Evelina already knew the answer in her heart. Just as she'd known it when Blackburn told her, no matter how strenuously she denied it.

She just couldn't understand it.

CHAPTER 2

Vaughn sat in his study the next morning, staring at the state of his desk. He'd always been a tidy person, taking care of his duties as swiftly as he could and immediately filing or discarding the papers that went along with them. But in the last six months, that had changed, along with every other part of his life. His desk was piled with papers now, almost all to do with his divorce. There were so many parts to the complicated act of severing a marriage so that it no longer existed. So many disapproving and demanding people to respond to so that he could receive permission from church and sovereign and family to pretend as though he and Florence had not spent five years as man and wife.

It was an expensive endeavor, as well. He sometimes felt he was bleeding money. He supposed that was part of how the world discouraged such a scandalous act. Make it impossible financially, socially and even physically.

There was a rumble of thunder that shook the windows and Vaughn started as he looked up. He hadn't even realized it had started raining. Well, it was appropriate. The gloomy dark clouds fit the tumultuous emotions in his heart. And a raincloud tended to ruin everyone else's day, too, so that also seemed to match his current situation.

He thought, and not for the first time, of Evelina Comerford at the hell the night before. Her expression when he revealed the truth about Southwater had been…broken, even if she called Vaughn a liar and stormed out. He'd hurt her, and it would only hurt more when she realized he was right. It gave him no pleasure that he'd been the one to tear her last vestiges of belief about Harry down.

He'd always liked Evelina. She had only ever been kind and bright all the times he spoken to her over the years when she'd been his former best friend's lover.

"Bollocks," he muttered to himself. It seemed all he could do lately was destroy.

There was a light knock on the door and he looked up as his butler cracked the door. He hesitated there and Vaughn could hardly blame him. He'd been such a grumbling ogre lately that all the staff avoided him, which was even more proof of his wretchedness.

"Yes, Langley?" he said, trying to sound warmer than he had lately.

"I beg your pardon, my lord, but you have a visitor." He extended a card as Vaughn got up and came around the desk to receive it.

Evelina Comerford

The card was a scrawl of delicate filigree and gold leafing that made up the swirls of her name. He found himself tracing those peaks and valleys with his fingernail.

"She…she's here?" he asked in shock. Since he'd just been thinking of the woman, it almost felt as if he'd conjured her.

"Yes, my lord. I would have sent her away as you've requested to be done to all visitors in the last few months, but the lady was very insistent. She has put herself on one of the benches in the foyer and refuses to leave. What should I do?"

Vaughn let out a shaky breath. He'd thought Evelina wouldn't wish to see him again after the last encounter that weighed so heavily on his mind, but it seemed he was wrong. He could only imagine why. Did she wish to share the pain of her betrayal with another person? He could hardly manage his own.

But then again, *he* had been at least part of the cause of her hurt, so he should do the gentlemanly thing and see her.

"Tell the lady that I'm in residence. And take her to the blue parlor." He hesitated and wrinkled his brow. "Is the blue parlor ready for guests?"

He'd closed up so many rooms in this big house lately, but Langley inclined his head. "Indeed, it is the parlor we keep prepared for unexpected arrivals and to receive…er…"

"Solicitors and representatives of the church who come to demand penance and pennies?" Vaughn couldn't control the bitterness in his tone now. "Yes. Good then. The blue parlor. Oh, and offer her refreshments. I'll join her shortly. Thank you."

"Very good." The butler executed a small bow, then exited the room, closing Vaughn back into his solitude. He paced to the window, staring out at the rain and then back to the fire. He repeated that path a few times as he tried to calm himself without success.

Why had Evelina come here? Was it to shout at him again? Or perhaps to give him news about their erstwhile lovers? Or did she want to blame him for what had happened now that she understood it? God knew he did that often enough to himself.

"*Bollocks*!" he repeated, only this time louder. He looked at himself in the mirror above the fireplace and smoothed his hair, straightened his waistcoat. He wasn't wearing his jacket, though he didn't recall taking it off. He glanced around but didn't find it, so he left his shirtsleeves rolled to the elbow and forced himself to leave the relative safety of his study and head down to the blue parlor to meet his guest.

When he entered the chamber, he found her at the fire, staring into the flames with a deep frown on her face. As he closed the door, she started and turned fully toward him.

She was lovely, even with distress on every line of her face. Not as flashy as she had been last night at the hell when she wore her full regalia as a courtesan, but still alluring. Although, as he stepped toward her, he could see that she'd been crying. Her brown eyes were red-rimmed and a little puffy. He flinched at the evidence of her heartbreak.

"Miss Comerford," he said.

This time she didn't correct him and ask that he continue to call her Evelina. She only inclined her head. "My lord."

"I-I wasn't expecting you," he said, and motioned to the chairs before the fire. He glanced over and saw the sideboard was empty. "Didn't they bring you tea?"

"Your butler offered, but I refused."

That she would refuse his hospitality didn't bode well. "I see. Please, won't you sit?"

He motioned again to the chairs and this time she moved to take one. He sat in the other and for a moment they just stared at each other. Her expression was unreadable, he hoped his was the same.

She folded and unfolded her hands in her lap for what felt like forever before she finally drew in a shaky breath and then said, "I-I know you weren't expecting me. Probably you didn't want to see me after my outburst last night."

"I felt no such thing," he said, and found that the politeness wasn't entirely false.

She continued as if he hadn't spoken, as if she feared to stop talking or else she might lose her nerve. "Either way, it was very rude of me to not send word ahead."

She stopped and her fingers continued to clench and unclench in her lap as she inched to the front of her chair. She seemed to struggle with what to do or say next, with how to approach this untenable situation.

The thunder rumbled again, even louder than it had been in his study and she jumped.

He met her stare, hoping to soothe her a little. "Please, I can see your struggle. What can I do for you, Miss Comerford?"

"Oh." She sighed. "I was so shocked last night when you told me what you think Harry has done."

"I don't think it, I know it," he said.

She stiffened. "Yes, I believe you think you do. But it seems so outrageous. You two were so close. He would never—"

Vaughn refused to listen to such a defense of his former friend and interrupted. "And yet he did."

She shifted, her cheeks pinkening, and he could see she was getting upset again. The flush to her cheeks and flash to her eyes revealed both hurt and anger. She was truly lovely in both, though he never would have wished to see her so broken.

"I can see how you would be upset because of the divorce," she said carefully. "Such a thing must be so shocking and horrible. But to accuse your friend…"

He folded his arms. "And what would it take for you to believe it, Evelina?"

She stopped short and opened and shut her mouth a few times. "I-I don't know."

He thought for a moment, his mind going over and over things that he often drank away, tried to forget. Things that had seared the truth into his mind so he could no longer deny the truth as she was trying to do.

He pursed his lips. "Would seeing them together help? At your old home?"

Her mouth dropped open. "My old home? The one Harry let for me? No, he let that go after I moved out. He…he…"

"He kept it," Vaughn said softly. "And moved my wife into it last week, apparently. It is where he will keep her until he can make her duchess."

Her lower lip trembled slightly as she swallowed. "My—my little house?"

He nodded, though the smallness of her voice was so broken that he wanted to turn away from it. "Yes, I'm afraid so. I can take you there now if you'd like. I'd wager they're together. They've hardly been anywhere else if my sources are to be believed."

She didn't respond for a moment. He could see her fighting with herself, fighting the desire to know the truth versus the protective instinct to keep it away as long as possible. But at last she nodded. "Yes."

He stood. "Then I'll arrange for my carriage to be readied. I'll return shortly."

He left her, forcing himself not to look back at her. It didn't matter that he didn't. He knew she was shrinking into herself. He knew even more that what he was doing was wrong. That it was certainly not his finest hour, to drag this poor woman to the proof of her betrayal so that…what? That he'd have a partner in pain?

And yet he didn't stop himself as he called for Langley to ready his carriage for the journey ahead.

Evelina had to focus on the act of breathing for it no longer seemed automatic. In and out, slow and steady so she didn't lose consciousness as she sat across from Blackburn in his fine carriage rushing across the city toward…

She didn't want to think about what the two of them were rushing toward. Blackburn was so quiet and grim, his green gaze locked on her though his expression was unreadable. To focus herself, she examined him. She knew the man very little, just in passing as Harry's friend. But she'd always seen him as light, an entertaining and bright gentleman who had always treated her with respect, which was not a given in the men of the *ton*.

But now he was shadow of what he'd been before. He was made up only of frowns and pain that bubbled so close to the surface that he couldn't hide it. It was sad to see and also terrifying. He wasn't pretending this grief and betrayal, of that she was almost entirely certain.

And that meant she was very likely about to uncover exactly what she was praying was a lie. A misunderstanding. A nightmare she would wake from.

The carriage slowed and she realized Blackburn's driver had brought them not just in front of her old house but into the little park across the street from it. She looked out the window and flinched at the sight of the pretty gables and bright blue door. She had loved this house. Harry had promised her it would be hers forever, *their* home even if propriety dictated he marry a woman of his station and produce his heirs and spares.

She had expected it to be dark, perhaps not yet inhabited since she had vacated it less than a month before and these things usually took time. But the lights were bright in the windows, the curtains pulled back to allow her glimpses into the life that had once been hers.

"I think I ought not do this," Blackburn said softly, perhaps more to himself than to her.

She started at the low resonance of his voice. She'd been a little distracted in her own world and now she was dragged back into his plan to prove Harry's betrayal.

"Why?" she asked.

He shook his head. "It's cruel to you. I don't want to be cruel."

"No. It's not cruel. If this is true, I want to see it for myself so there will be no question. And if it's not, perhaps we'll see something here that will give us both ease."

He didn't look convinced but sighed. "We'll have a better view if we leave the vehicle. It isn't raining anymore," he said, and pushed the carriage door open. He stepped down and reached back up for her. "May I?"

She stared at the outstretched hand, gloved, but that didn't hide the lean strength of the man. Nor the slight shake of his fingers as they hung there between them.

"Thank you," she managed to gasp out, and took his help to get down. She followed him to a line of waist-high bushes just beyond the park entrance and he stopped there and reached into the inside pocket of his great coat to retrieve a spyglass.

She arched a brow as he extended it and handed it to her. "You come prepared."

"I wish I could say I hadn't come here since I heard the news about the affair. That I wasn't trying to make sense of it by watching the life that is no longer my own, but I'm too exhausted to pretend otherwise. You'll be able to see into the main parlor from here."

She caught her breath and lifted the spyglass. He was correct, she could see into the main parlor just off her foyer, almost as clearly as if she could open the window and step inside. The room was empty, though, there was no ringing proof that Harry had broken the bonds of friendship and the promises he'd made of a future. She was about to lower the glass and tell Blackburn so when the parlor door opened and the world stopped.

Harry stepped inside, talking over his shoulder to someone who had not yet entered the room. Evelina was shocked by his expression in the bright light of the parlor. He looked so...*happy*. Almost excited. When was the last time she'd seen that look on his normally serious face?

She didn't have a chance to think further on that question when Harry's companion followed him into the room. The person was, indeed, Lady Blackburn, who Evelina had seen a few times at the opera and in Hyde Park. She was a very pretty woman, with curly blonde hair and a slight figure.

She reached back to close the door as she entered the room and moved to the sideboard, which was slightly out of view of the spyglasses reach for it was beyond the window. Evelina leaned forward, trying to see, but was further blocked when Harry stepped in her way and showed her only a view of his broad back. She huffed out a breath but then stopped breathing entirely when the couple moved together back into the view of the window.

They were locked in an embrace, a passionate kiss that answered all the swirling, horrifying questions she'd been trying not to answer for the last twenty-four hours. That ones that broke every last vestige of what she'd believed to be true.

This woman was in *her* house with *her* Harry. When they parted from their embrace, Lady Blackburn reached up to touch his cheek and there was an intimacy that couldn't have been born in a few days or even weeks. It went far deeper.

The spyglass slipped from Evelina's hands and made a broken crunch on the path at her feet. The rain began again, as if on cue in some cruel play, but she could hardly feel the cold sting of it as she spun on her heel and staggered into the deserted park.

She couldn't see as she walked into the darkness, she could barely hear the earl calling her name behind her. It didn't matter now. Not anymore.

She was heading toward the entrance on the opposite side of the park. Where she would go once she reached it, she had no idea. She was far from Arabella's old home with no vehicle and no money since she'd foolishly left her reticule behind at Blackburn's. She didn't care, though. All she wanted was to get away.

"Please!" Blackburn's voice was closer now. "Miss Comerford!"

She continued to ignore him, tears blurring her eyes as she exited the park and stumbled forward into the street.

"Evelina!"

The earl caught her arm and yanked her back just as a carriage rumbled by, sending water splashing up on her skirt. She stumbled against his chest and then looked up at him in the flickering lamplight. The rain continued to pour down, washing over both of them as they stared at each other in grief and pain and...and *anger* that she tamped down. If she let that loose she might never stop.

Blackburn stepped back from her, steadying her gently before he tucked her hand into his elbow. "Come, I'll take you home."

She didn't fight him as he started to take her back around the perimeter of the park to the vehicle they had abandoned. All she could do was let out a humorless snort and whisper, "There is no home. Not anymore."

CHAPTER 3

Vaughn rubbed a towel through his hair and stared at the parlor door, just as he had been every two minutes since he had returned Evelina Comerford to her home. Well, it was her sister Arabella's old home, as Evelina kept correcting him, even as she looked through him with that hollow, hurting stare.

The one he had caused because he needed her to know the truth, somehow. Why? Because he wanted a partner in his pain? Because he couldn't stand to let her be happy with her misaligned memories? What a bastard he was.

The parlor door opened and she entered the room. She had changed from her earlier gown and her hair was down in damp curls around her shoulders. She had a little more color in her cheeks than she'd had on the ride back, and for that he was grateful.

She gave him a grim look and then crossed to the sideboard and poured them each a whisky in glasses far too tall for the drink. She handed one over and motioned to the chairs before the warm fire.

"Tell me everything," she said after she'd taken a long sip.

He gripped his own glass in his hand without taking a drink. "Miss Comerford—"

"Please!" she interrupted, her voice sharp. "Please tell me."

He nodded. "Very well. You deserve that after what I've just shown you. I suppose I must start with my marriage."

He blinked after he said that last sentence. Talk about his marriage? He didn't do that with anyone. And yet here they were.

"It was arranged, of course," he said, practically forcing the words from his mouth because it was so difficult to make them fall naturally. "I was twenty-five when I realized my father was dying and twenty-six when he brought me to his side and told me that he would see me married before his death. They had even chosen the lady for me, should I approve."

"And you did," Evelina said softly.

"I did. Florence was the eldest daughter of the Marquess of Estridge. It was a good political and social match. She was four years my junior, so not so young that we had nothing in common. And she was…*is*…lovely to look at."

Evelina turned her head, but before she took another drink she conceded, "Yes. There is no denying that as much as I might like to do so in this moment. It seems you were drawn to her."

He hesitated. "Nothing repelled me. And as it was the great wish of my family, I agreed to the match and we were married before that summer was out."

He stopped talking then, trying not to let his mind spiral to what had come after those first heady months of marriage when he and Florence had tried to forge a bond beyond duty. He thought they had sometimes when she slept in his arms or laughed at some silly quip, but now nothing in any happier day felt real. Not when her smiles had so swiftly turned sour and her pleasure had gone in other directions.

"What changed?" Evelina pressed. "Divorce is almost unheard of in any set, but certainly not in the Upper Ten Thousand. How did you move from all the hopes of an arranged union to now?"

"Florence was…restless," he said. "Even from the beginning. She wanted more, always more. When my father died and I became earl, I thought she would be sated, for we had access to all the funds and she had a great deal more to do as countess than she had as mere viscountess. She embraced it all. She redecorated every home I own, she bought gowns until the wardrobes burst with them, she hosted parties and more parties."

"Did you like all that?" Evelina asked.

"I didn't *dislike* it." He said the words and felt how false they were even as he forged ahead in the explanation. "I thought we had a reasonable marriage, truly. It was difficult not to like her, with all her spark and laughter and drive. Sometimes I thought I might even..." He drew off with a shake of his head. "Well, she never returned any feelings toward me, but she wasn't unkind. And she never turned me away when I asked for her company."

He hesitated because this raw confession felt so odd. He'd never said any of these things to any other person in his life, not a friend, not a family member. And yet now that he'd begun to speak, the intimacies of five years of marriage came spilling out. He hated himself for not being able to keep them in.

"There were no children," he continued, now more slowly, for the pain was coming and he wanted to hold it off a little longer. "I wanted children, not just because it was my duty to provide them, but because I thought I might like being a father."

She tilted her head, as if that sentiment surprised her. "Most men of the *ton* hardly notice their off spring."

He shrugged. "And my father hardly noticed me unless it was to his purposes. But I wanted to be different. When it didn't happen, I tried my best not to pressure her to try more often. After all, my cousins are the best of men. They would carry on the family name admirably."

She wrinkled her brow. "Was it the children that broke it?"

"No." He cleared his throat. "The first time I realized she was being unfaithful, I was shocked."

She caught her breath and he felt her surprise. At least there was that. "When did it begin?"

"Two years into the marriage." He shook his head. "The man was her childhood friend. Someone I supposed she always cared for and had been separated from. I did confront her. She cried. Apologized. Told me that she had not intended for things to go so far. I forgave her and asked her to be more prudent. She said she wouldn't do something like that again. I believed her. Until I found out about another lover a few months later. And another. And another."

Her eyes widened. "Gossip about such things usually reaches us first, but I admit the courtesan network never said a thing. Not until the divorce became public did anyone even suspect the marriage was troubled."

"After she was caught the first time, I suppose she became more careful. But she never stopped. And there was no longer the excuse of an old love who she had been unable to resist. These were men she hadn't known before, ones she didn't even care about."

"What did you do about it?" Evelina asked. "You must have been livid."

"I was humiliated and yes, occasionally livid." He clenched his hands against his thighs. "I confronted her, over and over. At first there were more apologies and tears, but as the number of lovers increased, she stopped pretending to be sorry. And what could I do?"

"There are ways some men handle a wife like that," Evelina said.

"You mean a mad house?" Vaughn shuddered. "I could never be so cruel. She wasn't mad, she just wanted, like passion could fill some hole in her. And she was cruel, because flaunting it to me, if no one else, became part of the game. I chose to ignore it as much as I could. Many lords and ladies live separate lives within the confines of their marriages. Many more ignore the dalliances of their spouses in order to save face. It was not what I'd hoped for, but I came to accept that it was part of life."

"Then what led to the divorce?"

"She did." He sighed. "She began asking for it, demanding it, nine months ago. She would scream and weep and tell me she couldn't go on like this. That the scandal couldn't be more painful than the life she was leading. I didn't understand why she wanted such a shocking thing, but now I do."

"Because she was with Harry," Evelina said softly. "Because he offered her the life of a duchess."

Vaughn downed what was left of his drink and nodded. "Yes. For a woman who always wanted more, that was the ultimate carrot to dangle above her."

"They cannot imagine they'll be accepted by Society after all this is done."

He snorted out a humorless laugh. "I've no idea what they imagine, but when it comes to the scandal you needn't spell it out to me. I've been colored with the same brush. And yes, I cannot I imagine how they will spin this tale to make it palatable. Perhaps they're truly in love. Perhaps none of this matters to them and all they need is each other."

Evelina pushed from her chair and crossed the room away from him to stare out onto the street below. When she didn't move for a while, he cleared his throat. "I'm sorry."

"No." She didn't face him but continued to look outside. "It's good to know it."

"What will you do about it?" he asked.

She did turn then and looked at him in confusion. "Do?"

"You've been betrayed."

Her lips thinned. "A courtesan cannot be betrayed."

He got up and took a few long steps toward her. "Whatever else happened in the end, Southwater and I were once friends. I know what promises he made to you. You *were* betrayed, Evelina. Don't diminish it."

For a long moment their gazes held there, locked together. The soft brown of her eyes, sparkling lightly with unshed tears gave him a sensation he hadn't had since the nightmare of this divorce had begun all those months ago. He felt seen. Heard. Felt. And there was peace to that release of the loneliness of the separation and all the humiliation that had followed.

She broke the stare and the comfort went with it. The raw, dull ache of his anger and embarrassment and hurt returned.

"I will admit that when I looked into my window...*my window...* and saw them together, there was a moment I wanted to hurt him like he'd hurt me. To confront him and go to battle." Her cheeks turned pink at the admission and her gaze returned to his. "I can see you understand that."

He nodded. "When she demanded the divorce from me, when she begged me to set her free, I did everything she asked."

"Why?"

He tilted his head in confusion over the question. "Why?"

"You could have simply pushed her from your home, made public your displeasure, cut her off even. She could have lived her affairs and you could have washed your hands of it rather than throw yourself into the fire even more."

He pursed his lips. "I suppose I couldn't stand to make us both so miserable. And she threatened me if I didn't give her what she wanted. Yes, she would be separate from me in some ways if she was pushed out and I washed my hands without severing the marriage. But she still would have wielded enormous power with my name. She told me she would make her affairs as fully public as possible. She would spend money in my name. She would do everything in her power to ruin me."

"God. What an evil...evil...bitch."

She said the last in a whisper, like it softened it. And he, fool that he was, still felt this strange desire to defend Florence. He fought it and shrugged. "Whatever she is, it became clear it was better to give her what she wanted. The cost, in the end, would be lower. So I have. I've done my part by petitioning for the divorce. I've paid for it, in more ways than one, and given her an allowance and access to another home in London. I would have walked away without ever seeking retribution until she and Harry made their liaison public. Until I saw that she had betrayed me with a friend. Worse, that *he* had betrayed me. And then I admit I wanted to hurt him. Hurt them."

He realized he had his empty glass in a white-knuckled grip as he spoke. Evelina made no mention of it but moved to him and slipped the tumbler away. She walked back to her sideboard and refilled both their glasses. When she returned to him, she took a sip and said, "But not *physically* hurt them, surely."

He shook his head instantly. Oh, he'd thought about punching Southwater as hard as he could, but anything more than that? Of course he would never harm them. "No! I mean a humiliation that in some small way reflects what I've felt. What *we* have felt. To make them care about what they've done. That would be the fantasy."

She lifted her gaze again at that word and once again he was lost in the depths of it. But this time there was no peace. No, instead he felt something entirely different. He felt the hatching of the tiniest kernel of a plan. An itch in his mind that whispered that this woman could be the key.

"I don't know how we could do that," Evelina said.

"He..." He hesitated.

"What?" she said when he didn't finish his thought.

"I've hurt you enough already."

She arched a brow. "That wasn't you, my lord. Harry hurt me. What do you have to say about him? Let's get it all out, for we are the only two who could ever understand what has happened."

He nodded slowly. "Very well. He was always proud to have you as his mistress. He bragged about you."

He didn't add that sometimes Southwater had done so rudely and with great detail to leering friends. It had always turned Vaughn's stomach, for he didn't imagine Evelina would have liked to be spoken of in such a way.

Her cheeks pinkened. "Well, some good that pride has done me."

"He liked that other men were jealous of your attentions. He liked that you were willing to be with him, even if he eventually married. He saw that as some proof of his prowess and his power over you." He shook his head. "I'm sorry."

"Stop saying that," she muttered, and she slugged back more of her drink. "He told you that?"

He nodded. "And it makes me wonder if he might not be annoyed if you were to quickly enter into a new arrangement. Something public and passionate." Her eyes widened, but he didn't stop. The kernel was growing now, flowering. "Something with a friend of *his*. With…with me."

And there it was, out. Something he hadn't fully thought out, at least not intentionally. But perhaps the moment he saw her at the hell the night before, walking toward him, it had begun to fester, this idea. And it did make sense.

"I beg your pardon," she said, her nostrils flaring and her gaze flitting over him with…perhaps it was a touch of disgust at the idea that all this was some sloppy way to try to bed her. "You want to sleep with me?"

"No!" he said, but though his tone sounded certain when he said the word, he felt less so. It had been a long time since he took anyone to his bed. And Evelina was lovely. He'd always found her so, though he never would have pursued that little flicker of desire because of a thousand promises that had meant so little to those to whom he'd made them.

"Thank you," she said with dry humor.

He smiled despite the topic. "I apologize. It is not for your lack of attractiveness. I'm just not talking about us *truly* becoming lovers. We only want Florence and Southwater to *think* that we are. To let them see us together, see us flaunt our supposed passion and happiness as if what they've done to us is meaningless."

She blinked and he couldn't tell what she truly thought of his suggestion. "That's mad."

"Is it?" he pressed, and then sighed as exhaustion washed through him. "I don't know, perhaps it is. Perhaps it's just too much whisky and pain talking." He walked away and set his half-full glass on the sideboard. When he faced her again, he smoothed his jacket and tried very hard to become the proper Earl of Blackburn again. "I don't know much, Evelina, but I know I blew your life apart tonight, or at least your perception of what your life once was. The actions of others may not be my fault, but my own are and I'm sorry for the hurt I've caused amongst all the others. I'll go now."

She seemed to consider that statement and then she slowly nodded. "Thank you, my lord. For both helping me see the truth and for your apology. It's rare to receive one, let alone one over and over, for ladies of my station. And once again, let me say how sorry *I* am that you've been hurt so deeply."

He inclined his head. "Don't trouble yourself to see me out. Good evening."

And with that he pivoted away and returned to her foyer where her butler hustled to meet him and then called for his carriage. But as he awaited the arrival of his vehicle, he couldn't help but occasionally look back toward the parlor where he had left Evelina. She never exited it, but he was fully aware that she was so close.

And that somehow they were now bound by the betrayals of their former lovers. And by the anger they had found safety enough to express in each other's company. He welcomed that, but he also feared he might not ever find an outlet for it again.

Because no one else in the world could understand his grief except for the woman he was riding away from. And the two of them hardly knew each other at all.

CHAPTER 4

Evelina hadn't been able to find a way out of supper with Silas, her sisters and their beloved aunt Caroline two nights after her strange encounter with Blackburn. If she could have, she would have, because her mind spun with thoughts of the man and his suggestion that if the two of them pretended to be lovers, it would hurt their former partners.

Why did that keep her up at night? She'd never been a vengeful person and yet the idea gave her a lightness that had been lacking since Harry ended things. What kind of monster was she?

"Evie."

She started as she realized her aunt was speaking to her. She glanced up to find her reaching across the table, covering Evelina's hand. Her expression was lined with pity, just as everyone else's at the table was. God, but she hated that. It made her want to jump out of the closest window and run into the night, never to be seen again, even if she knew they all only had her best interest at heart.

"Dearest," Aunt Caroline said. "I cannot bear to see you like this. I've remained silent on the topic in the hopes you would recover on your own, but I think we *must* address what is happening."

Evelina blinked. When she and her sisters had been forced to run from their abusive father and eventually had each become courtesans, they had embarked on a world very different from the one their aunt inhabited. Caroline was a lady, a widow with means enough to be independent, but one still bound by the strict rules of Society. Caroline embraced those same rules, so the sisters only rarely discussed the reality of their experiences with her.

But now her aunt held her gaze as if she truly understood and Evelina glared at first Arabella and then Julia. "You told her?"

Before either could answer, her aunt squeezed her hand again. "No. Neither of them said a word. The scandal with the divorce of Lord and Lady Blackburn is part of my world as much as it is yours. And this new development involving the Duke of Southwater's part is spreading like wildfire now that they've made their *amour* public. Though how they think they can survive such abominably wretched behavior is beyond me."

Arabella wrinkled her brow. "*Abominably wretched behavior.* That's the same turn of phrase Simone used when she verified to me that Harry and Lady Blackburn were together."

Caroline shrugged, though her cheeks grew a little pinker, perhaps out of embarrassment that she would speak like a celebrated courtesan even in a small way.

"Well, your friend is very wise. What those two have done is social suicide from every direction, I think. I hope." Caroline pressed her lips together. "But the more important matter to me is how much it's clearly hurt you, Evie."

Evelina sighed. Now that she'd talked to Blackburn, she felt strong enough to broach the subject here. How that was possible, she didn't want to explore too much. "I wouldn't sport with the intelligence of anyone at this table and deny it. I was fool enough to believe everything Harry...*Southwater* ever said to me. To take each promise as gospel and never prepare for any other life than the one where I was his true, if hidden, love who would be protected financially and physically. Foolish, foolish girl."

"You aren't truly saying that you consider this your fault," Silas,

Arabella's husband, said as he tossed his napkin beside his empty plate.

"Whose else could it be?"

He arched a brow and the sudden intensity of his stare made Evelina catch her breath. He was often so silly and fun, but when he speared a person this way she was very clear on why Arabella was obsessed with the man.

"It's that poxy prick Southwater's fault," he said, and then glanced toward Caroline. "Apologies, Caroline."

Caroline was blushing like a plum at the words, but still nodded vigorously. "Silas is right, as colorful as his language is. If you believed in a man who told you he loved you, that is on him, not you. And he deserves every fragment of pain or suffering he will endure over the rest of his awful life."

Evelina worried her lip. There it was again, that intrusive thought about Blackburn's suggestion of a way to get revenge. To cause a little of the pain and suffering her aunt was describing.

"What is that look?" It was Julia who asked and she arched a brow at Evelina.

"What—what look?"

"Oh, yes, *that* look!" Arabella leaned closer. "It's very wicked and I rarely see it on your pretty face anymore. What are you thinking about?"

"Nothing at all," she lied, and pushed her half-full plate away. "You two are seeing things."

"Liar, liar!" Julia said in a sing-song tone. "It's evident you're thinking of something specific. Tell us."

Evelina looked around the table. She trusted her sisters without hesitation and she had very little doubt that Silas would do anything in his power to protect her. And he seemed the kind of man who would enjoy a revenge plot.

But then there was Caroline. Once again she was concerned about exposing her to a life she never would have chosen.

"Er, Aunt Caroline, I don't want to offend—"

Her aunt folded her arms. "Please. I may not have taken the same path you and your sisters took, but I'm not some complete innocent."

"No, indeed not," Julia said with a little look at their aunt that Evelina didn't understand.

Evelina chose to ignore it. "Of course you aren't an innocent, you were married and you are well-aware of society politics. But what I'm about to say is about…it's about something far seedier."

Caroline's brows lifted and she smothered a smile. "Then I *definitely* want to know. Yes, you might shock me, but who doesn't like a little shock? It isn't the same as causing offense. And if it would help, I would hear you tell me *anything*, no matter what it was. Tell us."

Evelina let out her breath and waited a moment while the servants brought dessert. Her favorite, a lemon tart, heaven love Arabella. But even as she looked at the dessert, she couldn't think of eating it as she tried to find a way to explain her tangled thoughts.

"I already told you about Blackburn taking me to see that his wife was in my house, with Harry…Southwater."

"Yes," Silas said. "And I'm still deciding if I'm happy that he ripped the plaster from that wound so swiftly or angry that he put you through that."

"You don't have to be either," Evelina said with a little smile. "I'm capable of taking care of myself."

He inclined his head as if conceding that point. "Of course you are. Go on."

"Well, I didn't tell you something else that happened that night." She shifted slightly. "After we had talked about the situation. Commiserated about betrayal, I suppose is a better way of putting it. Well, after that he made a suggestion about how we might… might get back at Harry and Lady Blackburn."

"Get…get back at them?" Arabella repeated slowly. "What did he mean by that?"

"Blackburn believes that Harry used to take some kind of brutish pride in my apparently foolish devotion to him. And that it would rankle him if I very swiftly entered into another arrangement, especially a public one. And as for Blackburn's wife—"

"Wait, are you saying he wants to be your protector? To enter into an affair with you?" Julia burst out, her eyes wide.

"Gracious, am I so easy to read?" Evelina asked. "Yes, that's exactly it. Well, no. Not truly. A pretend affair. Nothing real."

"Oh, well, that's disappointing," Caroline said, and all of them stared at her. She bent her head, cheeks even darker than they had been after Silas's swearing. She took a long gulp of her wine. "I realize you inhabit a very different reality from my own. And Lord Blackburn *is* a fine specimen of a man."

"No one could deny that he's very handsome," Evelina admitted, and found herself thinking of him briefly with those intense green eyes and angled features. She shook that away. "But neither of us is ready for something like that. No, this would only be to tweak our previous lovers. To make ourselves look a little less pathetic."

"You aren't pathetic," Arabella insisted. "I'll duel anyone who says otherwise, including you, so be careful."

Evelina couldn't help but smile at that playful defense. "I think you would, thank you for that."

"So you said yes to him?" Silas asked, gently steering the conversation back to matters at hand.

Evelina shook her head. "I was so shocked by the suggestion, I don't think I said anything. He left soon after with a great many apologies and I haven't seen the man since. But I also haven't been able to stop thinking about that proposition. And I suppose I would like some opinions on it. From all of you."

There was silence at the table for a moment as her family exchanged looks. There was concern, but also interest, and happily, no judgment.

Julia spoke first. "What would the terms be?"

"We hadn't gotten that far," Evelina admitted. "But if they weren't good terms, I wouldn't agree."

"How long would it go on?" Silas asked.

She shifted. "Goodness, it seems I can offer no information one way or another. Again, we didn't dig into the specifics. It was an offhand suggestion made while he was telling me I deserved my feelings of hurt and anger."

"Which you do, so at least we know he isn't a complete waste," Arabella said. "Silas, what do you know about Lord Blackburn? You two were in school together briefly, yes?"

"We were," Silas said. "We weren't mates, exactly, but I never had any negative feelings about him. He was a fun fellow, always telling jokes and playing pranks, but never cruelly or at another's expense. As far as posh pricks go, you could do a great deal worse. And you have."

Evelina bent her head with a little smile. "Your impression of him is the same as my own. Before everything happened with his wife, I used to actually look forward to encountering him. He was always friendly and polite. And he never spoke to my breasts, which is what most of Harry's friends did, even if the duke was standing right next to me. Blackburn is changed now...broken, I suppose. But there still isn't a sense of abject cruelty or violence to him."

Arabella shifted her attention to Caroline. "And what are your thoughts on the man, auntie? He is in your circles, after all."

"He's much younger than I am, but I did know his father, who was nothing but gentlemanly." Caroline shrugged. "I've encountered the new earl a few times at gatherings here and there over the years and I've always judged him much the same way as you all have. He seems a friendly, jovial man with a sharp intelligence. I've never heard him spoken of in any negative way until the divorce scandal."

"And what about his wife?" Evelina asked softly.

Her aunt met her gaze. "There were always a few little whispers, unproven suggestions that she was untrue. And I always found her to be very proud when I met her, and not in a good way. She likes her title and she likes attention. Those things alone don't mean anything, but she isn't a very nice person, especially if she believes someone around her is beneath her."

Evelina nodded as she picked at her lemon tart. "And do you think that starting some kind of public affair with me would hurt Blackburn more than he's already been hurt?"

"You care about that?" Caroline asked.

There was a question. Care about that, care about him? She barely knew him.

"I'm not sure the man is thinking straight," she said slowly. "and one of us must consider the consequences. Even if I can't hurt Harry, having a public affair will raise my worth when I'm truly ready to go back out into the courtesan market. But if it's going to hurt the earl in some way, I must be the one who is reasonable."

Caroline considered the question as she took a bite of her tart and chewed. "When the divorce was first announced, the shock was powerful and the blame and disgust seemed to be equally spread. But these last few days when Lady Blackburn's affair with South-water became public? Sympathies have strongly shifted to Lord Blackburn. I think if he were to engage in an affair with you, it certainly wouldn't hurt him. And I suppose that a few well-placed whispers could only help."

"Well-placed whispers?" Evelina repeated. "Such as?"

"People will ask me about it, as our relationship is not secret," Caroline said. "They always ask me about you three. And I can say how both of you were wronged and are taking comfort in each other. How he's helping you when you were so cruelly abandoned. How much he deserves a little pleasure after being so strong and kind during the worst betrayal. In the end, it might actually limit the damage being done to him in the public eye."

Evelina took all that information in. It certainly gave an altruistic turn to what was otherwise an act of vengeance.

"I still have such a hard time believing Harry would be so abjectly cruel," Julia said with a sigh and a frown.

"I don't," Silas said softly, and looked down the table at Evelina.

She knew what he was thinking about, that night when she had begged Harry to help Silas find Arabella only to have him refuse for fear of a scandal.

And here he was, courting one ten times as terrible for some other woman. Her chest ached with that fact and she dropped her gaze back to her tart.

"Perhaps before I do anything to claim vengeance I should…I should talk to Harry," she said softly.

That brought everyone's silverware to clatter against their plates and when she looked up she found the table full of staring eyes and gaping mouths.

"You cannot mean that," Arabella said first. "It cannot be wise."

"I don't care about wise, I care about safe," Silas said.

Safe. There was something she'd always believed herself to be with Harry. She shook her head. "I-I cannot imagine Harry would bring me physical harm."

"You couldn't imagine a great many things, my dear," Silas said, the words harsh but the tone gentle.

She shut her eyes. "He cannot be a complete monster. He cannot."

"If you must see him, let me be with you when you do it," Silas said. "I'll stand by, I won't interfere. I just want to be there in case."

"Fine," she said softly. "I'll write to him and see if he'll even meet with me and then ensure you are there to chaperone. But now I'm tired of lamenting my situation. Can we speak of something else? Aunt Caroline, do you have any interested gentlemen this Season?"

Her aunt's cheeks darkened a shade, just as they always did when her nieces teased her about the subject of her love life. That was, of course, why they all did it. "Er. No."

"That's shame," Arabella's eyes danced with humor. "You deserve as much wicked fun as your nieces have!"

"You're a widow, auntie," Julia added with a laugh. "You could get away with so much."

"I could arrange something for you. Simone would help, I'm sure," Arabella continued.

Caroline covered her cheeks with her hands. "Lord, let us not involve Miss Stanhope. Please, this is too much, even if I know you're all in jest. Can't we talk about Julia's new gentleman instead?"

The eyes of the table shifted to Evelina's younger sister, who was blushing almost as darkly as their aunt. "Lord Castleton is a fine protector thus far. We attend the opera each week and supper at my place every other Thursday."

"Sounds like a font of passion," Arabella said with a roll of her eyes before she took a sip of her drink.

"Not everyone gets your fairytale ending," Julia said. "And it's fine enough for now."

They continued their conversation, teasing each other, playful together as the sisters had always been. Silas and Caroline fit right in and for a moment Evelina felt peace. It was fleeting, of course, just as it had been for a flash of a moment two nights ago when she'd gripped Blackburn's arm and felt the same.

Perhaps one day she'd get back to peace. But first she had to write a letter to Harry. Fully resolve things, understand him, and then walk away, perhaps without needing revenge for the wrongs he'd committed.

That seemed slightly less terrifying than diving into some kind of pretend affair with Blackburn.

CHAPTER 5

Vaughn no longer went to White's. The attention he received there from gentlemen who looked down their noses at him and turned away when he approached was a humiliation he wished to avoid. He had come to appreciate a different club, Fitzhugh's, a great deal over the last few months. It was run by a man who no one would label a gentleman, but who behaved with more care and thought than most men in Vaughn's acquaintance. And the company kept there was far more varied and interesting as a result.

Still, as he sat before one of the big windows overlooking the street below, he occasionally heard his name in the air, usually accompanied by his wife's and Southwater's. His stomach burned with acid at it, even as he tried to remain outwardly unmoved.

"May I buy you a drink?"

He glanced up at the question to find Silas Windham sliding into the chair across from his own. He had known the man a little when they were children. Windham was the bastard son of the previous Marquess of Penteghast, though he'd been raised amongst the legitimate children for some odd reason. They'd gone to school together a few years and Vaughn had always liked the intelligent, if wild gentleman before him. And yet he didn't understand the approach and braced himself for all the reasons he might be making it.

"That would be kind," he said carefully.

Windham raised a hand and when the room attendant came he asked for whisky. While they waited, they watched each other. He could feel Windham reading him, just as he was doing the same. In the end, he decided to simply launch the conversation in an attempt to control it.

"It's good to have you back in London. You went to…to America, didn't you?"

"Yes, for almost five years," Windham said as he they took their glasses from the tray when it came and then clinked them together. "I returned when my brother took ill, became reacquainted with Arabella and the rest is history."

Ah yes, the man had married Evelina's older sister, the infamous courtesan Arabella Comerford. Which made Vaughn wonder if his recent interactions with Evelina were actually why he was being approached now.

He proceeded with caution. "I extend my truest felicitations on your marriage. I've seen you two together here and there. It seems a love match."

He said that with great difficulty, for it brought up ugly emotions about his own life. Windham, of course, had no idea of the conflict in Vaughn's chest and smiled broadly. "It is that. Thank you for the thought. It's much appreciated."

They were silent for a moment and then Vaughn sighed. "Do you come to find out more information about my divorce for the courtesan network? Or is it to address my recent interactions with Miss Evelina Comerford, which I'm certain you've heard about?"

Windham arched a brow, but didn't look angry. "I've always liked a direct man. You can pick one or the other, I'm interested in both. Though not for the courtesan network. They can find out their own information—they don't need me."

Vaughn pursed his lips. "I suppose not. I really don't want to discuss my marriage, thank you."

"I understand that. Honestly, I wouldn't have any interest in that topic at all if your marriage, or the end of it, didn't directly affect my sister-in-law and in turn, the happiness of my wife."

Vaughn downed his drink in one long gulp and set the glass aside. "Then say whatever it is you wish to say."

"You revealed the truth about Southwater to Evelina."

There was no emotion tied to that statement of fact. Vaughn couldn't tell if Windham was relieved or upset or furious about his interference with Evelina's awareness of her former lover's behavior.

"I did. Accidentally at first. I thought because of her connections she must have heard about the scandalous connection of my wife to my former best friend. But once it was clear she didn't, I felt it was important for her to hear it so that she'd know what kind of man she'd lost."

"Not much of a loss in my estimation," Windham said, and now his flash of anger was dark and intense, even if it was brief. "But she *was* hurt by finding out the truth in such a blunt manner."

Vaughn bent his head. "Yes. I know. Perhaps I went too far. I seem to be doing a lot of that lately."

"I suppose that's understandable, considering the circum-stances." Windham sighed. "I think the family is only concerned that Evelina isn't hurt further. Even a pretend liaison could cause very real pain."

Vaughn lifted his brows. "Ah, so she told you about that, as well."

He wasn't sure what to think about that. It implied she was considering the notion, even if she had been hesitant about it a few days before. Why did that give him such a thrill? He knew he was being ridiculous to even suggest such an imprudent thing.

"I suppose," Vaughn said slowly when Windham didn't fill the gap in conversation, "that although I understand the concern of you and her sisters, I must point out that Miss Comerford…Evelina…is of sound mind and of age. I haven't put pressure on her when it comes to the idea and I won't irrespective of whether she reaches out to me about it or not, nor regardless if she refuses me or not."

"Ah, so it's none of my business," Windham said, a little hint of laughter in his tone.

"I wouldn't go that far. But the answer is hers to give, if she *is* considering the suggestion."

Windham sipped his drink, a troubled expression flickering over his face. "Well, she is, so that should lighten your mood. Only first she wishes to do something that I fear might be more foolish than taking up your idea at revenge."

Vaughn wrinkled his brow, surprised by the concern that filled him at the statement. He had no real relationship with Evelina to worry about what she did and yet that was the emotion. "What do you mean?"

"She is reaching out to that poxy fuck Southwater and trying to discuss what he's done to you both first. I suppose to give him a chance to prove he's not a bastard of the highest order, even though he is most definitely that."

Vaughn recoiled slightly at the idea of Evelina speaking to his former friend. "I don't think she'll like his answers."

"Nor do I. But I'm more concerned about how he'll behave if he's alone with her. I suppose you're biased, but do you think he could be…*aggressive* if directly met with accusations?"

It would have been easy for Vaughn to immediately say yes, to weaponize this man who looked like he knew exactly how to throw a punch against the friend who had betrayed him. But as much as he longed to do so, he found himself shaking his head.

"No. I cannot say he won't be cruel. But I can't picture him putting a hand on her. He's a different kind of…what did you call him?"

"A poxy fuck," Windham said easily.

"Yes, that fits nicely. Southwater is a different kind of poxy fuck than that."

Windham's brows lifted as if he were surprised Vaughn hadn't given the worst possible version of Southwater. But then he nodded. "That's good to know. She's supposed to reach out to me when her meeting has been arranged so that I can be there just in case she needs protection despite your belief."

Vaughn nodded, but he still felt more concerned about Evelina's heart over her body. The idea of directly addressing the person who had caused such pain sounded fine enough, but he knew from bitter experience that there would likely only be more heartbreak to come from it. Southwater could be so cold, so hard, when he no longer cared about a person. Vaughn had already seen Evelina crumple once. Christ, she'd nearly been run down in the street because of it. He hated to think of her doing the same again when the very man who had broken her spirit would get the pleasure of seeing her collapse.

"And now I think we've dug into this wound more than enough," Windham said. "Why don't we talk about something else? Do you still go to Ripley's to box?"

"Yes, every Thursday morning like clockwork. It's been a welcome release."

"I'd say so. I think I'll start going again now that I'm back in Town. My middle brother, Reg, goes and cannot stop talking about it."

They continued the conversation about the boxing club and its owner and Vaughn was happy for such normalcy. But he couldn't stop thinking about Evelina and her plan to speak to Southwater.

Perhaps he should call on her. Try to dissuade her. After all, he already knew the cost of such a thing, why shouldn't she be helped so she wouldn't have to pay the same? He owed her that, perhaps, after being the one to spring the awful truth on her.

~

Evelina paced her parlor floor, alternating wringing her hands before herself and smoothing her skirt over and over. She kept glancing at the clock, counting down to the time she was waiting for and the arrival she anticipated. Harry would be here soon.

She had dressed for battle, of course. She'd learned that from Simone Stanhope and Arabella over the years. Her fashionable and somewhat revealing green gown was cut to perfection to remind a man what he'd once had and lost. Her hair was exactly as he'd liked it best. She even wore a piece of jewelry he'd once given her, a jade amulet that hung between her breasts to draw the eye.

It wasn't seduction. No, that was a different kind of war paint. Today she dressed for regret. To remind him of his if he felt any part of it.

A carriage turned into her drive and she caught her breath. He was early, which was against his character. Harry was never early, which could only mean he was anticipating this meeting as much as she was. She hated that the fact gave her hope. She wasn't trying to reunite with the man, after all.

After a moment, there was a light knock on the door and she clutched her hands together as the butler, Parsons, stepped in. "You have a visitor, Miss Comerford."

"Show him in!" she gasped out without waiting for further announcement.

Parsons stepped aside and allowed the gentleman behind him to enter. But it wasn't Southwater—it was Lord Blackburn. She tried to school her expression, but she felt her face fall as her hands dropped to her sides.

"I...oh, Lord Blackburn!"

He inclined his head. "I know you weren't expecting me, though it seems you are expecting someone."

She glanced at the clock again. There was less than ten minutes before Southwater was supposed to arrive and here was Blackburn, his mortal enemy, in her parlor.

"I am, I am expecting someone," she said. "You—you shouldn't be here."

His brow wrinkled at her rude response and then his eyes went wide. "I thought you were supposed to make sure Windham was here with you when Southwater came to call."

Her mouth dropped open in shock at that casual statement. "What are you—how do you know that? I realize you park yourself outside of my old home watching there, but please tell me you aren't stalking *my* door, as well."

There was a flicker of annoyance that moved over his face. "*No!* I saw your brother-in-law at my club earlier today and he mentioned your intended meeting."

She folded her arms as frustration bubbled up in her. "That little —I don't appreciate being talked about behind my back."

"Oh, trust me, I understand that," Blackburn retorted, his eyes flashing now in a most interesting way. He was usually so controlled, just showing hints of emotion when it became very high. This was something more focused and direct. "But your family is concerned about you and when I heard about your plan, so was I. You should not lower yourself to see this man."

She stared at Blackburn for a moment, the anger she so often suppressed rising in her chest. "And what right do you have to give your opinions? I *need* to see him."

"Why?" He took a step closer, filling the room somehow with his presence. "He is an arse. He doesn't deserve to shine your shoe, let alone to have you greet him looking so beautiful and with your eyes so bright."

She blinked at that unexpected compliment. Slowly, she smoothed her skirts again and wished her cheeks weren't getting hot. "It isn't your business, Blackburn."

He might have responded, but at that moment another carriage turned into her drive and she recognized that this time it *was* Southwater, on time exactly, just as he always was.

She moved forward and pressed her hands to Blackburn's chest.

His surprisingly firm chest. "You must go! Oh God, it's too late to go. You'll encounter each other."

"Good," Blackburn said, folding his arms and setting his jaw, which only seemed to make it a sharper line.

"Christ, you are frustrating," she muttered. "What to do...go into the room across the hall. Hurry. You can wait there for us to finish."

"Evelina—"

"Please!" she gasped out, and then shoved him backward.

To her surprise, he didn't fight her, but lifted his hands in surrender and strode out of the room and across the hall just as she heard Parsons open the front door and greet Harry.

She shook out her arms in the hopes she could calm herself, but her chest felt like a thousand birds were fluttering around in it as her servant escorted the duke into the parlor.

She didn't hear him being announced because she was staring into the face of the man she'd once loved. She'd loved him, hadn't she? The hurt and anger were so strong now she could hardly recall what had come before.

He looked the same. Tall, broad shouldered, handsome with his blond hair in perfect place and his cheeks smooth. His bright gaze, which had once flitted over her with desire, now moved over her from head to two and reflected...nothing. There was *nothing* in that stare. Like he didn't even know her.

"Harry," she whispered.

He stiffened at the familiar address she had promised herself she wouldn't use. "Miss Comerford. I have come as you requested, though I'm not sure what we have to say to each other. You've been settled generously. I have no intention of giving you more if that is your hope."

She wrinkled her brow. "You—you think I've called you here to demand money?"

He shrugged. "I assume a woman of your position isn't above asking for more."

"A—a woman of my position?" she repeated. "What does that mean?"

He stared down at her, his expression cool and almost blank. "You're a courtesan."

Her nostrils flared and the anger she kept trying to tamp down rushed up at his dismissal. "Yes. I was. I *am*, I suppose. And you liked that when it suited your purposes. You also told me I was more. You promised me a future."

"Men will say a great deal to keep a woman in his bed," he said with a shrug. "As you say, it suited my purposes. You couldn't have been foolish enough to believe that I would truly maintain you for life. That I would forgo a great love for *you*."

"A great love?" she repeated. "Are you talking about the wife of your best friend? *That* great love?"

Now *his* anger flashed, hot and quick, and in that moment she was happy Blackburn was across the hall in case she needed help. But no. No, she didn't believe Harry capable of violence against her. That was ridiculous.

"Watch your tone," he said, too softly to be anything but dangerous. "That is my future wife you are talking about."

"You are outrageous," she said with a shake of her head. "I thought if you came here, I would see that this is all a mistake, a terrible misunderstanding. That the man I thought I knew, the one who wouldn't hurt his friend, still existed and could explain all this somehow. But that man doesn't exist, does he?"

He shook his head. "Calm yourself, you're being overwrought and dramatic."

She ignored him and continued, "Because if you did, you would feel *ashamed* for what you did to Blackburn."

Southwater let out a little snort. "He didn't tend his own garden as well as he should have and *you* were a body to warm my bed. How could I feel shame about taking advantage of either of those things? This is a waste of my time. I came here to tell you not to write to me again. Our transaction is complete and that's all it ever was."

She opened and shut her mouth, trying to find words to respond to that cruel dismissal but unable to find any. Then the door behind Harry opened and words fled even further as Lord Blackburn entered the room. Horror flooded her as time turned to slow motion. Harry turned back to see the intruder. His eyes widened and there was that flare of emotion again. He was clearly shocked to see his former friend. He was *angry*.

And as he jerked his gaze back and forth between her and Blackburn, he showed something else. Just a flash of that passion he had denied her since his arrival. He looked...*jealous*.

"What the bloody hell is this?" Southwater said. "Wh-what is *he* doing here?"

"As if you have any call to question Evelina's actions after you discarded her so callously?" Blackburn folded his arms, one fine brow arched in challenge.

"And what do you know of it?" Southwater retorted, his cheeks darkening to a deep red. His fists gripped at his sides. "Why the hell would you insert yourself in this, a private moment between us?"

Evelina almost scoffed out loud. After dismissing her as nothing more than a grasping, idiot whore, he now implied his friend had interrupted an intimate moment between them?

Without thinking, she stepped up to Blackburn and slid her hand through the crook of his elbow. "He is here because I asked him to be. Because I wanted him to be present when I told you the other reason why I asked you to join me this afternoon."

"And what is that?" Southwater's tone was rough and she hated herself for reveling in it.

But she didn't stop. Instead, she forced a smile that felt as tight and unnatural as a mask. "I wanted to tell you that you needn't be concerned about my future, not that you seem to be. But if you ever had a care for me, you'll be happy to know that Blackburn is taking care of that, and of me, very well."

What happened next was something she hadn't truly intended nor planned to do, but the drive for it was too powerful to resist. She turned toward the earl, cupped the back of his neck and pulled him down. He didn't resist her though his expression was shocked before she closed her eyes against it and he was stiff when her mouth found his and she kissed him.

CHAPTER 6

Vaughn had been too shocked to deny Evelina her kiss, and the entire endeavor ended too swiftly for him to really feel it. She released his neck and tucked her arm around his waist, pulling herself up close to him. He looked at Southwater, his former friend, his most hated enemy, and he saw the bright anger and jealousy in the duke's stare.

Oh, how he loved to see it. Loved to see even a fraction of the pain that this man had created in his selfish wake be revisited on him. He put his arm around Evelina in return and smiled broadly.

"You said you were a courtesan," Southwater hissed out, his voice a little sharper. He seemed to have more emotion about this than what Vaughn had overheard when he was dismissing Evelina with such cruelty. It was why Vaughn had felt driven to intervene. "But I think I'd call you far worse based on this. Don't send for me again, either of you."

The duke pivoted on his heel and stomped from the room. The front door slammed just seconds afterward and immediately Evelina shrugged from Vaughn's embrace and paced to the window, watching her former lover's carriage leave. When she looked back at Vaughn, her hands were shaking and her cheeks were pale.

"I'm sorry, my lord. I shouldn't have sprung such a thing on you."

"Well, we did talk about it before," he said softly, still trying to process what had just happened. "It was even my idea."

She shook her head. "But we never agreed to it. It was a violation of your consent and I know better than most what a betrayal that is."

He wrinkled his brow and wondered what had happened to her in her past. Had Southwater violated her consent or someone else?

He cleared his throat because the answers to those questions were none of his business. "Did you see his face, though?" She hesitated and then a small smile just barely tilted her lips, like she was fighting any pleasure. He leaned a little closer. "He was *furious*, Evelina. Seeing us together drove him mad."

The smile on her face grew wider. "Oh, I'm the worst person, but I admit seeing him finally moved after everything that has happened was satisfying. But perhaps I went too far. Did too much."

"After the way he treated you?" When she began to shake her head as if to dismiss that, he continued, "Evelina, I heard everything he said to you. He deserved a little cruelty. More than a little, in truth. And you must admit I was right when I suggested we pretend a connection. He was bothered by you moving on and especially moving on with me."

"He was," she admitted slowly. "Almost in the same breath that he dismissed me as nothing, he was wound up that someone else would actually want me."

"If we continued on, that feeling would only be worse, you know," Vaughn said. "He would think about it, even when he was with *her*. He would know people were talking about it, just as they've been talking about what the two of them did to us. It's not justice, not truly, but it is something, isn't it?"

She worried her full bottom lip. "You can't really mean to continue."

"Why not? You just told him we were together, didn't you? The lie is set in motion. Why not let it play out a little while? Not for long, of course, just enough to make both Southwater and my wife uncomfortable. Just long enough to make them stare at each other over a supper table and know that they didn't win."

He could see Evelina pondering that. Perhaps even playing it out in her mind, watching the possibilities come to fruition. Then she let out a long, shuddering sigh. "As you say, I already set the wheel in motion. If we abandon the deception, I suppose it would only make it worse, especially for you."

He flinched as he thought of the other thing he'd overheard a moment before. Evelina had chided Southwater for his behavior toward Vaughn almost more than she had about what he'd done to her. And it had…mattered somehow to have a champion. Which was entirely foolish.

"Don't do it to protect me," he said swiftly. "That isn't your duty. Do it because…I don't know…we're both just petty enough to want the tiniest hint of revenge."

"I will admit I'm feeling very petty after watching his reaction," she said. She paced away, worrying her hands in front of her, shaking her head. He waited for her to decide and finally she stopped and faced him. "Oh…*yes*. I agree to continue. But we must come to terms."

He almost wanted to crow, to pump a fist in the air like he'd won a hurling competition. But he calmed that reaction and tilted his head. "Terms?"

She nodded. "Yes. This is an arrangement that may not be exactly like the kind I normally come to, but certainly there is business to it. Coming to agreed-upon terms is one way to avoid disappointment or hurt when it ends." She hesitated. "Not that any terms I put in place did that when it came to Harry. But that's different. You and I aren't talking about sex or love."

He felt a flicker of disappointment in his chest when she said that, but nodded. "You're correct. As we discussed, this would all be an act, a falsehood. I have no expectations that you'd take me to your bed and I don't think either of us is ready in any way to take someone to our hearts."

"No, I'll never do that again," she said softly.

He wrinkled his brow, unexpectedly bothered by the idea that she would surrender any hope of love in her life so easily. Southwater didn't deserve to have taken that from her. But it wasn't his business.

"You are the expert and I'm sure you're right," he said.

"Very good." He watched her walk to the bell at the door and she rang it. When her butler appeared she said, "Parsons, the earl will be joining me for supper."

"Very good, Miss Comerford," Parsons said with a slight incline of his head in Vaughn's direction. "I'll let the staff know. We shall serve in about half an hour."

"Good." When he left, she faced Vaughn again. "May I offer you a drink?"

He nodded and watched her move to the sideboard. Now that they had agreed to this odd arrangement, he felt something had shifted in her. There was something more sensual in her movements, something more certain like she was back in her own skin after wearing a costume for too long.

She really was lovely.

At the sideboard, she looked at him over her shoulder. "What do you like? I have cognac, brandy, a very fine whisky."

He arched a brow. "*He* liked cognac, didn't he?"

"He did."

He smiled a little. "Then I'll drink that. It would serve him right."

"I asked what *you* like, my lord."

He stared at her a moment, feeling her even gaze on him. She said nothing else, but waited for him. He shifted and at last said, "Brandy."

"Very good." She grabbed for a bottle and poured him a snifter. As she handed it over, she said, "Every part of this doesn't have to be for revenge. You should have what pleases you."

He broke his gaze from hers and found his voice was thick as he said, "Well, that would be something, wouldn't it?" He took a sip of the drink and smiled at her as the flavor hit his tongue. "That's lovely."

"Good." She poured herself a madeira and took a place on the settee. She motioned for him to join her and he did, watching her every move like she was a mesmerist in the park. It was impossible not to be drawn in.

"We'll discuss the terms over supper shortly," she said. "But I thought perhaps you'd like to know the kind of person I am. So that you're certain you wish to affiliate yourself with me. After all, you told me some painful things about your marriage, it seems only fair."

He flinched. He *had* done that. He tried to forget about it when he thought about Evelina. Tried to pretend like he hadn't spilled himself out like that with a stranger.

"I cannot imagine I would think less of you no matter what you tell me. But I admit a curiosity about you. You are difficult to read, Evelina Comerford."

She gave a flash of a smile. "The best courtesans are. I forgot that for a while when I pretended it could be more."

Her smile fell and he reached out to cover her hand. They both stared for a moment and he pulled it away. "That wasn't your fault."

"Perhaps not, but I must correct it now," she said with a sigh. Then she shook her head. "Let me focus. My past, yes? I was born to Albert and Rebecca Comerford. I don't remember my mother—she died when I was just two and a half, trying to have the son my father insisted she bear for him. She had four pregnancies in just as many years and it broke her body. Arabella recalls her a little—flashes, she says—but when someone says the word *mother*, I'm afraid Julia and I have just a blank there."

"I'm sorry," he said softly. "What about your father?"

She stiffened. "He was a gentleman, but he never acted like one.

My mother was nothing more than a broodmare to him, his daughters disappointments and convenient targets for his anger and occasionally his violence. Arabella took most of the brunt of it, trying to protect Julia and me. When she ran away, went to London to be a courtesan, I took up her role."

He shook his head. "I'm so sorry, Evelina. That's terrible. He died recently, yes? Wasn't it an accidental shooting when he was in his cups?"

She hesitated a moment, like she was pondering that statement. He could see her deep discomfort and then she said, "That's the story, yes."

"It's not true?" When she didn't answer, he reached across and took her hands again. This time he didn't let go because she seemed to need the comfort. "You don't owe me any answers."

She stared into his face a moment and then let out her breath in a shaky sigh. "I suppose I don't. But somehow I want to give them to you, again so you can make the best decision for yourself."

He watched as she downed the rest of her madeira in one gulp. "Take your time. I'm in no rush."

She nodded and seemed to gather herself. Her voice was strong as she continued, "He came to London hellbent on harming Arabella, who he blamed for his fall from grace. He kidnapped her. He wanted to kill her. But in his madness, he turned the gun on himself instead. It was a suicide. Silas's brothers were kind enough to cover it up with the authorities."

He shook his head and squeezed her hands gently. "Oh, Evelina. That's terrible. What you three have been through."

"He knew."

He blinked in confusion. "He? He who?"

"Harry," she whispered. "Harry was with me that night when we discovered Arabella had been taken. Silas was mad with fear and I begged Harry to go with us to search. To help me save my sister and he—he *refused*." She let loose a humorless laugh. "He told me he wouldn't involve himself in something that could cause such a scandal to his name."

Vaughn stared at her, a blind rage lifting in his chest. "That bastard. Fucking hell, that arse."

She blinked and he realized there were tears in her eyes. "It changed things between us. Obviously it was only a few months ago, I know now that he was already with Lady Blackburn, but it was never the same. I don't know if that was part of why he decided he would throw me over and put all his energy into her, but if it was then—"

He realized where she was going with that sentence and shook his head. "If you apologize for the actions of that prick, I will lose my senses. He owed you more. Full stop. And this information only makes me despise him all the more."

She looked a little confused at that statement. "Oh. Well, thank you. Thank you, Blackburn. At any rate, it isn't very likely that the truth will come out, but it is ammunition that I suppose Harry could use against me and us, if we're pretending a relationship. So I thought you should know about it to protect you from any scandal that might follow."

He found himself laughing, and for the first time in a long time it was real. "Along the scale of scandals currently happening in my life, this would rate very low, I assure you. I would only care he did it because it would hurt you. But I'm guessing he wouldn't want to tangle with Silas, who seems the kind of man who might rip a man's arms off if his wife was harmed."

Evelina's smile seemed brighter at those words. "He is that. He is the best of men and I'm so happy to have him as my brother-in-law. At least one of sisters is happy and for that I'm grateful."

There was a light knock at the parlor door and the butler returned. "Supper is served."

"Thank you, Parsons," Evelina said, and stood. Vaughn held out his arm and she didn't hesitate before she took it. The feel of her fingers folding along the inside of his elbow was warm and gentle and he let out a long breath as they started out of the room.

"Thank you again for telling me," he said. "And now I look forward to the negotiation of terms, Miss Comerford. For I have a guess that you'll bring a nerve of steel to such things."

He was happy that she laughed as a response, something musical that lightened the mood between them. And after the last few months, having anything lightened was something miraculous, indeed.

Evelina observed Blackburn carefully as their food was served. He was an interesting man, of which she had always been aware in their occasional interactions, but it went deeper than she had suspected. Oh, she'd seen him as intelligent and witty. And no one could deny he was handsome.

But there was so much more below that surface. He was kind. Kind to her servants, kind to her. This drive for vengeance seemed to not be in his normal character, but borne from deep pain, betrayal and grief. She understood those things. She'd experienced them not only in the situation with Harry, but in the life she'd led under her father's thumb.

Somehow she was glad Blackburn knew a little about that now. They understood each other better, so they would be less likely to cause each other pain.

"And now that you've been lured in with fine brandy and a fricassee that I promise you is to die for, I think it's time we discussed those terms," she teased.

He laughed as he took a bite of said fricassee and then jerked his gaze toward her. "Oh, you are right. That's delicious. You don't play fair, Evelina."

"I'm a courtesan. We seduce the senses," she said, and then heard the tone of her words. "Oh, obviously I don't mean seduce as in erotic seduction. Not with us."

He hesitated, she wasn't exactly certain of why, but then inclined his head. "Yes, I think we have both agreed to that term already. This is not meant to be a true affair. I won't have an expectation of being in your bed."

"Good." She said it but had an odd sensation of brief disappointment. "Good. Then the terms are more about duration and expectation outside of what a normal protector and courtesan would do together."

"As well as agreeing to what I'll provide," he added.

She blinked. "What you'll provide?"

"I'm keeping you from the courtesan market," he said. "And asking you to pretend to be mine. I don't expect that will come without some financial cost. Your sister owns this house, yes? Does she charge you rent?"

"No, of course not," Evelina said.

"Then I'll deposit what a place like this would let for into your accounts as compensation, along with a small amount of pin money. What do you say to a hundred and fifty pounds for each month?"

"I say that's far too much money!" she gasped. "I doubt Arabella would let this place for more than thirty a month and another ten or twenty at most for pin money would be more than generous. Fifty pounds when I'm not even bedding you is the maximum."

He folded his arms. "I'm not sure you understand what negotiating means, Miss Comerford. You're supposed to be getting the *maximum* for your effort."

"No, that's not accurate. A fair price is what a negotiation should be. Fair to both parties."

He tilted his head and for a moment he seemed confused by that notion. "Very well. Then let us meet in the middle. A hundred pounds, paid up front, for each month we will spend pretending to be lovers." She opened and shut her mouth, because it was still far too high a sum, but he held up a hand. "I will brook no refusals. A hundred pounds is my final offer and not a ha'penny less."

"Blackburn—" she began.

"Evelina," he interrupted.

She bent her head with a laugh at the playfully stern expression on his face. "Well, when we end this arrangement and people ask me about you, I will say generous to a fault and it won't be a lie. A hundred pounds a month is very kind. And since you seem hellbent on the sum, I won't refuse you."

"Very good, our first accord," he said with a playful wink. "And now to the next item to be determined. I believe you mentioned duration."

"Yes. I'm not sure how long a person needs to enact revenge by pretending to be attached to someone new. What are your thoughts?"

He pondered for a moment, stroking his hand over his chin. "A good question. Not too short or else it will only cause more scandal. But not too long for I don't want to keep you from finding a true protector who will provide more fully for your future. Why don't we agree to discuss the topic each month before I make my next payment to your accounts? And we assume that we will do this no more than…three months?"

"It would get us both through the end of the Season," she said. "And will your divorce be finished by then?"

His frown pulled down. "I hope so. We're in the final negotiations, trying to get the permissions from church and sovereign."

"Then the timing will be right. I agree to those terms."

"We're very good at this. What else should the terms include?"

"What to expect. If not sex, then how would we work out the pretended affair so that others know it's happening? I have some thoughts on that."

He sipped his wine. "I long to hear them."

"I propose we attend one public event together each week and share a suggestively long supper once a week, as well."

"So people think we're doing the thing we aren't doing," he said.

She nodded. "Exactly. And if we decide we want to do more or less, then we can agree to that on a case-by-case basis."

"You mean if we go to the opera but then there is some art showing I think you'd like the same week," he said, and leaned closer. "Do you enjoy an art showing, Evelina?"

"I think it would be a poor mind that didn't enjoy a good art showing," she teased back. "Though it does depend on the artist."

"I think we might be agreeing to be friends," he said after a moment's consideration. "Is that what we're agreeing on?"

She leaned back. "Friends. Goodness, I've never been friends with a man before. What a concept. But I suppose we are. We have a very sad thing in common, but that doesn't mean we can't enjoy each other's company even as we…well, I suppose act in bad faith."

"*Lightly* in bad faith," he corrected.

She laughed. "Are we agreed then?"

"We seem to be," he said, "And now I'd like to eat this fine food and talk about something that isn't my wretched wife or your wretched former lover. It will be our first suggestively long supper, after all."

She smiled and after she'd taken a bite of her food, the first bite that had tasted of anything at all for months, she asked, "Have you read any good books lately, then?"

His gaze lit up. "Oh yes! I'm reading the most fascinating biography about Cook's time in the Pacific." He frowned. "Is that too dry?"

"The biography of an explorer?" she said with a laugh. "Not at all. I'm fascinated by such things. Please, tell me all about it."

He did, making her laugh and gasp in equal measure as he told her adventurous tales of the explorer. And the supper was long, probably suggestively if anyone was watching but seemed to fly by. After their dessert plates were cleared away, he leaned back and smiled at her.

"That's the longest conversation I've had in an age about anything that wasn't my divorce."

There was such a lightness when he said that, a flash of the man she'd vaguely known during her time as Southwater's mistress. The one who had been fun to be around. There he was and he was very attractive. The kind of man some high society lady would forgive for his tortured past once time and gossip had moved on. He could be happy again. She hoped he would be.

"I'd be happy to be practice for such conversations," she said. "And get you ready to return to good company at some point."

She was teasing but their eyes met and suddenly there was a little thickness to the air. Like they'd hit upon something real in the midst of all the games and lies and schemes.

"Good company," he repeated with a shake of his head. "That sounds dreadful."

"Oh, you'll like it again someday, I just know you will." She sat back, as if a little added distance could lessen the unexpected weight that talking to him had. "Speaking of which, should we plan our first public outing?"

He shifted. "I suppose we should. What about the opera?"

She considered it. "It's a good idea. People expect to see men at the opera with their mistresses. But I think we need to do something a little less obvious to begin. Are you a member of Lady Lena's Salon?"

He nodded. "Yes. I was invited a few years ago. I don't go as often as I once did, but I always enjoyed it."

She worried her lip. "Is it a place you went with your wife? I'm sorry to be so direct, but I want to make sure that anything I suggest doesn't cause you further pain."

His expression softened a little at that statement. He cleared his throat. "Florence had little use for intellectual salons. Not because she isn't clever, she very much is, but because they didn't have the kind of social standing she liked to cultivate. She never attended with me, so there is no association with her for me in that place."

"Good, that will be perfect then," she said. "Two nights from now there is a gathering there. I believe there will be a discussion about astronomy led by Miss Herschel. I think she'll talk about all of her comets."

"Fascinating," he breathed. "I've always wished to hear her speak. What a coup for Lena Bright and Harriet Smith. Do you know them well?"

"The owners of the establishment? Very little. I like them both a great deal," she said. "They're brilliant. I always enjoy my time there. And it's a good place for us to be seen without making it as obvious."

He nodded slowly. "Very intelligent, not that I expected anything else. What time shall I fetch you?"

"You won't," she said. "I think it would be better to be a bit coy about it. We both attend and then be seen talking, deciding to sit together, perhaps being a little too wrapped up in each other's company. Let the world see what they think is the beginning of something new and have it be reported back to Southwater and Lady Blackburn."

"But he thinks he knows that we're already engaged in some kind of affair," he said.

"And he'll think that his discovery of us together is the reason why we decided to start to be public. Let him stew. Let him seethe." She couldn't help a little smile. "Gracious, I sound so Machiavellian."

"Very wicked, indeed. I find I quite like it in my partner in...well, it's not exactly crime. I like this idea. The salon usually begins at eight, I will be there a few moments before and make sure there is a place for us to sit together. When you arrive...fashionably late, one must assume, we will begin."

She nodded and got to her feet. He followed, just as a gentleman should and glanced at the door. She tilted her head. "Are you thinking it's time to make your escape?"

"I've enjoyed our time together very much, truly, Evelina. But I've a great deal to think about."

She motioned to the door. "Let me see you out."

They moved together to the foyer and chatted about nothing at all while his carriage was brought. He took her hand before he left her, squeezing it gently as he said his goodbyes and rode off in his fine carriage. She sighed as she closed the front door and leaned back on it.

She liked this man insofar as she had gotten to know him. *Truly* liked him. Which was a dangerous thing, indeed. And one she'd have to be very careful of as they navigated the waters of deceit.

CHAPTER 7

Just as he'd told Eveline two nights before, it had been months since Vaughn had attended Lady Lena's Salon. Those kinds of public outings had become too difficult to bear as the heat of the gossip surrounding his divorce grew worse. Eventually, he had locked himself away almost entirely, cutting off everything but the well of his own pain, anger and humiliation. Wallowing had become his pastime and he was very good at it even if he hated himself for such self-indulgence and missed the more nuanced man he once was.

So tonight, sitting at the crowded salon, watching the door for Evelina's arrival, he couldn't help but feel a little out of sorts. There was so much energy in the air from the people around him, so much anticipation of what would be discussed by Caroline Herschel, who had once been in the inner circle of George III. That was long before the king's decline, and the rise of his thoughtless, frivolous son as Regent.

Vaughn looked at the lady in question. She was older, in her sixties, he would wager. If seen on the street, some might dismiss her as merely an old woman in an unfashionable white lace cap and drab dark blue gown, but one only had to look at her bright eyes as she chatted with one of the salon's owners, Harriet Smith, to see the golden glow of her intelligence.

In that moment, he thought of Evelina and her spark. He supposed she must also be often judged by her appearance, though in the opposite direction. Men looked at her curves and her suggestive dresses and her pleasing mask and thought her one thing. Certainly, he'd heard many men over the years speak of her as only one thing, including Southwater.

But after just one evening with her, Vaughn was beginning to realize just how deep those waters went. It was a fascinating thing.

"Lord Blackburn."

He jolted as he realized the lady in question had arrived while he mused about women in general being judged for their outward appearances. Evelina now stood beside his chair and she smiled as he jumped to his feet and tried to recall what he was meant to pretend about their meeting here.

"Miss Comerford," he said, and let his gaze flit over her. She was dressed less provocatively than usual tonight. Her blue-gray silk gown was draped and arranged to accentuate amazing curves, but not flaunt them. She wore fewer gems than the last time he'd seen her, too. There was something so lovely about her that it put him to mind of spring. A season full of newness and possibility.

"What a pleasure it is to see you, my lord," she said, extending a gloved hand.

He took it and lifted it to his lips briefly. He caught a whiff of her scent as she stepped a little closer. Cherry blossom, if he wasn't mistaken. Another hint of spring after his very long winter.

"I didn't know you were a member here," she lied, meeting his eyes with both a clear message and also a little concern.

He supposed he had earned the second because he must look as off-kilter as he felt. Honestly, he had to get his head in the game they were playing. After all, people *were* looking at them as they interacted so publicly, watching them with evident interest. He had to take advantage of what the crowd would think and assume about them. Be mindful that everything he did from this moment forward would also likely be reported to their former partners.

"Yes, it's been a while since I attended," he managed to get out without much difficulty in finding the right words once he began. "And I suppose we must have gone on different nights if we never saw each other before. What a delight to know we share this common interest."

Evelina glanced toward Miss Herschel at the front of the room and her expression brightened with what seemed to be true happiness. "It is. Tonight should be fascinating. Miss Herschel discovered five comets in her own right, you know, while working for the King." Her lips pursed slightly. "One must wonder how many of her brother's discoveries were more than merely *assisted* by her."

He frowned as he followed her gaze and observed the older woman again. "I'm sure more than one. I suppose that's how it is for many women of an intellectual bent. To be taken seriously they must be merged into the academic lives of a brother or husband. It seems very unfair."

He looked at Evelina and found she had turned her face toward his and was watching him with great intent. She shifted slightly, as if she was a little stunned, and then she nodded. "I agree. It's interesting to hear a man, especially a man of your rank, understand or acknowledge that sad and frustrating truth."

He smiled a little. "I do try not to be an entirely obtuse arse. I fail a great deal, I'm certain." He motioned toward the chair he had been guarding until her arrival. "Would you care to sit beside me during the presentation? It seems we share a great deal in common on this subject."

She jolted, like she'd forgotten this exchange wasn't exactly real. They'd planned it, after all, it wasn't as natural as he hoped it seemed. But then again, it wasn't as false as it could have been, either. Just like at her home for supper two nights before, he felt the real spark of interest when it came to his exchanges with her. She was a captivating woman, after all. He *did* want to know her thoughts on astronomy and exploration and music and all the other interests he'd nurtured privately when Florence had shown them no interest and even disdain.

"I would be happy to join you, my lord," she said.

They didn't get to talk anymore after that and the attention that had been paid to them by those in the crowd around them faded, too, as Lady Lena, the face of the salon, stepped to the dais in the front of the room and began a spirited introduction of Miss Herschel. For the first time in months, Vaughn relaxed into nothing but enjoyment of the event.

And enjoyment of the company he was lucky enough to keep, regardless of the motives he and Evelina had developed when they first arranged to meet here.

Evelina's hands hurt from clapping so hard when the evening came to its end. She had come here as part of a ploy arranged with Vaughn, but she had truly enjoyed every aspect of the night. Miss Herschel was a clever, amusing presenter and her observations about the stars and revelations of how she had meticulously mapped them were enthralling.

She looked to her right and found Vaughn also clapping vigorously. All night she had been just as drawn to him as to the astronomer. He had listened with as much rapt attention as she had. His interest hadn't been pretended either, for at the end of the formal presentation, when Lady Lena had called for participation from the audience, he had asked some of the same questions Evelina herself had had during the evening.

It was clear that the man was as intelligent as he was handsome and rich. That wasn't always true of men like him, of course. Many of her lovers in the past had rank but no sense. And many of the interesting men she met had sense but no purse. To find one with all of the above felt a little like spotting a unicorn. Rare and...well, sleek and beautiful weren't the worst descriptors for her companion.

Blackburn turned toward her with a wide smile that lit up his face. "That was sublime," he said. "Did you enjoy it?"

"Oh yes!" she gushed. "When she talked about finding her first comet, I admit I was almost brought to tears. What a feeling that must have been. And it seems we judged her brother a little harshly earlier tonight. I adored that he always called it 'my sister's comet' when he presented about it to the king."

"Yes, I also love that he was her champion," Blackburn agreed. "And still is, it sounds like."

She sighed with pleasure. "Oh, it was such a fine night."

He offered her his arm and she stared at it a moment. This was what they'd planned, after all, to show a small connection that others could gossip about before they made their bigger splash where it might be obvious they were lovers. But somehow the act of taking his elbow felt like it had deeper meaning. Like it was truly stepping into something new, not merely some act.

She blinked and pushed that foolish thought away, then forced her fingers to close inside his outstretched elbow. As he led her toward a table with petit fours and punch, she couldn't help but be fully aware of the lean strength of him. If they had truly planned to be lovers, she would have been excited to unwrap him from all that propriety and find out what was underneath.

But she'd never see the impressive muscle she felt. She had to stop being silly about it. They had an agreement and it was best to leave the business they were conducting separate from anything real.

A woman near them whispered behind her fan to a gentleman and the two of them looked at her and Blackburn. She forced herself back into reality and edged a little closer. Into his orbit just like the stars they'd been hearing about all night.

"Lord Blackburn, I think you know they're all watching," she said beneath her breath, fluttering her lashes a little.

He swallowed and nodded. "They've been watching all night. You were spot on in that assessment. Not that I'd expect anything less, clever as you are."

Heat filled her cheeks at that compliment. In this setting where it was obvious he was the kind of man who appreciated intelligence, it felt like it had more meaning. "I suppose we should make our exit before many others leave, then. Just so they can watch us go and see our slightly more than formal farewell."

"And what would that entail?" he asked.

"Perhaps you hold my hand a little too long?" she suggested. "Watch my carriage drive away with a look of longing on your face?"

"You should be on the stage, natural performer that you are," he teased. "But I can easily do both."

"Good." She let him lead her toward the exit of the salon. It was situated above Mattigan's, the city's best bookshop, and they came down the stairs and around to the front of that shop. Inside she could see a cozy fire burning and the bookseller chatting in an animated way to several patrons.

Blackburn raised a hand to have her carriage brought and they stood together as other patrons from the Salon meandered out onto the street for their own exits. They were definitely being watched and she once again leaned just a fraction closer.

He cleared his throat. "Would you still like to attend the opera? They're performing Rossini in three days at Drury Lane Theatre."

"Ah, very romantic. Perfect for our own show," she said. "I would be pleased to join you."

"Excellent. I'll send all the details and pick you up that night," he said.

Her carriage arrived and he lifted her hand to his lips, lingering there a little longer than he had when he first greeted her. She knew it was all for show but when he lifted his green gaze to hers as he brushed his lips over the silk of her glove her heart made a very real rate increase. She didn't have to pretend her blush or the way her hand shook as he released her and waved off her footman to help her into the rig himself.

"Goodnight," he said before he closed the door and allowed her to depart. She pushed the curtain away from her window and found he was, indeed, watching her as she rode away. If she hadn't known it was all an act, she would have thought he truly had an interest in her.

She shoved back into her seat and folded her arms. "Absolutely not," she chided herself softly. "This is an arrangement of a very different kind and a very good way for you to practice not getting lost in a man just because he's handsome or witty or fascinating."

She said the words, but it was harder to feel them. Which meant she had to be very careful as they moved forward in this bargain. She didn't have much of herself left to lose. She couldn't give it away to a man who clearly still had feelings for his wayward wife. A man who had made it clear he was only using her.

CHAPTER 8

A few nights later, Evelina stared at herself in the mirror, in her full finery for the opera. It had been a long time since she'd worn the complete costume of a courtesan. Even before Harry had cut her off, he had been critical of her being too flashy, especially if they were going out to someplace that might be considered proper.

But the dark green gown she had donned for the evening had always been one of her favorites. It had been gathered and tucked with exquisite attention to detail, from the way the fabric lay to the little dark yellow cloth flowers that adorned the neckline and capped off the sleeves. It was low cut, of course, revealing a bit more bosom than a proper lady might have dared to do. She'd always considered it the perfect combination of seduction and elegance.

What would Blackburn think of her?

She cut herself off from that thought immediately. *That* was the thought of a woman entering an affair in truth and that was not her. If she kept having thoughts about Blackburn it wasn't because she wanted him or longed to be wanted *by* him. This was about the arrangement and nothing more. That had been made clear by their lack of contact since they'd last met at Lady Lena's, beyond a quick note to inform her what time he would pick her up tonight. It had been warm but formal, nothing to confuse matters and so she refused to let herself become confused just because he liked astronomy or was kind to servants and probably children and little animals, too.

She sighed at her reflection in the mirror and got up to walk to her window. The garden behind the home was dark, but she could make out a few shadows of the trees and bushes. Would it be wrong to climb down the trellis and bolt into the night? Change her name and go live beside the sea?

Sometimes that seemed like the perfect answer to all her problems.

She heard the bell below and shrugged off her worries. She also tried to ignore how her hands shook as she smoothed her gown one last time and then moved to the door. Her maid arrived in mere moments to tell her of Blackburn's arrival and Evelina made her way to the stairs to go meet him.

To her surprise, she found him waiting at the bottom of those stairs as she turned across the landing to come down the second flight of them. He was leaning on the banister, staring up at her, and her breath caught.

The last few times she'd seen him, including at Lady Lena's, the man had been slightly disheveled. His hair had been a fraction too long, his cheeks slashed with stubble like he'd forgotten to shave. He'd looked like a man with troubles.

But tonight, dressed in full formal attire and cleaned up, he looked…well, he was very handsome. His gaze flitted over her from head to toe as she stepped from the last step and it was in that moment she realized her gown matched those eyes perfectly. Had she done that on purpose when she was choosing between this dress and a wine-colored one that would have been just as perfect for the opera?

She didn't think so. That was something a courtesan did when she was truly lovers with a man, not when she was pretending.

"Good evening, Evelina," he said, taking her hand and lifting it to his lips briefly. The brush of his mouth was soft on her bare skin and sent unexpected tingles up her arm.

"My lord," she managed to gasp out in response.

Those green eyes lifted to hers and he smiled. "Well, that won't do at all now that we've reached this moment when we're about to reveal ourselves as entangled. If we were truly lovers, you wouldn't be so formal, I don't think."

He was right, of course. But as she struggled to think of what to call him, heat rushed to her cheeks. "I-I just realized I don't know your given name, Blackburn."

"Vaughn Courteney," he said with a slight bow. "Seventh Earl of Blackburn, at your service."

"Vaughn," she repeated, letting the feel of it settle on her tongue. "It suits you."

He lifted his brows. "Does it? I admit I rarely hear it, for everyone in my acquaintance calls me Blackburn or my lords me into oblivion."

"Even your wife?" she asked.

She saw the flicker of his reaction at the mention of Lady Blackburn. The tightness of his lips and the way the life dimmed in his eyes made her wish she hadn't asked.

"Florence called me Vaughn at the beginning, but not for years now," he said.

"It's shame men of your station don't get to use their given names very often. Blackburn is a title, it's been owned by many men. You become anonymous in a way when it's all you're known by."

He drew back a little. "You're right, of course, though the observation isn't one I've heard anyone else ever make. I suppose the anonymity is part of the point. I'm meant to be a position rather than a man."

She shook her head. "Well, I think it's sad."

"It's a costume, like what you're wearing now."

She glanced down at herself. If he'd been surprised she'd called out the anonymity of his position, she was equally surprised he noted the performative aspect of her own.

"I suppose the benefit of both our costumes is that they offer protection," she said. "But if you'd like me to call you Vaughn, I'm happy to do so. And you may continue to call me Evelina. Or Evie, if it suits."

He nodded. "Evie. I like that. I never heard Southwater call you that."

"He only did once or twice, always when drunk." She frowned, for the fact the duke had only ever accidentally used her nickname had always stung a little. To her, Evie was an expression of love and affection that her sisters often used. Harry hadn't wanted to do so, he'd said as much whenever pressed.

"Then all the better reason for me to do so, *Evie*." They stared at each other a brief moment and then he offered her his arm. "Shall we be off? We'll be just beyond fashionably late for the opera now and I think that's perfect if our goal is to be seen."

She pushed away any tangled thoughts the topic of names had created in her and took his arm. She was off to battle now, but at least she had a good ally in the fight. One she hoped she could help as much as he helped her.

As the carriage bobbed along the busy streets toward the Drury Lane Theatre, Vaughn found himself watching Evie. She would have looked entirely serene, if not for the fact that she kept working her hands together and her foot tapped beneath her skirt. They were subtle tells, of course, but there nonetheless.

"You seem nervous," he said softly.

She jolted as if surprised he'd noticed. Her dark brown eyes dropped away from his for a moment and then she sighed. "I suppose there's no reason to hide it, given the nature of our relationship. It's...it's the first time I've been out to such a large event since Southwater ended things last month. Unlike at the gambling hell or Lady Lena's, there will be little avenue for me to escape if the crowd's attention becomes too intense. And even if I could, I don't want to let you down by acting incorrectly."

He tilted his head. "Let *me* down? I must make it clear, Evie, whatever the nature of this arrangement we've made, I don't see you as a tool. I know how impossible all this is. When I see them together, it hurts. I'm not so much a fool as to think you would feel differently. If you need to escape, we'll leave. And if it hurts...you can take my hand."

She stared at him, surprise evident on her lovely face. For a moment he wondered how rare it was for her to be offered kindness or gentleness, understanding that she was as full and real a person as he was, that she had a heart and emotions.

If she hadn't been granted those allowances, he was angry on her behalf.

"Thank you, Vaughn," she said at last. "And the same goes for you."

He smiled as they came to a stop before the Drury Lane Theatre. It had burned down several years before and only been rebuilt and opened for performances less than a year before. He stepped down from the carriage and held out a hand to help her down. There were few people on the street in front of the building, as they were late. Together they stared up at the plain, rectangular façade with its portico that welcomed patrons.

Together they said, "I miss the old building."

He looked at her and they laughed that they'd said the same thing at the same time.

"The brickwork was just prettier before. And the statue of Apollo?" she said.

"Yes, it was all just so much grander," he agreed. "I used to get a thrill just looking at it."

He took her arm and together they entered the majestic hall. "This, at least, is still very fine," she said. "The rotunda is so lovely."

"It is. And the productions are reasonable, no matter the look of the place."

There were more people in entry hall and as they moved toward the entrance to the boxes, he noted when the others began to recognize them. There were stares and a few whispers as they went past and Evie's hand tightened in his elbow as she tugged herself a little closer to his side.

"Look down at me adoringly," she whispered.

He jolted and then did as she requested, staring down into those dark eyes for a moment. There was something calming about her even stare and his heart rate slowed a little as he drew a long breath. "It's going to be more intense once we enter the box. Especially if my sources are correct that Southwater and Florence are in attendance in his box."

"Oh," she said, and her throat worked as she swallowed. "I wondered if he might be here. And I suppose he would bring *her* now that they aren't hiding things anymore."

He leaned closer. "Is it too much?"

She shook her head too quickly and any worry she'd shown was erased. "Of course not. His box is directly across from yours. It will almost be a showdown."

"We'll win the showdown by pretending not to care. Are you ready?"

She nodded as he helped her into the small hallway behind the boxes and maneuvered her to where his was located. A footman held back the little curtain and they stepped into the box.

The gazes of those around them pivoted to them, both below in the main gallery and in the boxes surrounding the stage. The buzzing crowd quieted a moment and then a burst of whispers began again, this time pointed and without trying to hide her name or his. He looked at Evelina and found she was staring across the way. He followed her look and saw that her gaze was pinned on Southwater's box. When he let his eyes move to the same spot, he found the duke was there and Florence was with him.

As for their former partners? Well, both were also staring at him and Evelina. Southwater looked just as enraged as he had a few days before when he encountered Vaughn at Evelina's new home. His face was actually red and his hands fisted at his sides. Florence kept looking up and then back into her lap. She was too far away to make out her expression, but her posture was tight and unhappy.

Vaughn wanted the thrill at that fact to be stronger and more pleasing, but it left a raw emptiness in his chest instead.

"Staring should be theirs, not ours," he suggested gently.

She started. "I hadn't realized I was staring," she whispered.

He felt her hand slide into his and he put all his focus onto her. She smiled up at him, her eyes brimming with tears but her expression calm. No one would know about her pain. She was remarkably strong, it only made him like her more.

"Why don't we sit?" she suggested. "Try not to look at them again, just keep focused on me."

He arched a brow as they settled into their places and the lights of the theatre flickered to tell the crowd that the opera was about to begin.

"That won't be difficult," he said. "My companion is the loveliest woman in attendance."

She laughed lightly and placed their still-entwined hands into her lap. "That's very convincing."

"It's very *true*," he said. "You really are beautiful in that color."

He reached out and brushed a stray curl from her cheek. Her breath caught at the motion. None of this was real, of course. He knew that even if it took a little reminding. But she *was* certainly gorgeous.

The lights went down in the house and they didn't talk anymore, but focused on the opera. But even though no one could see them anymore, he was keenly aware that she kept his hand on her lap through the entire show, their fingers intertwined. And he made no attempt to separate them.

~

Evelina wished she could have said that she lost herself in the opera. She actually loved the art and was enraptured most of the time. But she hadn't been able to focus all night, not when she knew Harry and Lady Blackburn were across the way, cuddled up in the very box where *she'd* once watched opera with him. She'd been far too aware of them. And also very aware of Vaughn beside her, his lean, strong fingers tangled with her own. How was he feeling? And was this a good idea, to lean into their worst impulses in order to tweak those who'd harmed them?

She didn't know the answer, but as they made their way through the slow crowd after the performance, she tried not to think about it too hard. She'd lost track of Southwater and Lady Blackburn at some point and hoped she'd not see them again.

A hope that was denied when she and Vaughn moved toward the door and there the other couple was, just ten feet away in the milling crowd.

She froze in her place, causing Vaughn to come up short next to her. He followed her gaze and she felt him stiffen, his posture reflecting what his unreadable expression didn't.

Lady Blackburn really was beautiful up close, with perfect blonde hair and pretty, bright eyes, not to mention her elegant brocade gown. She was also wearing a large, brightly bejeweled necklace. Evelina's stomach turned when she realized it was a piece Harry had given to her and demanded back a month ago.

The other woman leaned up toward Harry and they spoke for a moment, then she looked back at Evelina and she…she *smirked*. The bright rage Evelina rarely allowed herself in this untenable situation rose up in her and she tugged Vaughn's elbow gently.

He looked at her and she smiled even as she whispered through clenched teeth. "Kiss me. Now. Kiss me."

His eyes widened, but he glanced toward the other couple for a brief second before he cupped Evelina's cheek and slowly his lips descended to hers.

Their first kiss had been brief and impulsive. There hadn't been much time to analyze it or feel anything from it. But this...*this* was something else. His lips brushed hers, gentle, even somewhat hesitant. They were soft, firm, fuller than one might have expected. His fingers bent a little against her jawline and the pressure of his mouth increased, became more real. She found herself resting her hand against his chest to steady herself as all her thoughts faded and she was left with just...this.

This kiss. This man. This moment. It was public, far too public. It was meant to upset, not to soothe, and yet somehow it did just that. She felt calmer with his mouth touching hers, and she also couldn't deny the sizzling heat of awareness that rushed through her whole body as he drew back, his green eyes dilated and stunned.

She was a little dizzy as he lowered his hand from her. "Well," she said softly. "That was lovely."

He laughed roughly and only then did he glance up. She looked, as well, and saw that Southwater and Lady Blackburn were gone. She had to imagine they'd seen the embrace. Certainly the gawking crowd would be sure to give them both the details if they hadn't stayed for the entire exchange.

Vaughn's hand moved to the small of her back and he guided her through the crowd and out where the carriages were coming. It was a crush, but soon enough their vehicle arrived and he helped her up into it. They settled into place across from each other and after they began to move, he merely stared at her in the dimness.

"Did I offend you with my demand?" she asked when he didn't speak or move for what felt like a lifetime.

He shook his head. "Not at all."

He was silent once more and she shifted. "Because there's a tension now. One I hope won't spoil things between us."

He swallowed and then he let out his breath in a shaky sigh. "I suppose I must be honest about what I was thinking. I simply realized that both times we've kissed, *you've* been the one to run it all."

"Oh," she said. Was he getting bigger? That wasn't possible, but as they spoke he seemed to fill the space more.

He shifted to the front of his seat a little and draped his elbows over his knees. It was a casual pose, really, but it felt anything but in that charged moment where he seemed to pin her with nothing but a focused stare.

"And it makes me wonder what would happen if I just..." He hesitated a fraction, his gaze breaking from hers, then returning with no less intensity. "What would happen if *I* kissed you. Not because you pulled me in or ordered me to do so with such a fire in your stare that you could not be denied."

"I didn't have fire in my stare," she interrupted, feeling her cheeks heat. God, she was a courtesan and yet this man made her blush over and over.

"Oh, you did. Impossible to refuse you when you take charge like that." He was teasing, but she didn't feel light. Or at least not entirely. There was just too much tension between them to do so.

"So are you saying you want to...to kiss me? *Really* kiss me?" she asked.

He nodded slowly. "I...I do."

CHAPTER 9

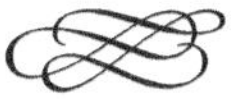

Evelina could have said no. This was outside the barriers of their false arrangement. No one was watching—if they kissed now it would be real.

But she didn't want to say no. She wanted, as she looked at this handsome man, to be kissed by him in a way that wasn't for anyone but her.

She crooked her finger and he made a rumble deep in his chest that felt like it ricocheted through every nerve in her body. Slowly, he leaned across the space between them, pressing one hand into the cushion beside her thigh and the other against the wall near her shoulder.

She was caged in as she looked up at him, his body heat swirling around her and the clean, woodsy scent of him filling her senses. Slowly he leaned in, his mouth hovering above hers for a moment before he met her lips and kissed her.

Oh yes, this was different, even from the first moment there was no denying it. There was no distraction, no negative emotion clouding the moment. All there was was the pressure of his lips on hers, the feel of him as she lifted a hand to his shoulder and gripped him like she could keep herself from being washed away on delicious sensation.

But she could have tied herself to a tree and it wouldn't have stopped that from happening. This kiss was a wave and she was being pulled out to sea.

The pressure of his mouth increased and then he gently probed her lips with the tip of his tongue. She opened without hesitation and he delved inside. With that, the tenor of the kiss changed again. He made that delicious rumble in his chest again and now the hand he gripped against the wall behind her moved to sweep around her back and tug her against his chest.

The passion spiraled, lifting ever higher as tongues crashed and hands gripped. It was all unrestrained passion and reckless abandon and her body felt like it was being lit aflame with every passing moment.

The carriage began to slow as it took the turn onto Evelina's drive. Only then did Vaughn back away, returning to his carriage seat where they stared at each other for a moment as charged as the unexpected kiss had been.

If she asked him to come inside, she had no doubt he would say yes. That he would go upstairs to her bedroom and make love to her until they were both dizzy from pleasure. But she couldn't seem to make the words form, not when her mind was reeling so entirely.

As if he read those thoughts, he cleared his throat. "Do you think we should renegotiate our terms?"

She caught her breath. "You're talking about becoming lovers."

He hesitated and then slowly nodded. "Yes." The footman came to the door and opened it, standing by at the ready to help her from the vehicle, but for a moment they only continued to look at each other. Then he smiled. "Think about it. We can discuss it when we next see each other."

She gave one bob of her head before took the footman's hand to exit the vehicle. "Good night, Vaughn."

"Good night, Evie," he said, and then the carriage door shut and he was off into the night, leaving her with questions and a desire she hadn't felt for a very long time.

Vaughn's hands were still shaking when he reached his home a quarter of an hour later. He greeted his servants absently as he made his way through the house and straight up to his chamber. He paced the room, thinking about Evie and the taste of her lips when she'd sighed shakily against him.

He wanted her. That was patently clear by his body's reaction. Even now his cock still throbbed whenever he thought of the way her fingers had clenched against his shoulder, the way she'd tasted of mint and sherry and honey sweetness, about the way she'd looked at him, gaze glassy and soft with desire when they'd parted.

He hadn't expected such a thing. After all, their arrangement had only been pretend, but here they were. He moved across the room, unwinding his cravat as he did so. He should call his valet to help, but he wanted to do something else first.

He collapsed on the settee before the fire and unfastened his fall front. Since Florence had left, he had been in too much of a spiral into hell to ponder pleasure. In this moment, he craved it like air. He shut his eyes, remembered Evie's gasp once again and began to stroke his half-hard cock.

Everything in his life had been muted for months, filtered through the awful pain of the end of his marriage. Now his pleasure was sharp and crisp, rushing up his cock as he stroked and pictured Evie, her mouth, her tongue tangling around his own, her body lifting toward him with as much need as he felt.

He could picture what could have happened next if the carriage hadn't turned into her drive or if he asked her if he could come in. He could easily imagine them smashing together, mouths seeking, hands tugging clothing. He wanted to feel her soft skin pressed to his, watch her ride above him with that silky dark hair swinging around her shoulders and her head thrown back in pleasure as she came with great waves gripping his cock.

He grunted as his own pleasure streaked hot as fire and he came with sudden, jolting gasps. He went limp on the settee as his cock slipped from his hand and then he stared up at the ceiling.

There was something calming about allowing himself to come undone like that. Of fully surrendering emotions he'd been tightly controlling for months. They were softened now, despite the fact that he'd seen his wife out in public with the man he'd once called friend.

Strange that he hadn't been obsessing over that fact, but rather Evelina's lips. Now, though, as he tucked himself back together, he did think of Florence and Southwater. He'd recognized the shape of his wife's irritation when she'd looked across the opera house and seen him with Evie in his box. But he'd also seen other things. He'd glanced over toward them many times to find them with their heads close together, talking.

It made the facts of this awful situation all the clearer. Florence had made her choice and didn't care about the consequences to herself or to him. The only thing that mattered to her was being with Southwater. She would burn them both on a pyre to do that.

Had *they* ever shared such a connection? Had his wife ever been willing to do anything to be with him? Not at first, of course, when the marriage had been arranged, but after they'd been together for a while. When things had been happier, had she ever looked at him across a room or a table and felt the thrill of affection and desire and a willingness to sacrifice everything to be closer?

He had tried, at least. He'd thrown himself into the marriage with a hope it could become warm, even loving. That they would produce children and a future and a life that gave him satisfaction when he reflected upon it at the end of his days. But it had always felt like she was pulling away, even before she turned to others to find her pleasure and her thrills.

He squeezed his eyes shut. All pleasant feelings from coming had fled now. He got up, went to the basin to wash his hands, and then rang for his valet. He'd have a drink and go to bed and hopefully everything would be clearer in the morning.

Because right now the cloudy combination of regret and desire was confusing, indeed.

~

"I heard you went to the opera two nights ago."

Evelina jolted from her distracted thoughts and looked toward her sister. She'd been having tea with Arabella this afternoon and trying to keep her thoughts focused and failing.

"I did," she said, wishing her voice sounded a bit steadier. "Lord Blackburn took me." She hesitated and then said, "Vaughn took me."

It was an odd thing that she didn't feel strange calling the man that to his face, but the intimacy of using his given name with her sister felt far more vulnerable. Arabella's raised eyebrows didn't lessen that sensation.

"*Vaughn*," she repeated. "So you and *Vaughn* came to an agreement after all."

Evelina worried her hands in her lap. "We did. You seemed supportive of the idea before—have you changed your mind?"

"I don't think I *seemed* to have one opinion or the other about it." Arabella tilted her head.

"So you don't approve then?"

Her sister was quiet a moment, which was a rare enough occurrence that Evelina's chest tightened a fraction as she awaited the response. At last Arabella sighed.

"I...think..." she began slowly, "...that the mere concept of pretending a relationship for the sake of revenge and show isn't the worst idea. Certainly many courtesans are on the arm of a man to prove some point—it's part of the life. This is little different. In theory."

"I know you too well not to understand that you have a different take on the actual practice of such a thing."

"Not necessarily. There are ways this could happen where no one would have to get hurt, where everyone could benefit. But you're my sister, Evie. I've watched you go through hell this last month or so and it's broken my heart, been the only blemish on my otherwise very happy new life. I am experienced enough in such matters to know you could still be hurt. And that indulging in ruminations over the past might not be the healthiest way of overcoming a broken heart."

Evelina stared at her hands again. "You could be right, of course. There are certainly ways where I might come out of this situation even more damaged than when I came in. But you must understand that we do have rules. And Vaughn is very kind. He isn't just using me to hurt his wife and friend. He knows I have feelings in this, as well, and he isn't trying to run me over."

"That's good." Arabella sipped her tea. "And what are the terms?"

"We know how often we'll spend time together, how we'll interact in public. And..." She trailed off because the other rule she was about to tell her sister was the very one he'd suggested they change after that heated kiss in the carriage two nights before.

"Will he fuck you?"

Evelina jerked her head up. "Gracious, leave it to you to be so damned direct about it."

Arabella shrugged one shoulder lightly. "It's part of my charm. Will he?"

"Well, at first we agreed that wouldn't happen. That we would be only friends and partners in this deception. But then...then something happened after the opera."

"Something?" Arabella's brows lifted. "Is it the something I think it was?"

"We didn't go to bed if that's what you're thinking." Her sister looked almost disappointed but didn't interrupt. "But we did kiss.

Not for show like it's been before…but a real kiss, in the privacy of the rig."

"I see. And how was that?"

"It's been a long time since someone kissed me like that. Like I was breath, do you know what I mean? Like he might starve if he couldn't devour me."

Arabella smiled gently. "I do know. That's a hell of a kiss for two people who aren't going to mix business and pleasure."

"It was," Evelina agreed. "Afterward, he asked if I wanted to renegotiate the terms of our arrangement. He left me to think about it and said we could discuss it the next time we meet."

"Which is?"

"Tomorrow night," Evelina said. "We're going to a soiree at the home of a mistress of one of his friends. He sent me the details yesterday."

"With any pressure to consider making your connection more than a kiss?" Arabella asked.

"None at all," she said. "But I think I must have an answer when we next meet. So that we don't get things mixed up and one or both of us gets even more hurt than we already have been. So it is real or not real?"

Arabella wrinkled her brow. "It's very rarely real for women in our position, you know. We build sandcastles around it, we might even enjoy it and truly care for the men we align with, but Evelina, most of us don't expect a future. You had something different with Harry, but that was rare."

"And very much a lie," Evelina said with a shiver.

"All I'm saying is that you don't have to choose sex or pretend. You can have orgasms and fun and still have it be meaningless beyond your desire to the same end. It can be brief and leave you unscarred."

"I was never very good at that part," Evelina said.

"No. For a variety of reasons scarring seems like it's always been part of your journey." Arabella covered her hand. "And Julia is little better. She's been chasing a fairytale since we rescued her from Father's traps and brought her here into the life."

"Funny that you, the only pragmatic one, is the one who ended up with the fairytale," Evelina said.

Arabella blushed now and it was such a rare thing that Evelina caught her breath to see it. "It *is* a fairytale," her sister agreed. "Sometimes I think I don't deserve it. But it's mine and I won't return the life Silas and I share."

"Nor should you." Evelina sighed. "I know you're right about the passion part. That I can have passion without love, or the hope of a future."

"If that's what you want," Arabella stressed. "So is it? Do you want him?"

Evelina shivered because the question set off a cascade of reaction through her body that she had no control over. "Oh, Arabella, I haven't wanted anyone but Harry for so long. It almost feels like betraying him to say yes. But yes. *Yes*, when Vaughn kissed me all I wanted was for him to ask me to go upstairs. To press me against any surface that would bear our weight and just take me until I could forget all the pain and heartbreak of the last six weeks."

"That sounds like as good a reason to do it as any." Arabella smiled. "It will certainly make your outward appearances be more genuine. The passion will look real between you because it will be real."

"So you're advising that I tell him I want to change the perimeters of the agreement?"

"Yes, so long as you can separate your heart and your body, why not? Have orgasms and fun and not just revenge. In fact, perhaps the orgasms and fun would be the better revenge for both of you."

"I'll consider it," Evelina said, and then shook her head. "Oh, but I can't talk about it anymore. You mentioned a moment ago that Julia was little better than I am about love. What do you think of her viscount? I've only met him in passing."

Arabella rolled her eyes. "Oh, you know how men like that are.

Silas and I bumped into them at a club and he was fine. Rather like a potato, but not entirely unpalatable. She seems like she's keeping her head about herself, but I'd like to keep monitoring her if you don't mind doing the same."

Evelina nodded and she and Arabella began a conversation about the logistics of how to act as nursemaid to their youngest sister without it being too obvious. But even as they did so, Evelina couldn't help but wonder how much she, herself, needed an angel over her shoulder so she wouldn't forget herself.

She'd done it once and she had to be careful never to do it again, no matter what she decided when it came to Lord Blackburn and his drugging, seducing kisses.

In the three days since he'd last seen Evelina, Vaughn had not stopped thinking about her and that charged moment in the carriage when their lips had met and it wasn't for anything but pleasure. She had been the star of his vivid fantasies, as well. So as his carriage arrived at her home so they could go together to the gathering of a few friends and their mistresses, he had both a spring to his step and a little embarrassment in his heart. He was going to have to look at her and try to pretend that in his dreams he hadn't undressed her with his teeth.

Not to mention she would likely have an answer to his suggestion that they renegotiate the terms of their arrangement. If she said no, he would have to hide his disappointment and recover. After all, this thing between them was never supposed to be about connection or sex. If she didn't want those things with him, he could manage that.

And somehow stop fantasizing about it so their affiliation wouldn't become uncomfortable.

When he got out of the carriage and went up to her door, he was greeted by her butler. Unlike when he'd taken her to the opera, he was escorted to a parlor and found she was already there waiting for him.

She turned from the fire as he entered and he caught his breath. She truly was lovely. The dusky pink of her gown matched the bright color in her cheeks and the lines of it accentuate her gorgeous curves. Her hair was done loosely tonight, with pretty little ringlets arranged to highlight the angles of her face.

"Aren't you a vision," he murmured, and it wasn't a lie.

She smiled, that blush going even darker than the dress. "You are too much of a flatterer, I will get a swelled head at this rate."

"I say nothing that isn't true. Certainly, I cannot be the first man to give you compliments. They must line up to do so."

Her lips thinned a little and he realized he'd hit upon a point of true pain for her without meaning to. "Not exactly," she said.

He shook his head in disbelief. "Southwater wasn't free with his compliments? Even when he got to regularly see you looking like this?"

She shrugged, but the dismissive action didn't match the emotion on her face. "Not in the last six or seven months we were together. I realize now he must have been saving those compliments for someone else."

Anger flared in him, but for the first time in this situation, it wasn't for himself. Right now it didn't matter that perhaps Southwater had been complimenting Florence instead, it was only how the removal of his affection had hurt Evelina.

He stepped a little closer and caught her hand, lifting it to her lips. "The fact that he couldn't only see you in any room is proof enough of what a fool he is. You are stunning, Evie, truly a sight to behold and any man who doesn't track your every move and breathe out the word *goddess* in your wake is an idiot."

Her gaze darted down and her cheeks pinkened even further. "You see, entirely swelled head."

"I doubt that," he teased. "And now, shall we go?"

She nodded and they moved into the foyer together where she

retrieved her wrap from her butler and then they were off to the carriage. He helped her into her seat and they rattled into the night toward their destination.

She shifted as they rode, her hands crossing and uncrossing her lap. "Er, remind me what friends we're visiting?"

"The Marquess of Ravenscroft and his mistress—"

"Matilda," Evelina provided with a smile. "Oh, I like her."

"Good. And I believe the Earl of Thistlebury will also be in attendance."

"Thistlebury." She seemed to search her mind for a moment. "Harriet Benson," she supplied at last. "She's a very experienced courtesan and I don't know her well, but I've always respected her."

"Then it shall be a very fine evening," he said. When she nodded and then her gaze darted away, he sighed. "Evelina, it appears you have something that is weighing on your mind. The ride is more than a quarter hour to go, won't you clear your thoughts and tell me?"

She huffed out a breath. "Very well. Yes, I've something to say. To ask. To discuss."

A frisson of anxiety made his arms tingle momentarily. She didn't sound pleased and he feared she would, indeed, deny him. Somehow he managed to keep all that emotion from his voice as he said, "Go ahead."

"I've been thinking about what you said the other night after we kissed in the carriage. That we could renegotiate the terms."

He arched a brow and metered his breath. "Have you now?"

Her expression tightened. "Oh, please don't play games with me. If you've changed your mind about…about what you want…then just be direct."

He stared for a moment. Her upset made him realize that she had been just as afraid he didn't want to change the trajectory of their affair as he had been. Here they were, two idiots who would have probably had a great deal of fun days earlier if they'd just been brave enough to have this conversation.

He leaned closer and caught her hand. "I wouldn't ever play games with you, Evie. At least not this kind. I would very much like to renegotiate terms with you. That kiss is all I've thought about, in detail, since it happened."

Her lips parted and then a little smile tilted them. "Oh."

"And what about you?"

"Oh yes," she whispered. "In great detail."

All he wanted to do was launch himself across the carriage, gather her up against him and finish what they'd started in that exact position two nights before. But the vehicle was slowing as they reached the home of his friend's mistress and he forced himself to remain just where he was.

"You've no idea how much I want to start these 'negotiations' with you right now, but it will have to wait since I think this evening could further both our goals for the future."

She nodded and then inched forward on her seat, her knees invading his space and the soft cherry blossom scent of her curling into his nostrils like a drug that made him lose all control.

"Well, some people say the waiting is the best part." She stroked a fingertip along his jawline and electric desire seemed to follow in its wake.

"That is absolutely not true," he said with a tense laugh. "If the waiting is the best part, the man is definitely not doing something right."

She laughed along with him and dropped her hand as the carriage door opened. He stepped out and waved off the footman so he could reach back for her. "May I help you down, my dear?"

Her smile faded a fraction and he actually watched the moment when she put back on the mask of the courtesan. She was going to play a role tonight of his lover, the woman who was making him forget all the betrayals that had cut open his soul. It was their game, no matter what happened next.

He knew all that and he was still shocked by how much it bothered him to see her pull away from whatever real connection they were developing. He shouldn't want that. Desire was one thing but that…that was something else.

He shook all those thoughts away as she slipped her hand into his elbow and he guided her toward the house. He was not going to let anything get in the way of having a good time tonight, both for show and for reality.

~

Evelina hadn't been entirely sure how this night would go, but as supper ended, she had to admit she'd actually had…*fun*. The courtesans in attendance were lovely, their protectors influential men but also seemingly decent. They were all kind to Vaughn, at any rate, and that was all she wanted. He had smiled a great deal as the meal went on. He was very handsome when he smiled, truly smiled and it went all the way to those stunning green eyes.

The man had also flirted with her shamelessly. He was always letting his hand linger on hers or locking eyes with her for a little too long. She found herself squirming in her seat all night, thinking about what would likely happen when the gathering was over and they were alone again.

"Shall the ladies retire to the parlor while the men share some port?" Matilda said as she and Lord Ravenscroft rose and smiled at each other.

"That's a fine idea," Lord Thistlebury said. "I haven't played a round of billiards with Blackburn for months and I am owed the chance to best him after the last routing."

"I'm rusty, so you might get your wish," Vaughn said as he helped Evelina from her chair.

The couples started from the room together, talking and smiling before they'd part ways in the hall. Vaughn took her hand and lifted it to his lips before he whispered, "Just a short time now and we can go back to my home and…negotiate. Be prepared, I think I shall want to negotiate all night."

She shook her head and swatted at his chest playfully. "You are terrible. But…I am looking forward to doing some negotiating."

They followed the others and Vaughn kissed her hand again before he let her trail off into the parlor where the other courtesans had gone before he hustled to catch up with the two gentlemen.

The two women were already at the sideboard, pouring wine and spirits. "Harriet is having a scotch, wicked thing," Matilda said as she turned to Evelina. "What will you have, my dear? I've a wonderful madeira."

"Madeira is my favorite, I'll have one with you," Evelina said, and walked to the fireplace. She smiled at the miniature of the marquess that was perched there. "You and Ravenscroft seem well matched," she said. "You've been with him for what…a month or two?"

"Oh yes, is he still making your toes curl in every room in this wonderful little house?" Harriet asked.

Matilda laughed and shook her head. "You two are terrible. And Harriet is spot on. It's wonderful when the sex is actually good, isn't it? Makes the entire endeavor much easier."

Evelina nodded along with Harriet, even though the question about toes curling made her treacherous mind go to Vaughn and whatever would happen tonight. She couldn't imagine he wouldn't be incredibly talented in bed. His kiss alone had set her off kilter and she'd noticed he was a fine dancer over the years. That was usually a good sign.

"Why won't you bother Evelina, anyway?" Matilda continued. "After all, she's the one everyone wants to know about."

"Oh Lord," Evelina said with a playful roll of her eyes. "Go on with it, then. Ask your questions."

They sat together, Evelina on the settee with Harriet beside her and Matilda across from them on a chair.

"It's all the talk of London, of course," Harriet said. "When you and Blackburn stepped out together at the opera…the shockwave could have brought down a building. With the very man whose wife *your* former lover stole?"

Evelina somehow managed not to flinch but didn't have to speak because now Matilda interrupted, "It's practically Shakespearian. What revenge!"

Evelina considered her next words carefully. Revenge was, of course, the way of their plan, but to say it would give it less power. She wanted this conversation to drift back through the ranks of both courtesans and those of influence, all the way until it burned the ears of Lady Blackburn and Southwater.

"Oh heavens, revenge is hardly the thing on my mind when there is such a man," she said, lightly fanning herself with the hand that didn't hold her drink. "Of course I knew he was *that woman's* husband, but that wasn't why we began. I'd always liked Vaughn, found him interesting, and of course he's handsome as sin."

"As sin," Matilda repeated with a little sigh. "Those eyes."

"That arse," Harriet added, and all three women laughed even though Evelina felt a shocking tremor of…was that jealousy? Great God, she was beginning to believe her own stories if *that* was cropping up.

"That everything," she said with a suggestive waggle of her eyebrows. "He is…magnificent. And good company. I couldn't be happier with my choice. In fact, there's part of me that thinks I should write poor Harry a thank-you letter. If he hadn't behaved so badly, I never would have had this chance."

There, that ought to do it. She'd waxed poetic *and* a bit vulgar. She'd implied Vaughn was a stunning lover and a good protector. And it had been easy to do so. Too easy, perhaps. After all, she did actually like spending time with him. He was witty when one got past the dour emotions of his loss and regret. And he was kind. She could talk about those things for hours and not have to make up a lie.

"Well, I must say I'm glad to hear it," Harriet said, and sipped her drink. "Obviously this whole divorce business is shocking beyond belief. I read every single word about it in the gossip rags."

Evelina felt her smile fade a fraction. "I suppose that's to be expected."

"Does he ever tell you anything about it?" Matilda pressed, and the light in both the women's eyes made Evelina's stomach turn. They both so wanted to take a strip of Vaughn's pain and carry it around like a badge that said they knew more than anyone else.

"It doesn't come up," she said softly. "We're too busy doing other things with our mouths than talk."

"Oh." Matilda sighed, and there was no hiding her disappointment at not getting any insider information.

Harriet was a little more subtle. "I'm glad to hear it, Evelina. After all, it sounds like the duke and his new paramour have moved on entirely, if the rumors of the reasons for their becoming public are true."

Evelina drew back. "What reasons?"

Some of the color left Harriet's cheeks and she exchanged a look with Matilda. "Oh, nothing."

"No, you cannot imply something so enflaming and then keep it to yourself." Her hands gripped at her sides, almost against her will. "What do you mean? Why would Harry—Southwater—and Lady Blackburn become public in their affair now?"

"I just heard a little rumor, nothing out in the open yet. But it might be that the duke and his lover may not be entirely…careful with their amour. That perhaps they have fear of a child and want to rush through the end of the divorce and marry as soon as possible in case his heir is about to become obvious."

The lovely supper Evelina had so enjoyed now rose to her throat and she swallowed back bile and tried to maintain her composure in the face of such horrific rumor. "And where did you hear such a thing?"

"Maids talking to maids, you know how it is." Harriet shifted. "It's probably all nonsense."

And at that, it might be. At the same time, courting the massive public disapproval of making their affair public had never seemed right to Evelina. But a rush to make the relationship palatable and use Harry's influence to finish the long process of severing the ties...

A potential child would be a very good reason for that. And so it might be true. Which meant that she now knew something devastating about Vaughn's countess. About her potentially giving another man the children he had so longed for. That was yet another heartbreak on a pile of heartbreak so high that it teetered precariously. If it fell...

Well, she worried it might crush the man in its wake. And she hated that she might be the one who'd have to set that fall in motion.

Vaughn didn't play billiards well that night. When the marquess and the earl teased him about it, he kept saying it was for lack of practice lately, but in truth, he kept thinking about Evie. She had been an amazing companion over the evening. She was intelligent enough to keep up sparkling conversation, she had a kindness to her that drew everyone around her into her sphere.

And she looked a treat in that dress. Sometimes he caught himself watching and wondering how long it would take to remove it. It was such a shocking thing. He hadn't played the rake since before he was married. He'd assumed that part of him was long dead and yet here he was, fantasizing in the middle of the billiard room.

Ravenscroft moved to stand beside him as they watched Thistlebury take a shot. "You look well, Blackburn. Better than I've seen you in months."

Vaughn stiffened. Here it was. If the ladies were known for their gossip when the men went to have port, he knew for a fact that the gentlemen were often just as bad.

"Well, I'm rejuvenated, it seems," he said.

Thistlebury glanced up from the table. "That's good. It's a rotten business, this. I still can't believe Southwater would behave in such a manner. His wealth and influence will save him in the end, but it's going to be a while before he goes into a room and everyone doesn't turn away."

Vaughn didn't respond. Everyone did the same to him, after all, and he hadn't fucked anyone's wife. But that was the way of the world.

"And what a reason to be rejuvenated!" Ravenscroft said, clearly wishing to change the uncomfortable subject as much as Vaughn did. "A Comerford Courtesan, that's a landing if I've ever seen one."

"Yes, she's lovely, isn't she?" Thistlebury took his shot at last. "I've always been with another lady when she was available, so I'm desperately jealous. Now, tell us…how is she? Are all the rumors true? And have you convinced her to bring her sister in on the fun?"

Vaughn turned his head slightly at the lewd suggestion. It wasn't the first time over the years that he'd heard someone suggest that a man could bed all three sisters at the same time. Now, though, he wasn't just disgusted at the idea, but he felt protective. How many times had Evie had to hear such a thing and hold her head up or smile even though it made her stomach turn?

"Evelina is charming in all ways," he said evenly. "And I wouldn't be so crass as to discuss private matters."

"Oh, come on," Thistlebury chuckled. "She's a courtesan. It's not like you're discussing your wife."

There was a moment where that sentence hung in the air between the three of them, a knife Vaughn didn't think Thistlebury had actually intended to throw and yet here it was.

"I won't be discussing *her* either," he said.

Ravenscroft cleared his throat at the uncomfortable silence and motioned toward the door. "Well, I'm sure the ladies are missing us. Why don't we return? We could play charades."

Vaughn pushed his shoulders back and inclined his head. "I'm certain we'd enjoy it."

He didn't wait for the marquess to leave the room, but led the way instead. He could hear the two men whispering behind him and ignored it as he entered the parlor where the ladies had been left.

When they came into the room, both Matilda and Harriet went to their gentlemen and Evie got up from her place on the settee. She smiled, but it didn't seem to fully reach her eyes, leaving him to wonder if the conversation in this room had been any more pleasant than the one in the other.

He moved to her, instead and she shook her head like she was waking from a dream before she lifted up on her tiptoes and pressed a kiss to his cheek. The feel of her eased a fraction of the sting and he smiled.

"Everything is well?" he asked so the others wouldn't hear.

She shifted and he could see even further discomfort. "It's…it's fine," she said, and touched his face briefly. "And you?"

"Eh, you know. They all want to wheedle their information out. But it was fine, as well."

"Good." She took his hand and they turned to face the others.

"Ravenscroft says that he suggested charades," Matilda said. "That would be a wonderful laugh, shall we?"

Evelina tucked herself in closer to Vaughn and pressed a hand to his chest. "I believe the earl and I must cry off. I haven't had him alone all day."

"Ah, the romantic beginnings," Harriet cooed. "Of course we understand."

They said their goodbyes and when he found himself before Thistlebury, the earl shook his hand a little longer than necessary. "My apologies, Blackburn. I wasn't thinking."

He inclined his head. "Don't trouble yourself, my lord. I'm accustomed to it. Good night."

Evelina drew him away then and they found their carriage already waiting thanks to the quick actions of the marquess as the farewells were being drawn out.

They both waved from the window as they were driven away

and then Vaughn collapsed back against the seat. She moved to his side of the carriage after a moment and took his hand between hers.

"What did Thistlebury say that made him apologize at the end?" she asked, her voice laced with tension.

He shrugged. "Oh, it was nothing. He made some offhand comment about my wife and froze the room. How was your evening with the ladies?"

"You'll be happy to hear I let them know we can't get enough of each other and you're amazing in bed. That ought to get back to any interested parties."

He laughed. "Well, I seem to have done the opposite. When they asked about you, I refused to tell them any details."

She tilted her head and for a moment he could see her surprise that he would be discreet. "I think it's rather romantic that you would demand privacy and *that* might be the worst thing to get back to those same interested parties."

"It seems we did the opposite of what is perceived to be a societal norm," he said.

She shrugged. "Oh, no. The courtesans always talk about the men. Compare notes. Compare cocks."

His mouth dropped open. "You do?"

"What do you think the courtesan network is?" she laughed. "It's not just gossip, but information about all aspects of the men we partner with. A courtesan might not refuse to affiliate with a gentleman who didn't know how to use his hips properly when he fucks, but at least she'd know what she was getting into so she wouldn't expect orgasms."

"Well, I hope I end up on the correct side of *that* discussion in the end," he said, and met her stare evenly. "Assuming you still wish to change the tenor of this arrangement."

Her breath hitched ever so slightly. "I do. Vaughn—"

Before she could say anything more, he wrapped an arm around her waist and tugged her flush against him. Her curves molded to his like they were meant to do so and she let out another shuddering sigh as his mouth took hers and he forgot every other thing in the world but this.

CHAPTER 11

Evelina had intended to speak to Vaughn about what she'd heard from the other courtesans. She hadn't wanted to, but she felt she was obligated to do so. But when his arms came around her and his mouth claimed hers, everything else in the world became fuzzy and unimportant. There was only sensation and oh, how she wanted that.

He was such a good kisser. Perhaps the best she'd ever experienced and that was saying something. He devoured and claimed, giving her no doubt to how much he wanted her without being too rough or, God forbid, drooly. And when his hands clenched at her back while he kissed her? She felt like she was falling, or perhaps floating like a feather was a better description. Just fluttering down on the softness of the desire that began to build in her.

He pulled away and there was the same stunned expression on his face that she felt on her own. "God, I needed this," he whispered. "How did I not know how much I needed this?"

His words made her think again of what the courtesans had told her about Lady Blackburn and Harry. It was the only thing that could bring her out of the haze. She needed to tell him. But not right now. Not when he actually looked happy for the first time in months.

Right now was the time for pleasure and nothing else.

"I'm very happy to give you what you need," she murmured, and returned her mouth to his as she pressed a hand to his chest. Even though the layers of clothing, she could feel his heart throbbing, feel the heat of him increasing. She glided her hand down, testing the shape of him through his clothing and grumbling with pleasure at the firm muscle hidden there.

When her hand dipped lower still, smoothing over his hip, he let out harsh gasp against her mouth. "Evie."

Her name was a warning and a plea all at once. She smiled against his mouth and cupped him, measuring the size of his half-hard cock. Well, he wasn't going to disappoint in *that* department, even if it was more how the man used what he had that brought pleasure.

Somehow she doubted he could be anything but magical.

She stroked his length, memorizing how his breath hitched as he went from half-hard to fully hard in a few strokes. She wanted this man freed from his trousers. She wanted him in her mouth. She wanted him buried inside of her, bruising her with his fingers as she shattered around him.

She wanted him where she could take her time and fully enjoy him.

The thought had scarcely crossed her mind when they turned onto her drive and slowed to a stop before Arabella's old home. The light from the windows gave a little more illumination in the dark of the carriage and she looked up at him.

"Come upstairs with me, Vaughn."

"I couldn't deny you if there were wild horses trying to drag me away," he said, and reached past her to open the door. "Lead the way."

She let the footman help her down and when Vaughn joined her she took his hand, threading her fingers through his, and guided them up to the door. Parsons opened it just as they reached it. "Welcome back, Miss Comerford, my lord. May I offer you any—"

"Nothing at all, Parsons," she interrupted as she continued to tug Vaughn through the foyer. "I have everything I need right here."

Vaughn chuckled as they started up the stairs together. "In some households that would cause a scandal."

"There's no room for scandal in the home of courtesans," she said with a glance over her shoulder as they reached the big bedroom at the end of the hall. "The servants are accustomed to such things."

"I suppose they must be," he said, and then stopped as they entered chamber.

She knew what he saw. The room was enormous, done in sensual wine hues and velvet adornments. The bed was big enough for three if not four lovers to tangle in pleasure and the fire cast an ethereal glow over the bed.

"You…sleep here?"

She laughed. "Well, not every night. This was Arabella's chamber, but once she went to the new house with Silas, she told me I should take it over. Many nights I sleep in my old room, but sometimes I come in here and try to remind myself I'm a courtesan and a seductress."

He turned to face her and his gaze was hooded. "I can remind you of that if you'd like."

Her hands trembled as she wrapped her arms around his neck. "I'd very much like that."

His mouth was on her again, gentle but quickly giving way to passionate and more forceful. He backed her toward that wonderful bed, his hands drifting from her waist and around to cup her backside and lift her more firmly against him. She couldn't help the moan that ricocheted between them when he did so. His mouth moved away from hers with a chuckle and he dragged his lips to her jawline, feathering light kisses along down to her throat.

She dropped her head back and shivered at the electric pleasure he was creating with such simple touches.

"And now to take this off," he said, and his hands found the back of her gown where the line of buttons danced along her spine. She shook her head.

"They aren't real."

"What isn't real?" he murmured.

"The buttons."

He stopped and then brushed the back of her gown as if testing the veracity of the statement. "Why?"

There was a loaded question and a more loaded answer that she had no intention of giving. Not tonight. Instead she pushed out of his arms and stepped back.

"A courtesan may need to dress or undress herself," she explained. "And there's something so wicked, isn't there, about knowing the secret that this gown…" She found the hidden bow within the folds of fabric. "…is held together…" She flicked the bow open and unhooked a few additional hidden spots. "…by little more than a hope and a prayer."

As she said it she let the silk fall away in an artful pool at her feet. She didn't wear undergarments, so she was entirely naked before this man save for slippers and her stockings. It was curious how she'd been a courtesan since she was nineteen but in that moment she felt…vulnerable.

Vaughn stared at her from head to toe, then he swallowed hard and moved toward her. "Funny, because most of my recent hopes and prayers were you standing before me exactly as you are."

"Then I suppose it's time to let the fantasy become reality." She took his hand and placed it against her naked breast.

He let out that same possessive growl he'd given in the carriage before he kissed her the first time and her body clenched in antici-pation of what would happen next.

He didn't disappoint. He fully cupped the breast she had offered, stroking the pad of his thumb over her rapidly hardening nipple.

Waves of pleasure spread through her at that intimate touch and she lifted against him.

"You're so soft," he mused. "So exquisitely soft. And I wonder what you taste like."

She lifted her mouth and he took it yet again, delving deeper this time, washing her away on rapidly increasing waves that would not be calmed by anything but passion and pleasure.

"Mint," he whispered as their mouths parted. "Madeira."

He drew his mouth down again, across her neck, lower to her collarbone, then just skimmed across the top swell of her breasts. "Flowers," he said. "A little salt."

"Vaughn," she murmured, digging her hands into his hair and loving how the crisp locks curled around her fingers.

He glanced up at her and there was something filled with command that entered his expression. Like he'd just remembered how much power he wielded. She couldn't help but shiver at the sight of it as he said, "You aren't going to rush this."

"I wouldn't try," she promised.

"Now to taste the next, I think you should be seated. On the bed?"

She nodded and climbed onto the high mattress. She did it artfully, of course, giving him flashes of her sex as she crawled to the pillows and settled onto her back. She spread her legs and rested a hand between them, hissing pleasure at the pressure of her own hand even though she hadn't done anything. *That* was how excited he made her and it had been a very, very long time since that had happened. In that moment she realized how much she'd missed wicked anticipation.

She expected him to come to her, cover her, perhaps even take her fast and hard and over too soon. Instead he winked at her, as wicked as any gentleman could be, and shrugged out of his jacket. He tossed it aside and went to work on his cravat, unwinding it slowly before he let it fall with the jacket. She sat up a little, working her fingers over herself absently as he moved to remove the shirt.

She truly wanted to see what was under all that propriety. A few times when she'd touched him, she'd felt the shape of him, unexpectedly toned and muscled for a man of his station, but imagination and reality were often very different things.

He tugged the shirt over his head and she caught her breath. That body...it was a sin that he covered it. He should have roamed around shirtless all day long, just letting hungry ladies and gentlemen enjoy the view. He had broad shoulders defined by the curves of muscle and the arches of his collarbone. They tapered into trim hips and lightly defined abdominal muscles. And his arms. Lordy, his arms. Forearms corded with definition and biceps rippling when he slid his hands to his trouser buttons and lowered his fall front.

"Oh," she gasped, hating herself for being so missish and yet unable to be anything but because the cock was just as stunning and exciting as the rest he'd revealed. He was bigger than Harry, thick, and in his excitement his member curled toward his belly.

"I'll take that *oh* as a compliment," he teased as he pressed his hands to the bottom of the big bed and then began a slow crawl toward her.

He bent his head and rubbed the smoothness of his cheek against her calf, he edged up farther and cupped her knees with both hands, pushing them wider. She removed her fingers from between her thighs and stared as he settled on his stomach between them.

"Oh," he said with a wink up at her. "And *that* is most definitely a compliment."

She laughed somehow, even with her breath nonexistent and her heart throbbing. She felt like she'd spun around a few too many times and now she was dizzy and that sensation didn't get any better when he pressed his hands between her legs and gently peeled her open.

"And now what will you taste like here?" he mused, bending his head to press a closed-mouthed kiss to the quivering lips of her quim. "Earthy? Sweet?" He nuzzled her and she arched a little toward him.

He let his tongue stroke her once, twice, enjoying the full length of her slit with another of those possessive growls he sometimes made when they touched. The ones that made her insides turn to jelly in a way they normally didn't.

"Oh no, this flavor is just Evelina," he whispered. "Gorgeously Evelina."

She moaned and he smiled against her flesh before he delved into licking her without talking anymore. And oh, but he was magnificent. Unlike some of the men who had done this over the years, he seemed to truly enjoy tasting her. He was firm and certain with the strokes of his tongue and the way he sucked her clitoris to tease and torment.

He also seemed in no hurry. This wasn't just some quick way to make her wet for him, he was driving her toward release, drawing her step by step as the pleasure notched up bit by bit. She sank into the sensation of his tongue stroking over her, forgetting everything else but the ache that built inside of her. She gripped the coverlet with both hands, rising to meet him, reaching for every drop of desire.

Her legs shook, her heart throbbed, her moans echoed around the room as the pleasure peaked and then she fell over the edge of it and spiraled out of control. She dug her hands into his hair, holding him to her as she thrust her hips in wild time to the pulsating release that seemed to give her wings.

He gave her no quarter as she soared, continuing his torment until her voice was hoarse and her muscle sore from contracting in harsh, continued pleasure. It was only when she went limp, her only movements a few twitches here and there, that he lifted his head. He licked his lips like a satisfied cat and then continued his journey up the length of her body.

He settled herself over her sated frame and dropped his mouth to hers. She groaned, arms coming up around his neck, tilting her head so she could taste every bit of him, of herself and the pleasure he had drawn from her.

"I think you better finish what you started, my lord," she whispered, only barely parting her lips from his. "Because I need more."

He dug his hands into her hair, his kiss growing wilder and deeper. She wedged a hand between them and shifted, aligning that hard cock to her very wet entrance. He took her in one long, heavy stroke and she cried out against him at the lush sensation of being so filled.

"Fuck," he grunted, resting his head on her shoulder, his breath short and hard.

He rotated his hips and she jolted, rising to meet him in the most ancient dance of all time. He pulled his head back and they watched each other as he took her slow stroke by slow stroke, grinding against her aching clitoris every time their hips met.

She had always been a woman to find her pleasure easily, but this was something different. An exquisite sensitivity that ripped her control away and had her wailing out his name within a few expert strokes. When she gripped him with the second orgasm, the tendons in his neck tightened, he reared back more powerfully and the slap of their bodies echoed in the room.

She could see him losing control, feel him quake as his own orgasm approached. She lifted, matching his strokes beneath him, in wonder of the movement of him, the way he strained and his breath grew harsh.

And when he came? It was with a gulping cry before he pulled from her body and stroked himself to completion. The heat of him splashed on her thighs and she arched her back to lift toward him.

He collapsed over her, kissing her neck, her shoulders. She wrapped her arms and legs around him, reveling in his weight and for a little while in the quiet of that big bed, nothing mattered but the absolute shattering power of what they had just shared. Even if nothing else had been resolved at all.

Vaughn felt like he was coming from a fog as he lay with Evelina in his arms. He stroked his fingers through her hair, memorizing the way her body felt tucked against his, her hands moving over his chest in little patterns.

There had been pleasure before, but that…*that* had been different. Singular. And he felt both amazed by that feeling and also deeply guilty for it. He'd been married. In all technicality, he still was, even if his wife was most definitely not acting like it. But shouldn't he have felt this euphoric amazement with her, not Evelina?

"Oh, that look won't do," Evelina said, pressing a kiss to his collarbone. "You can't set a person on fire and then just float off in your mind, Vaughn. It's very bad form."

He laughed and was brought back to her, just as she wished him to be. "I suppose my thoughts *are* very scattered and you're to blame."

"Oh good. I do love to scramble a man's thoughts like morning eggs with my prowess. I'll make a notch on the bedpost to celebrate."

They smiled at each other and then he sighed. "I do wonder what this means for us. What now?"

She arched a brow and then leaned up on her elbow. "Didn't you ever have a mistress before, Blackburn?"

He nodded. "Of course, but this is diff—" He cut himself off. He couldn't say that. Wouldn't say it at any rate. He tried again. "We didn't exactly start this arrangement in the normal way, did we?"

"No," she said. "We didn't. But there's not really anything difficult to it, is there? You wanted to pretend an affair to tweak our former lovers. This will simply become a *real* affair and we'll still flaunt it."

"Is there a risk to that? Of everything becoming…confused?"

She tilted her head. "What is there to confuse? Sex isn't the same as emotion. If we want to enjoy each other, there's no reason that it has to go beyond that."

He nodded slowly. She was being entirely reasonable, of course. And if he felt a little disappointed in that pragmatism, it was probably because he had equated sex with love...or at least affection... since his marriage. And since Florence had demanded a divorce, he hadn't really wanted pleasure. Until Evie.

"The only questions we really must answer are the same ones all lovers must establish in a situation like this: How often would you like to do this and is there anything you don't want to do?"

"As far not wanting to do anything, I can't think of anything specific. Perhaps we can discover those things as we go." He let his hand trail along her bare sides. "And as for how often...well, as often as you'll let me touch you, Evie. I don't think I'll tire of this, of you, any time soon."

She smiled softly and shifted, straddling him in one smooth movement. She rocked back, letting his cock slide along her wet length as she balanced herself on his chest with both hands.

"Neither will I." She rocked back again and this time maneuvered so that he slid into her an inch. The tight heat of her enveloped him fully on the second stroke and he moaned as he reached up to cup her hips.

She rode him then, a glorious siren whose dark hair bobbed around her shoulders and back as she ground herself against him. And as he lost himself in her, in the pleasure, in the heat of this, the rest fell away and it was a welcome oblivion.

CHAPTER 12

I t had been two days since they'd first made love at her home. And though they'd moved to his estate at some point, other than that Vaughn had barely come up for air. It had been a long time since he'd been so tangled with a lover, unable to do anything but want to touch her, but Evie inspired that and he was vastly content to spend hours in her bed or his, exploring her body and every way he could make her twist and moan.

The door to the breakfast room opened and he blinked away the thoughts as he watched the woman, herself, enter. It was far too late for breakfast, of course. Almost noon, because it had taken them two hours to manage to get out of his bed this morning and make their way down.

"Good morning," he said, grasping the hand she offered to him and kissing her knuckles lightly. "I like your hair that way."

She reached up to touch the loosely bound locks and blushed very prettily. He did love to make her blush. "Thank you."

"There's whatever the poor staff could manage for a spread at this hour." He motioned to the sideboard and went back to his paper. His gaze flitted over the gossip section, blind items about those in Society, and smiled as he recognized one about himself.

Not about the divorce, but about his new mistress. Good. That was the point of this exercise.

Well, it didn't feel exactly like the point anymore, but he was simply caught up in the throughs of passion. When that faded, this would be left and it would help.

Evie took a seat beside him and began to pull apart the flaky layers of his cook's famous vanilla custard croissant. She licked a little of the custard from her thumb and he shook his head.

"We're not going to make it out of the bed long if you keep doing that," he said with a laugh.

She met his gaze and licked the same thumb again, this time while making eye contact, but then she smiled. "I am innocently eating my food, my lord. You really must learn a little self-control."

"Must I?" he asked, and pushed the paper away.

He sipped his tea as she went back to eating. This all felt so… easy. It had never been easy with Florence. Their marriage had been arranged, she'd never been comfortable when they were alone, always surrounding them with friends and family. He realized now in retrospect that it was a way to keep him and whatever feelings he felt for her at arm's length.

"Oh, your face just went very dark, that won't do," Evie said, and covered his hand with hers. "You know, it's a lovely day and you're so close to Hyde Park. Why don't we walk over and we can sit in the glorious sunshine on a blanket together and read from the Cook biography?"

"The one you stole from my bedside table the moment you entered my chamber for the first time?" he teased. "Little thief."

"You've caught me. My entire purpose in this arrangement was to obtain access to your room so I might take the book." She held up her hands. "You may take me away, lock me up for good."

There was such a brightness to her as she teased that he felt drawn to her. It was positively magnetic, unavoidable. He leaned in, cupped her cheek and said, "It's not a bad idea, having you all to myself." He kissed her before she could respond and tasted the vanilla custard on her tongue. Just as sweet as she was and he licked his lips as they parted. "What did you ask me? My mind is suddenly addled by a certain someone."

"Hyde Park," she said, her breath short. "Sitting on a blanket. Reading about Cook."

"Oh. Yes. That would be lovely. Finish your breakfast and we can go straight away since it's so late."

She nodded and the rest of the meal was shared in contented silence. He gave over half the paper, she read her bits and he continued with his own. If she saw the blind item about them, she gave no indication. Eventually, she pushed her plate away and smiled. "All ready."

"Excellent." He got up and offered her an arm. She took it and together they exited the breakfast room and down the hall. Langley met them in the foyer.

"May I get your carriage, my lord?"

"No, Langley, we're walking to the park."

"If it's not too much trouble, perhaps a blanket to sit on?" Evelina asked. "And we wished to take the biography on his lordship's bedside table, but I could fetch that."

"No, miss. I don't mind getting those things." Langley left them and was back in what felt like no time at all, a folded blanket and the book in his arms.

He handed them over to Vaughn. "Thank you. I assume we'll be a few hours, so perhaps tea around four?"

"Of course. Enjoy yourselves."

Vaughn inclined his head as he led Evie outside and into the rare sparkling sunshine of a late summer's day. He breathed in the air as he realized he had been locking *himself* away so often in the last few months that this brief sojourn out felt like freedom.

They took their time as they made their way down the lane toward the big park near the Thames, in no rush to see or be seen, even if that would be the result of this exercise.

"Your butler is very kind," Evie said at last. "Sometimes the servants don't approve when a man brings his mistress to his official home."

He wrinkled his brow. "Don't they? Well, Langley has been with me for a decade, he's a good one. I've never known him to be rude to anyone in his life."

"But he must…he must have feelings about the whole situation with Lady Blackburn."

He tensed. They hadn't spoken much about Southwater or Florence since they became lovers. It had been a nice respite, but this reminder brought him back to reality. "I'm sure he must. I'm not so naïve as to believe this isn't being discussed at length below-stairs. But I seem to have somehow won the loyalty of the servants, if nothing else in this separation."

"I think you were owed it," she said with a small frown. "And I'm glad you have it. At any rate, I appreciate the kindness. It makes my time in your home all the more comfortable."

"Did Southwater's servants approve of you?" he asked.

Her slightly pinched expression revealed all. "He…he didn't allow me into his house here in London. We always met at my—" She cut herself off with a quiet curse. "We met at the house he let me."

"The one where he now fucks my wife," Vaughn said softly.

"Yes." She shrugged. "I did go to his country estate for a week or two each summer while we were together. I liked it there, but I do admit the servants were cold. Their disapproval was evident."

"And he didn't speak to them about it?" Vaughn asked. "He didn't rush to your defense?"

She turned her head as if that question had struck a nerve and he felt her stiffen. She swallowed before she spoke. "He did not."

"Well, that's bollocks," he said with a shake of his head. "If any of my servants are ever rude to you, or my friends or anyone else while we're in this arrangement, I want you to tell me and I'll handle it."

Her lips parted slightly as she stopped on the path and turned toward him. "You—you would do that? Even though this isn't real?"

He stared into those dark brown eyes, lost himself a moment and then nodded. "I would. But I think we're past the arrangement not being real, considering I was perched between your thighs this morning, you gripping my hair and calling out for deities I've never even heard of."

Some of the tension left her expression and she laughed as they started into the park together. "You are terrible, Vaughn."

"I am, I really am. The most secretly wicked earl in all of London, no doubt."

"Oh, *secretly* wicked," she mused. "I like that. That means all that wickedness only belongs to me. I mean, for now. For a while."

He was about to retort when he caught a glimpse of someone over her shoulder. All thoughts and teasing ceased and the universe became entirely focused onto one person.

It was Florence. She wasn't with Southwater this time, but with her younger sister, Honora. The two women were standing on the grass together, watching out toward the river, but then Florence looked toward him and for the briefest of moments their eyes met.

"Vaughn." He blinked at the sound of Evie's voice saying his name and looked back toward her. She looked at him and then toward Florence and her expression softened with understanding. "This is unexpected, though part of us coming out was to be seen, yes?"

"I suppose it was," he agreed, wishing his voice didn't sound so raw. He glanced at his soon-to-be former wife again. She was not looking directly at him anymore, but she occasionally flitted her gaze in his direction.

And that wicked part he'd been teasing about with Evie, the one that he had pushed down and hidden over the years, returned to the surface. He looked at Evelina and smiled. "Miss Comerford, would you like to make a scene?"

~

Evelina was doing her level best not to react in any way to Vaughn's question. Her reason for coming here hadn't been this, but to truly spend a little time together that didn't involve tangled bodies and sweat-slicked sheets. But now it had turned back to reality and revenge. A stark reminder that sex was sex, but Vaughn still wanted to use Evelina for his own purposes.

She couldn't get that confused just because they now included orgasms and laughter in their arrangement.

"I'm never opposed to making a scene, Blackburn," she said with a forced smile. "Why don't we put our blanket here where we'll be sure to be in the correct sightline?"

His face lit up and he winked at her as he spread the blanket on the grass. She sat down, artfully arranging her skirt to fan out around her. Then she beckoned him to join her. He did so, taking a seat beside her.

"Oh no, my lord. If you truly want to make a scene, I think your very handsome head must go in my lap."

His eyes widened. "Er, here?"

She rolled her own eyes in response. "You know I don't mean face down, you cad."

He flashed her that quick grin and settled onto his back on the blanket, his head resting against her thighs. She looked down into that truly beautiful face and forced herself not to have a full-body shiver. Instead she began to thread her fingers through his thick hair.

"Oh, that's nice," he said, and his eyes shut. "We should come to the park and make a scene twice a week."

He was teasing, but she didn't smile. She found it was far too difficult to do so now that reality was back. All of it, including the secret she might know about the countess. The one she hadn't the heart to tell him when she was diving into passion and pleasure and locking out everything else. But here in the park wasn't the place to tell him about Florence.

She cleared her throat. "I've never met a man who didn't like to be petted like a dog."

He snorted at the quip but didn't open his eyes. "That's me. Your loyal bird dog. And you would be a sleek cat whose affection one must earn."

"But once one does, I hope it's worth the trouble."

Now his eyes did open and the green depths were truly impossible to look away from. "Very much worth the trouble."

She looked up to break the spell and found that Lady Blackburn was watching them. The countess *was* very pretty, with her perfectly quaffed blonde hair and a dark blue dress that was beautifully made from what looked like a gorgeous damask silk. At present, though, her lips were pinched. Even from a distance her frown was obvious. She shook her head and looked away as she realized Evelina was watching her.

"Oh, she doesn't like this," she said softly.

He lifted his head slightly. "No?"

She shook her head and glanced at the woman again. "She's not looking anymore, but her companion keeps glancing this way and folding and unfolding her arms."

"That's her sister, Honora. They've always been very close. Florence has financially supported her and her n'er-do-well of a husband a great deal over the years. With all the scandal, she must be calling in those favors."

Evelina blinked. "Oh. *Oh.*"

"Why oh?" he asked.

"It's silly, but I suppose I never think of *them* having family."

"Them?" he repeated, his tone laced with confusion.

She glanced again at the pair. Lady Blackburn's sister tossed her hair and snapped her gaze away and the two put their heads together for what looked like irritated chatter. Good. Let them fuss and worry after what that woman had done to Vaughn.

"All those proper ladies who are far too good for the likes of us. Of women like me or *my* sisters. The ones who judge us for the path we had to take to survive what they couldn't even imagine."

"Evelina—" he began, his tone softer.

She interrupted him, partly because she had information to convey and partly because she didn't want to be placated or pitied. "Lady Blackburn has stormed off to the path now though her sister remains and is just glaring at us."

"Wouldn't your sister do the same if she was watching someone you once cared for with a new love?" he asked.

She jerked her stare back to his face. "We aren't loves," she corrected. "And if Arabella saw Harry out with your wife, she might just scratch her eyes out. Or, more likely, *his*."

He gave just the flicker of a smile. "She's protective."

"Yes. She always was, before we left home and after. Even now." She smiled as she thought of Arabella. Her sister had nearly died for her and for Julia. But she was safe now. Happy. And Evelina's heart soared when she thought of it.

"I've met her," he said. "Briefly, years ago when she was still with Kentwood."

She smiled a little. "He gave her the house, you know. What was he...a marquess?"

His brow wrinkled. "A duke, actually. You don't recall?"

"They're not important. And once they're gone, it's better to forget."

"Even Southwater?"

She drew in a shaky breath. "I wish I could forget Harry," she admitted, and was frustrated that tears filled her eyes and her voice broke just a fraction. All those emotions she so tried to control were right at the surface and she hated revealing them to anyone.

Vaughn touched her face gently. "You will. Because one day you'll realize he wasn't fit to shine your shoe. That if he held even a sliver of your heart, *he* was the fortunate one, not you."

"Those are pretty words," she said.

"I mean them," he insisted. "I've been close to you for only a few weeks, but you are a remarkable woman."

She swallowed hard before she bent her head. He lifted to meet her and they kissed. It was brief, it didn't spiral into passion, but there was something so powerful in that public, gentle display. When they parted she was a little dizzy from it.

"Oh," she said as she became aware of her surroundings again. "Both Lady Blackburn and her sister are fully gone."

He started, almost as if he'd forgotten they were doing all this to annoy his wife. "Well, I suppose we did what was needed."

She expected him to push out of her lap and move on with their day, but instead he drew the biography they'd been stealing back and forth between each other from the inside pocket of his jacket and handed it up to her.

"Now, when I last left off he was just entering the islands of New Zealand."

"Oh, yes, I was almost there," she said, and took the book. "May I start a few pages beforehand?"

"Of course." He settled his head back into her lap and she began to read. But even as she lost herself to the adventures of the captain, she tried to remind herself how she needed to pull herself back from any emotions this man might engender in her. She needed to remember how to be a courtesan.

After all, it wouldn't do to make the same mistake twice.

CHAPTER 13

Mattigan's Bookshop was one of Vaughn's favorite places in the city, so much so that he almost didn't regret parting ways with Evie earlier in the day. They'd agreed to go about their regular business for a day or two. Let themselves recover from the marathon of pleasure. He actually felt sore from it and it was delicious.

He pushed the wicked thoughts away and went back to perusing the shelves. As he picked up books, he found himself in the Gothic Romance area. Evelina had mentioned her love of the genre a few times as they discussed and shared their reading habits. He tilted his head to look at the titles. She'd read that one. And that one. She'd discussed that one at length with him because he'd also very much enjoyed it.

He came around to the end of the shelf and looked toward the shop owner at his raised counter. "Mr. Mattigan, do you have any suggestions for new gothics? Or perhaps something that's harder to find? I'm looking for a gift for a special friend."

The shopkeep's eyes lit up at the question, just as it always did when one asked him about books. He was a delightful man, full of verve and intelligence and never disparaged any genre on his vast shelves. "Let me think." He pondered a moment. "You know, Mr. Kressley just released a new one last week and it's been flying off the shelves."

"I didn't see it there," Vaughn said, and stepped toward the counter. "I don't suppose you have one hidden?"

Mattigan smiled slightly. "For you, my lord?" He bent and when he straightened up he had a book in his hand. "I was holding this, but you're such a good customer, I know it will have a fine home with you."

"Ah, good man! That's wonderful. Wrap it up and I may come to you with more shortly."

"Of course, my lord. Excellent."

Vaughn left the man to do his business and returned to the shelves with a vigor in his step. He knew for certain that Evelina had been far too busy the last week to perhaps even know about this latest release of an author they had discussed several times. She had the theory that the writer was actually a woman, publishing under a pseudonym. Vaughn knew she would be thrilled when he presented the gift to her.

"Shopping for a *friend*, are we, Lord Blackburn?"

Vaughn turned, ready to encounter some gossipy person trying to invade his privacy and gather information. But to his surprise, it was Evelina's sister Arabella who was standing on the opposite side of the aisle, not a pushy stranger.

"Miss Comerford—er, Mrs. Windham," he said, stepping toward her. "I didn't realize you were in the shop."

He stared at her, for he could see all the features she shared with Evelina on her lovely face. Only they didn't draw him the same way. Her eyes were different, too, a dark blue where Evie's were such a rich brown.

"Nor did I until I heard you speaking to Mr. Mattigan," she said. "I know we've met before, but it was a very long time ago, I think."

She held out her hand and he took it to shake. She had a firm handshake and she partnered it with an even stare that made him feel like he was being assessed. But of course he would be. He'd no doubt Mrs. Windham was fully aware of not only his affair with Evie, but of the true nature of it. She was so close to her sisters, she certainly would have told them.

"It's nice to see you again," he said.

"And so you've bought Kressley's latest for Evie, it seems," Mrs. Windham said with a little smile that softened her expression considerably.

"I have," he admitted. "I know she's an admirer of his work. Or hers, if her theory is to be believed."

Mrs. Windham laughed. "I think it's a good theory, considering how well the female characters are written."

"I don't disagree. Are you also a fan of gothic romance?"

"Not as much as my sisters," Mrs. Windham said. "But I do enjoy them, yes. And if you're giving her that one it means I'll eventually get to read it, too, so I doubly approve of the gift."

He tilted his head. "And do you approve of everything else?"

Her brows lifted. "How very direct of you, my lord. Fascinating. Do you actually have concern about if I approve of your...arrangement with my sister?"

"Not for myself, but she cares for you and your youngest sister a great deal, it's evident in every way she speaks of you. So *that* matters to me."

Something in her expression shifted at that, softened. "Good. She deserves someone to care about her well-being this time. Even if it is...*temporary*, shall we say."

"I agree." He pursed his lips. "Evie deserves a great deal more than that. Certainly more than what she was given. She...she told me about the situation with your father. That Southwater wouldn't assist in finding you when you were taken. I was incensed on her behalf and on yours. And I'm happy beyond words that you weren't harmed, Mrs. Windham."

"Arabella. I insist," she said with a wave of an elegant hand. "I must say I'm surprised she told you that."

"Upset?"

"No. Evelina has her own feelings about that night, I'm sure. It's just that she doesn't speak of them very often, not even to me or to Julia. I suppose it's her way of protecting us from her pain."

"Then I'm happy to be an outlet if she has no other."

He shifted because he found that was true. And also that he felt a sense of…pride that she would feel safe enough to talk to him about something she kept close with others. It meant a great deal to be that for someone.

"Yes," Arabella mused. "My lord, we are having a little gathering tonight at my home. It will be my sisters, Silas and our aunt Caroline Banfield. Won't you join us?"

He started. "Invited to a family gathering?"

She nodded. "If you're interested."

"I am," he said. "That would be wonderful."

"Very good." She smiled at him and there was a warmth to it that hadn't been there before. "Join us at seven? I'll send over the address this afternoon."

"I'll be there."

"And now I must be off," she said. "Silas is expecting me and I don't disappoint him. Good afternoon, my lord."

He inclined his head. "Arabella."

She moved away, speaking briefly to Mr. Mattigan, with the shopkeeper's laughter booming from whatever she'd said to him on the way out. In her wake, she left a fragrant cloud of jasmine and vanilla and a little confusion. Based on the nature of their relationship, Vaughn hadn't thought he'd even be formally introduced by Evie to the other infamous Comerford sisters. He certainly hadn't thought he'd be included in one of their family gatherings. He found himself excited by the idea, though. To see Evie in an environment that wasn't about courtesans and secrets? He very much looked forward to discovering if there were layers to her that he hadn't seen.

Even though getting closer to her wasn't part of their arrangement. But things changed. They already had once. What harm could there be in it?

~

"And so you invited him?" Evie burst out as she paced Arabella's parlor, drink in her shaking hand and heart throbbing with unexpected excitement and anxiety.

Arabella watched her from a position on the settee, tucked into Silas's side. She didn't even have the decency to look chagrined. "Why wouldn't I?"

"Because we *never* include protectors in family supper," Evelina snapped. She looked toward Julia and her aunt in the hopes they would support her reaction. Neither seemed to do so.

"*I'm* invited to family supper," Silas said.

"Oh, you're not a protector! You're Arabella's husband. You know it's not the same."

Silas glanced at Arabella. "It's not the same," he said.

Arabella shrugged. "It felt the same when you and I were running all around London, doing very naughty things and upsetting all the apple carts."

"Oh, do shut up, both of you," Evelina gasped, and glared at them when they laughed together. "Why didn't you tell me earlier, at least?"

"Because I didn't think it would cause so much upset," Arabella responded, and got up to cross to her. "Gracious, you'd think I'd invited the queen to supper and you were in your nightclothes."

Julia nodded. "You really are very pink, dearest. It cannot just be the late notice."

Evelina took a few long breaths. Vaughn would be there soon, she had to pull herself together before then. And also because it was obvious she was revealing far too much not only to her family, but to herself. Why *was* she so worked up over Vaughn being there? Harry had visited with her sisters many times. Not with her aunt, but in the last few months Caroline had been far more involved in their lives, even the ones they'd once kept separate from her.

"I don't know why," she said softly, all the pepper going out of her. "I just—I just wasn't prepared to see him."

Arabella took her hands gently. "He isn't cruel to you, is he, Evie?"

"No!" she burst out. "No, he's infinitely kind."

"Good." Arabella let out her breath. "I didn't get that sense, but I never did before, either."

Evelina winced. Arabella was referring to a past protector who had been abusive to Evelina. One she tried to never think about. To put away where she wouldn't be troubled by the memories.

Julia got up and joined them. "If it's not cruelty, what is it?"

"It's just…it's not the same, is it?" she said. "He's *not* my protector, not truly. No matter what is happening between us in bed, it's not—it's not real. And to bring him into this part of my life, it only confuses things."

"Only if they have the potential to truly be confused," Arabella said. "Do they?"

Evelina didn't get the chance to respond, for Barnaby appeared in the parlor doorway. "The Earl of Blackburn, Mr. and Mrs. Windham."

Evelina's heart leapt and she feared that answered Arabella's question even before she'd seen Vaughn. When he walked through the door, ridiculously handsome in his evening attire, every crisp line of him in place, she almost stopped breathing. He found her across the room and his expression lit up.

Silas was already crossing to him, hand extended. "Blackburn," he said as the two men shook. "Fine to see you."

She watched them interact, hardly listening to the words exchanged. She watched him wish Arabella a good evening. Her sister gave her a hard look, like she was expecting her to join in, but she couldn't. It was physically impossible somehow.

So, frozen, she watched Arabella introduce him to their aunt and then Julia. He was friendly to both, treating them as equals even though men of their station would normally see Caroline as proper and Julia as something lesser. Not this man.

At last, he broke from her family and came to her. The rest stepped aside so they could have a private moment. "Evie," he said, taking her hand.

She swallowed, forcing her mouth to formulate words. "My lord."

His brows lifted. "So very formal," he said softly.

She shook her head. "Vaughn," she corrected herself. "I'm sorry, I'm just a little flummoxed to have you here."

"Oh," he said. "I'm sorry, I thought Arabella would tell you."

"She did. About ten minutes ago," she said, and now she laughed.

He didn't. "I'm sorry, Evelina. If I've intruded into a space where I'm not welcome-"

"Oh, they welcome you," she insisted.

He shook his head. "I wasn't talking about *them*."

She blinked up at him and in that moment all she could wonder was how his wife could be so foolish as to step away from him. How could anyone not want him, both for his beauty and his passion, but also because he was such a *good* man? Those were rare enough in the world. When one found one, they were something to be kept. Treasured.

"Evie? Should I go?"

She blinked as she realized he was expecting a response. "No. No, I'm *happy* to have you here." She squeezed his hand. "It will be great fun."

She knew that would be true. Her sisters would ensure it and Silas and Caroline would only multiply it. But she still found herself nervous. Thanks to Arabella's interference, this arrangement's hue had been altered. They were no longer merely partners in the annoyance of their former lovers. They were no longer simply lovers. This was yet another escalation into closeness.

"What will you have, Blackburn?" Silas asked as he moved to the sideboard. "I've a fine whisky that Arabella probably purchased from some smuggler."

Arabella laughed and her eyes lit up as she looked at her husband. "I'm not going to say you're wrong." She winked at Vaughn. "I was once a…a *friend* of a gentleman who made such arrangements and he's still kind enough to pass along a few bottles."

Evelina could see Vaughn was surprised by that admission and by the fact Silas just laughed and showed no jealousy. That was one of the things Evelina liked most about her brother-in-law. He never tried to stifle her sister's bright spirit and he never exhibited even a hint of annoyance at her past life.

"Well, I shall have whisky then," Vaughn said with a chuckle before he squeezed Evelina's hand and moved toward Silas. Silas poured the liquor and handed over the bottle to Vaughn so he could examine it. They stood together, chatting about the whisky and drinking it while they made orgasmic sounds of pure pleasure.

Evelina jolted as Caroline stepped up next to her and slid an arm through hers. Her aunt smiled at her. "Blackburn seems a good fit for Silas. He said they knew each other in school, didn't he?"

She nodded and continued to watch the men. Silas was often standoffish with men of rank—as a bastard he was as wary of them as courtesans occasionally had to be. But her aunt was correct that here he looked comfortable. For a brief moment, she could see a path where this could happen often. Vaughn could fit into their family circle with little effort.

Strange that she'd never fully pictured Harry in that circle. He had barely tolerated her family. When Silas had entered the picture, he'd said nasty things about him, talking about his bastard blood. And he'd *hated* the family gatherings and cried off from them even when she'd dared invite him and violate the *no protectors* rule.

She shook off those thoughts, they were only silly and dangerous.

"Yes, Eton, before Silas was kicked out, if I recall," she said.

Her aunt squeezed her arm a little. "Dearest, are you well? I know you've suffered and this whole situation is beastly."

She let out her breath in a shaky sigh. "It is. But time heals, I know it to be true."

"Is it just time?" Caroline pressed. "Or is it company?"

Evelina blinked up at her. "You know we're only pretending. I realize you must not approve, but don't get your hopes up about this being something more. When Vaughn is satisfied that we've made our point, I suppose he'll be done with it."

Caroline glanced at the earl, and in that moment he looked back and when his gaze fell on Evelina, he smiled. A bright, genuine expression that once again made her heart skip.

"If you say so," Caroline said. "I suppose you girls know far more about how to read a man than I do. And I don't disapprove. I understand. My only interest is that you don't get hurt."

"Well," Evelina said with a shake of her head. "No one can guarantee that, no matter what we do or don't do."

She meant the words, just as she meant the admonishment that the relationship wasn't real. Only sometimes that was hard to remember, especially when her traitorous mind tried to build futures out of smoke.

Was she just desperate? She'd believed she'd have a future with Harry, too, and that had been just as false. And yet she edged toward the same mistakes now and with a man who'd already agreed that couldn't happen.

She needed to toughen up. Put up her walls. Protect her heart even if she very willingly surrendered her body.

To do anything else was the height of stupidity.

CHAPTER 14

Vaughn had never been close to his family. His parents were like many people of their station—they had kept a respectable distance from their children. He didn't recall many moments of warmth or familial attachment. He had a sister, Emily, now a viscountess, but they hadn't ever been close either. She wrote him from time to time, they had supper once or twice during a Season and occasionally shared a holiday, but it was a cooler connection than even some of his acquaintanceships.

So when he sat in the parlor after a raucous supper with the Comerford sisters, Silas and their aunt, he couldn't help but be captivated by their bond. They were a delight to behold as a group. The sisters, especially, were enchanting. They could say a thousand words with just a look between them. They had personal jokes that made their eyes sparkle. And there was an intense protectiveness shared between them.

How lucky one would be to be invited into that sphere as Silas Windham had been when he married Arabella. Occasionally, he caught Windham watching the three sisters just as Vaughn was and he would smile like he enjoyed the exercise just as much.

The youngest sister, Julia, looked between the two men with a smile. "Now, I've heard you and Silas were once in school together, Blackburn. Did you get up to ridiculous antics?"

Silas grinned toward him. "Blackburn was a bit wilder back then, though not as wild as I was."

Vaughn chuckled. "I'd wager there were few as wild as you were. God, how much fun it was to watch you tweak every one of the beaks."

"Beaks?" Evelina asked with a shake of her head. "What's that?"

"Apologies, Eton has its own silly little language," Vaughn explained. "A beak is what we called the masters."

"The teachers," Silas supplied, and all four women nodded. "I did play my pranks and set my fires."

Vaughn snorted. "Metaphorical and once literal, yes?"

Silas bent his head. "To be fair, I didn't know the pamphlets would go up like that."

"Good Lord," Arabella said with a laugh as she came to link her arm through her husband's. She stared at him with pure adoration even as she teased, "You are hopeless."

"Entirely," he agreed. "And trust that I was punished for it. Lashings every Friday. I couldn't have my streak broken, could I?"

Evelina's lips parted. "They beat you?"

Silas's jaw tightened a little and Vaughn also felt the swell of anxiety at the topic of the school's infamous disciplinary system. "They did. Done by both the beaks and the prefects—those are the head boys who are allowed to mete out punishment. Always colossal pricks. You never became one after I left, did you, Blackburn?"

Vaughn shook his head. "No. Though Southwater did."

Silas arched a brow. "See, colossal pricks."

Evelina let out her breath and it was just a little shaky. "Harry used to speak fondly about his time as a head boy at the school. I had no idea about the beating part. It seems I knew very little, or perhaps purposefully ignored the signs out of foolishness."

Their aunt Caroline took Evelina's hand. "Dearest, as unsavory as it is, Eton is known for these things and always has been, at least quietly amongst those of the *ton*. And Southwater betrayed you in a great many ways, none of which was your fault."

"I agree," Vaughn said, and held her gaze from across the parlor. "*None* of it was your fault, Evie."

She blushed slightly. "Thank you."

Silas went to the sideboard and poured another drink for Evelina. As he handed it over, he said, "You three know better than most that men can be very good at hiding their true natures. I always thought Southwater was an arse. But he didn't show you that side until pretending it wasn't there no longer suited his purpose." He glanced at Vaughn. "Actually, Blackburn, I have to say I was always surprised you were friends with him both back then and even more recently. You never came across as much more than a *vague* arse."

Vaughn couldn't help but laugh, even though he'd guess that a man like Silas would very much see him as exactly that: a tolerable nob.

"I think that's about as high a praise as I can expect from you, Windham. So I'll take it." He sighed. "And as for Southwater…I suppose he was a bad habit after a while. As boys you don't often get to fully choose your friends. Our fathers were friendly, we were thrown together at gatherings and at school. We were of similar rank and age. It made sense. As we grew, I perhaps foolishly overlooked some of his worse impulses. I excused casual cruelties as him only having a bad moment."

"It's easy to do," Evelina said, and their gazes held. "We were both fools that way."

"But we never will be again," he said softly.

She nodded. "I suppose all we can do is grow from it."

He stiffened. It was a lovely idea that they would both become stronger or better people through this painful time. But was that what was happening? Was it growing to be playing games?

Pretending a relationship? Taking pleasure in tweaking Southwater and Florence?

He knew the answer. He hated himself a little for it.

Caroline Ashfield cleared her throat and Vaughn started. This conversation had become so much about just them that he'd all but forgotten the others in the room, watching them, reading them. "Arabella, why don't we play some parlor games?"

Arabella was still watching Vaughn, even as she nodded. "A capital idea! I hesitate to offer literary riddles because my dear husband is far too good at such things, but as long as he is on my team…"

The others laughed and it shook the heavier mood. Evelina came toward him and they didn't speak as they linked arms to ready themselves for the game. He glanced down at her. "My apologies, Evie. I shouldn't have gotten so maudlin."

Her brow wrinkled. "It isn't maudlin. And you don't have to apologize to me unless we end up being terrible at this game and have to endure my sister crowing about it and holding it over my head for the next twelve years."

"Twelve?" he repeated on a laugh.

"Oh yes," she said. "Don't ever mention the sack race we had as children, she'll never stop talking about how she bested Julia and me."

"Well, I will endeavor to act as your champion, my lady, and not let you lose again."

She smiled and for a moment he was dumbfounded by it. Like a ray of sunshine had hit some of the ice around his heart and it was thawing. He found he liked the sensation and he refused to back away from it as they launched into the game of riddles.

~

The evening was coming to an end as the clock chimed midnight and Evie smiled across the parlor at Vaughn. They'd ended up being very good partners in all the games played that night. They'd bested the rest several times and she found him to be as gracious a winner as he was a loser. She slowly moved to him.

"You've been lovely tonight," she said.

He smoothed a lock of hair from her face and that gentle touch sent reverberations of sensation through her body. "As have you. I know we came in separate vehicles and we didn't plan to spend the evening together but for Arabella's invitation, but would you like to come home with me?"

She couldn't look away from the green depths of those eyes and all the promises they contained. She nodded. "Very much so."

"Good." He leaned down and kissed her briefly. She blinked as she pulled away and then realized her entire family was watching the exchange. From the arch of Arabella's brow it seemed her sister had opinions.

Evelina wasn't ready for them tonight. So instead she said, "I'm afraid my energy is waning. I think Blackburn and I will take our leave. Julia, did you come in a carriage or do you need a ride?"

She found herself relieved when her youngest sister shook her head. "No. I'm staying with Arabella and Silas tonight."

"Good," Evelina said without thinking, and heat rushed to her cheeks at the slip. "I mean, that's lovely. You'll have a wonderful time."

Arabella arched a brow at her, but wasn't able to push her because Silas stepped up, hand outstretched to Vaughn. "It was good to see you, Blackburn. Perhaps we'll bump into each other over at Fitzhugh's. I sometimes play billiards there with the Earls of Delacourt and Ramsbury."

Vaughn lifted his brows. "Ah. Well, I'd be happy to join you. Thank you."

Evelina lifted up to kiss Silas's cheek. "Yes, thank you," she whispered, and met her brother-in-law's eyes as she said it. After all, she knew that every positive connection Vaughn made put him back on a path to acceptance once the nasty business of the divorce was finalized.

Silas squeezed her hands and then stepped aside so she could say her farewells to Arabella, Julia and her aunt. She did so, watching Vaughn do the same with as much warmth as he'd handled them all evening. Such a difference from Harry. She felt the weight of that all the more now.

Together they all moved to the foyer and she found Vaughn's carriage had already been called for. He helped her up and they waved as the vehicle started out the drive. As soon as it had exited onto the street, he caught her hand and drew her to his side.

She lifted her face to his and they kissed. It wasn't brief as their kiss had been at Arabella's. No, this was deep and powerful and passionate. He dug his fingers into her hair, she gripped her fist against his chest, their tongues collided and warred and when they parted her heart was pounding.

"Oh, I've been waiting to do that all night," he breathed. "The amount of self-control I've exhibited should be rewarded."

She shook her head with a laugh. "I can only imagine the kinds of rewards you'd request."

"You in a tub, me getting to lather that body up and then watch you ride me until we're both spent from coming?"

She blinked. "Well, that's a reward for both of us."

He waggled his eyebrows suggestively. "I'm very generous."

"I think you are at that," she said, touching his cheek. "And you were truly wonderful with my family."

"They're easy to be wonderful around. Your closeness is admirable and enviable. I wish I'd had the same, but you know how the *ton* is."

"Some of them," she said. "But yes, I've seen a great many families that were very much in name only. I do appreciate that mine is close. I couldn't imagine my life without my sisters and aunt. And even Silas, who has been such a welcome addition."

They rode together in quiet for a moment and then he seemed to recall something. His face brightened in the dim light coming from the street lamps rushing by outside. "I'd almost forgotten. I got you a gift today and brought it just in case I was able coax you into my carriage."

"No coaxing required, I assure you," she said. "But I do like gifts."

He reached behind himself to something that had become wedged in the seat. When he drew it out she recognized the shape of a book, wrapped in brown paper that looked like it had the stamp for Mattigan's on its surface.

"Oh, a book!" she asked, grasping it.

"Yes, I thought you might not have this one yet. It's all the rage, apparently, and difficult to find."

She unwrapped the paper and caught her breath as she read the title in the dimness. "*The Well of Saint Laurents*." Her mouth dropped open. "Kressley's latest! It *is* impossible to find. How did you manage it?"

"I'm a *very* good customer at Mattigan's," he admitted. "I hope I'll have a chance to read it when you're finished. Or perhaps we'll read it together."

She stared at the book again and was surprised that tears had begun to sting her eyes. "It's astounding to me that you like to read a gothic romance. Harry…Southwater, he always made fun of me for it. If I was too engulfed in a book, he'd even threaten to take it. *Burn them all*, he once said to me. He pretended he was teasing and that's how I excused it…but deep down I knew he meant it. He was always so jealous of anything that took my time when he demanded it."

She watched Vaughn's expression, which had been soft with delight at her excitement, turn harder. His nostrils flared. "Poxy fuck," he muttered. "Christ, I hate that I didn't see what a bastard he was. How he could treat you like that when you are so lovely and sweet and everything perfect is astounding to me."

She blinked at the compliments that seemed to flow from him with an ease. And better still, they felt genuine. Like this man, this remarkable man, could truly see her as something perfect. Something worth protecting and not just in the way that courtesans labeled the gentlemen they took to their beds. Most of *them* did very little protecting.

"You can't be real," she murmured even as she touched his face and proved to herself that he *was* real and here and putting his arms around her as the carriage slowed and turned into the drive of his home.

"Oh, I'm very much real," he said softly. "Come upstairs and I'll prove it, over and over if need be."

CHAPTER 15

Vaughn couldn't say how and refused to place why, but it felt like something had shifted between himself and Evelina as he guided her into his chamber, his mouth on hers, her hands gripping his lapels. There was still a heated desperation between them, of course, the kind that came with an irresistible drive to be together immediately.

But there was also something more genuine beneath that drive. He knew what pleasures they would share. He knew how to make her arch and moan and whimper his name, as well as all she could do to elicit the same response from him. He looked forward to all of that. But he also looked forward to how she would smile when they teased together as they made love. Or how her fingers would lightly touch him afterward while they talked. Or how she would fling a leg over his while she slept, like she was still claiming him even when she wasn't fully aware of her actions.

"Are you just going to stare at me, Vaughn, or do something about that?" She motioned toward the erection making itself very plain against the fall front of his trousers.

He chuckled as he let his hand stroke over it. "I'd like to do both."

She arched a brow, playful and powerful all at once. "I see. The gentleman wants to watch *and* play. I can do that."

She stepped toward him and wrapped her arms around his neck. She kissed him, driving the deepness of the kiss, sucking his tongue until he moaned against her. She lightly nipped his lower lip as she dragged her mouth lower, over his chin, down his neck until her lips met his cravat. Then over his still-clothed body. Lower and lower as she dropped to her knees and then looked up at him, the perfect combination of sweetness and spice as she unfastened his fall front and freed his very hard cock.

"Shit," he grunted, dropping his hands to her hair and tangling them in the locks like he had when he kissed her in the carriage. He loved the silky feel of them around his fingers and the way she let out a shaky breath when he touched her.

She looked up at him, all delectable sensuality in those gorgeous brown eyes, and then she took him firmly in hand and stroked her cheek against his cock. He braced so his knees wouldn't give out and watched the show she put on of teasing him. She nuzzled his length, teased him against her lips, even darted out her tongue to give him the lightest swipe.

"It's a very nice cock, Vaughn," she purred, her voice low and seductive. "And I'm an expert."

She proved that statement by taking him into her mouth, as deeply as she could, and swirling her tongue around him.

It was just one caress and he nearly blacked out from the pleasure of it. He groaned because he couldn't stop himself and tried to focus on watching her as she delved into sucking him to oblivion.

She was perfect, just as she always was when it came to passion. She paid attention, adjusting when he reacted, and the result was blinding, powerful pleasure that was unlike anything he'd ever known.

And it wasn't just the heat of her or the suction of her mouth, it wasn't just the way she used that talented tongue or worked with her hand the length she couldn't take. No, it was the image of her on her knees, looking up at him, in a position of submission, but with all the power in the world.

She had been slow at first, but as the pleasure built in him, she began to work faster, pumping her mouth over him in time to his flexing hips. He moaned as the pleasure streaked, building to something so powerful he almost feared the moment when the dam broke and he lost control.

He wanted that, of course. He wanted to lose himself in this woman's remarkable body, in her focused presence and attention. But he also wanted to feel her shuddering around him when he did. He wanted not just his own pleasure, but to feel hers, as well.

So just as he hit the edge of no return, he caught her under her arms and dragged her back up to her feet. "Oh no," he murmured as he kissed her. "I want more than just that."

When they parted from the kiss, she stuck out her lip playfully. "So unfair, Vaughn. So afraid to lose control?"

"Little minx," he purred as he unfastened one of those remarkable hidden fasteners that made her dress slide away so easily. "You think you have control? No, no, you were always mine for the taking."

To prove that, he caught the loose fabric of her gown and swiftly tugged it around her arms, lightly binding her in the silk so she couldn't move. He expected her to smile or moan or play along with the naughty idea of him tying her with her own dress and teasing her like he'd been teased. But instead she stiffened and the color drained from her cheeks.

"Vaughn," she gasped, and tugged against him. "Stop! Stop it!"

He released her immediately and she staggered back, her breath short and her hands shaking as she yanked her dress up to cover herself. She backed away from him like she had to escape. There was nothing teasing or playful or false about this reaction. He could see the pure terror on her face and his heart sank with it.

"Evelina," he said softly, gently, like he would with a wounded animal who needed care.

She shook her head and refused to meet his eyes. "I-I'm sorry. I'm sorry. Let me breathe and we can continue."

He drew back in horror. "Evie, I don't care about continuing."

She waved toward him, though she still wouldn't meet his gaze. "Of course you do, you didn't get to...to finish."

He stepped closer, carefully, not trying to invade her space or make her feel unsafe. "*Evelina*." At that she did look at him. "The last thing that matters to me is coming. Please, what just happened? Why did you react so strongly?"

She stared at him, still holding her dress up to cover herself and her struggle was evident. Her breath was short, her cheeks still pale as paper, her eyes sparkling with tears she kept trying to blink away. She opened and shut her mouth like she was trying to find the words. "I-It doesn't matter."

He shook his head. "You don't owe me a damn thing, so if you don't want to share it, that's fine. But understand this: it bloody well matters to me. Not only because I *never* want to accidentally do something that makes you look so devastated, but because I-I like you, Evie. I care about you."

She shifted back and forth and then she bent her head. Her breath was rough as she fought for words. At last they came. "The— the reason my dresses are designed like this, the hidden little fasteners, the way I can put them on and take them off on my own is because I...I never wanted to be trapped by needing assistance with clothing again."

"Again?" he repeated softly, his heart beginning to hurt even more for her. "Someone trapped you like that before."

She nodded. "My protector before Harry...he used to make sure I couldn't leave by refusing to help me with my clothing. He used that fact to trap me and—and make me do things I didn't want to do. And if I still refused—" Her voice grew rough and he realized she was hardly breathing anymore. "If I refused he would hurt me."

~

Evelina had told others about her past. Her sisters knew. A few other courtesans so that the network would be aware of her former lover's violence and issues with control. It was the way women like her protected each other, after all. But those had been brief conversations. She'd minimized even though she thought Arabella knew things had gone further.

But standing here with Vaughn, his green stare holding hers and offering some kind of peace, the words fell from her mouth and they burned like fire. Made her flash back to those awful times almost as much as the horrible moment when Vaughn had held her in the folds of her gown and she couldn't move.

She pushed at the memories to try to make them go away, but her body still shook. He took another step toward her, his hand held out. "Oh, Evie. Come, please sit."

She should have refused. She should have found some way back into seduction or even left his house, but her legs carried her to the chair before his fire and she all but collapsed, covering her face with both her hands as she tried to find her breath again.

She heard him moving around and then he returned to her. He took the chair next to hers and handed over a glass of water he'd fetched from the pitcher near the basin.

"You must think me a fool for reacting so strongly to something happened so long ago," she whispered as she took a drink.

He shook his head. "I could never think you a fool. Certainly not for this. As I said before, you owe me nothing, but…but if you want to tell me, I want to know."

She let out a little sob she hadn't meant to let escape and stared up at his ceiling as she tried to decide what to do. Even Harry hadn't known the full detail of facts. He hadn't wanted to know about past lovers, the good or the bad. He'd found it distasteful.

So should she pour out this story onto *this* man? The one who didn't even really promise any kind of future, short or long term to her? But then, perhaps he was the best one to tell when it was bubbling inside of her and trying to force itself out.

"Do you know how my sisters and I all came to be courtesans?" she asked.

He shook his head. "I don't."

"Everyone always focuses on what they see as fun. The idea of three sisters in the life feels like a play to them, a sparkling party. But we did this because we had to escape. Our father was horrible, an ogre."

"You said he tried to kill Arabella," he said.

"Yes, and that was just the culmination of decades of cruelty. Arabella ran first and chose this life. She always embraced it, reveled in it. She saw it as freedom."

His brow wrinkled. "You don't see it as the same?"

She hesitated. "I do. Please, let me be clear, I don't hate my choice. I've enjoyed the company of many of the men who have protected me over the years. And I enjoy sex and passion."

There was relief on his expression. "Good. I would hate to think that anything I've done beyond what just happened has been damaging."

"Oh no," she said. "*You* are a pleasure. A pure, unadulterated pleasure that I dream about and will likely dream about for a long time after it's over."

"It's the same for me."

"But as much as I accepted and grew to enjoy my choice, it's never been as comfortable as it was for Arabella." She sighed. "And my sister's ability to read people was never as fully developed in me as it was in her. So I didn't see the truth about...about *him* until it was too late."

"Who was he?" he asked.

She swallowed. "Normally I wouldn't tell you, but my list of lovers is public. You'd discover it on your own if I didn't share it."

"Not if you told me not to," he said.

She blinked. Here was this man telling her he wouldn't invade her privacy, despite her position in the world and his. "I think you wouldn't," she whispered. "That you are somehow so uncommonly decent that you'd keep your word."

"I don't know about uncommonly decent. My first thought when you told me someone hurt you was to find him and rip him apart limb from limb." He said it calmly, but she saw the flash in his stare, a protective darkness that said he would do that for her, too, if she asked.

It reminded her of Arabella and her protective streak.

"It wouldn't do any good except to make you more of a topic of gossip," she said softly. "His name is Gerard Brightling."

"Viscount Brightling's grandson?" Vaughn said.

She nodded. "Yes. On paper he was a good catch. Not in line to inherit the title, but a man of good fortune and breeding. He was young and charismatic, as well. Handsome enough. He liked to take me out to his clubs to show me off like I was a jewel in his crown. But when others showed any interest, he would go into jealous rages. Blame me for it."

Vaughn's nostrils flared, but he didn't interrupt, so she continued, mostly because the words kept pouring out, as if something had been loosened. "I realized it wasn't a good fit and I was trying to extract myself the first time he…he trapped me. We'd been at a play and my gown was very complicated. I needed a maid to get it fastened but he'd sent her away. Normally he'd help me dress, but he refused. I couldn't leave unless I wanted to run naked down the street, since he also refused to allow me the use of his carriage."

Waves of nausea washed over her. "So I stayed. And I did what he wanted and after a day he let me go home. There were flowers and apologies and promises and I was so humiliated that I couldn't move. Couldn't walk away. He was kind for a while afterward and I started to convince myself that I'd misunderstood."

Vaughn's eyes came shut and he reached out to take her hand. "But you hadn't."

"No. The next time it happened, I did try to dress myself against his wishes and he struck me. Hard enough that I bruised and couldn't go out for a week afterward. And then he—"

She cut herself off. The memories of that night washed over her, ripped through her, and it was like she was still there in that chamber that had looked so pretty and had been so horrible. She could recall everything that man had done to her and everything he'd said and called her while he did it.

"He forced you," Vaughn said softly.

She nodded. "Until he was finished and then he let me go again. I couldn't hide the bruise. Arabella and Julia saw it. Arabella used her protector at the time to help me get free. Brightling's grandfather was told of his behavior and apparently it wasn't the first time he'd harmed a lady. It was covered up and he let me go and went away to the continent for a while. And I moved on."

"So he harmed you and got a Grand Tour as reward," Vaughn said softly.

She shrugged. "Yes, I suppose that's the way of the world."

"It shouldn't be," he said, and his righteous anger for her felt good somehow. "My God, he should have been flayed for doing such a thing. He should have been shunned."

"It's a pretty idea that there would be consequences for such behavior, but sometimes that's not the way. The courtesans mostly avoid him, they know about him. He's married now, of course, no protecting *her*. But I hear she's put him deeply in debt."

"Sounds like she deserves whatever she spends to put up with him," Vaughn said. "I'm so sorry, Evelina. And I'm sorry that my playing tonight put you to mind of that horror. I would never have done *anything* to do that to you."

She stared at him a long time, drinking in every line of him. "No, I think you wouldn't." She sighed. "I suppose...I suppose what I went through is perhaps part of why I didn't see that Harry was untrue. He was my next protector after Brightling and he was so calm and steady. He also offered this grand future that looked so fine on paper. I wouldn't be his duchess, but I'd be his partner for life. I'd never have to risk another protector who could turn on me. And since he never once put a hand on me in violence, I ignored some of the other unsavory moments. I tried to push away the negative feelings."

His expression softened. "I understand that."

She dipped her head and now that all the pain was poured out, the humiliation that she'd allowed such a weakness rushed forward and took over. "God, you must be sorry you asked. A gentleman has a mistress so that he may be light and comfortable, not so that he can listen to her cry about her past."

Vaughn touched her chin with two fingers and tilted her face up so that they looked at each other again. "Even if that's a true expectation of some men when it comes to their lovers, that isn't mine. I already told you, Evie, I *like* you."

She had been told far more flowery and romantic sentiments over the years. Declarations of great love and passion from men who behaved like they were part of some romantic play while they waxed poetic about her eyes or her hair or whatever their preferred feature was until they bored of it all.

But this simple statement from this man felt like it wended its way past protective barriers. Worked its way around her heart.

"I like you too," she admitted. "And I suppose our arrangement isn't exactly the normal kind anyway. So perhaps there's more room for—for truth."

"I think we both deserve it after everything else," he said. His fingers smoothed across her cheek again, still so exquisitely gentle. "I want you stay, Evie. Will you stay with me tonight?"

She nodded and drank the rest of her water, trying to put herself back into the correct mindset. "Let me splash some water on my face and then I'll be ready to be the seductive goddess again."

She moved to stand, but he caught her hand. "You misunderstand. I'm not asking you to stay so we may finish what we started. I want you stay with me with no expectation."

"You don't want to make love?" she asked.

He let out a laugh. "I never said *that*. We'll do that again, I hope many times before we're finished with each other. But tonight I want to just…hold you, Evie. Just lie with you and be happy that you trusted me enough to share what you shared. And be happy that you survived it. Will you stay?"

She hesitated. All this was so intimate, far more intimate than any sex act they could share. She'd been warned against becoming truly intimate with a man. She'd also ignored those warnings in the past and been hurt.

But tonight she couldn't deny Vaughn. Perhaps more truthfully, she didn't want to, and so she nodded. He smiled like it mattered. They moved to his bed together. He helped her out of her half-unfastened dress and took off his own boots and shirt. They climbed under the crisp sheets and he opened his arms so that she could curl into him, his solid form and heat wrapping around her like a blanket.

And as she lay there, his fingers threading through her hair gently, she realized with a start that *this* man was who she'd always wanted Harry to be. Who she'd *pretended* the duke was, even if he wasn't.

And yet Vaughn wasn't hers, not really. He wouldn't ever be. A troubling thought to drift to sleep with, but she was so exhausted that it was the last thought on her mind before dreams took her.

Evie had been asleep for an hour and still Vaughn watched her in the fading light of the dying fire. He felt compelled to do so, to note her every movement and catch of breath. Her expression had softened over that time, earlier restless dreams giving way to deeper sleep as he cradled her. At least he could let her have that rest that she so richly deserved.

He smoothed a hand along her bare arm and she cuddled even closer with a murmur. He admired a great deal about her and always had. When she'd been with Southwater he'd always considered her intelligent and bright and fun to be around. He'd never delved deeper than that surface impression because she wasn't his and he was married and tried not to be a total lout, no matter what Florence did.

But in the past few weeks, he'd grown to know Evie on such a deeper level. Their arrangement had revealed more and more about her. Yet until tonight, until the gift of her shaky confession, he hadn't realized her greatest characteristic was her strength. With all her softness and gentleness and kindness, at her core was a steel rod of resilience. An ability to keep getting up even when she'd been knocked down by those who had vowed to protect her.

He wasn't certain he had half that quality. After all, he was so rocked by the betrayal of his wife and friend that he plotted revenge schemes and brooded in corners. Meanwhile, Evie built herself a life out of ashes and kept going even when it hurt.

He was humbled by that. By her. And found himself wondering more and more about her. Wanting to know more, to understand more. None of that had anything to do with Southwater and Florence or a false arrangement or even a very real passion that now connected them. It had to do with how remarkable this woman was.

Now he just had to start sorting out what to do about that. And with how he wanted this to continue.

Evelina set a plate heaped with delectable items at her place on Vaughn's right at the breakfast table and smoothed her skirt before she sat down. He had been reading the paper and he folded down the edge to look at her with a teasing smile. "I like to see a healthy appetite."

She laughed. "You do inspire it, my lord."

He joined her laughter and returned to his paper. The teasing wasn't a lie, of course. She hadn't left his home for two days. Not since the night when she panicked about being trapped in her gown and confessed her past to him. In that time, they'd shared a great deal of passion. The man still looked at her like he wanted to devour her and often followed through.

And yet things had also changed in that time. The relationship between them felt...gentler...somehow. Not like she was cracked glass that needed to be protected, but more like she was something precious. Together they read the book he'd gifted her and played games and walked in his lush gardens while they talked about nothing...and everything.

The one thing they hadn't talked about, though, was what Evie had heard about his wife and the potential for a pregnancy with

Southwater. It wasn't that she hadn't thought of it. She often had, dashing herself on the rocks as she tried to find the right words to share the rumor. But then he'd laugh or suggest they do something amusing or push her onto his bed and she couldn't take away the lightness from him. She couldn't destroy him, especially since she didn't even know if what she had heard was true.

Her desire to protect him was just as troublesome as the rest. This was all beginning to feel very real. That it was transforming again from a mere revenge scheme and later passion to something with more depth of feeling. Something that could cause an authentic broken heart.

She shook her head and pushed those thoughts away. She wouldn't be so foolish to allow that. "And what is on your agenda today, Vaughn?"

He folded the paper entirely and set it aside to fully focus on her. It was always startling when he did that, which he did often, because those green eyes seemed to see all. "I would love to tell you that my agenda was to stay here with you another day, try to best you at lawn darts for once and then make love to you in the orangery."

"You'll never best me at lawn darts, you must learn to accept the facts," she teased. "And the rest sounds very nice. *But…*"

"But," he continued, "I must unfortunately meet with my solicitor."

There was something about the way his expression fell and his tone became far more serious that made her lean closer. "About the divorce?"

He nodded, his lips pinching. "Yes. It seems that once Southwater decided to press forward with his influence and money to the situation, it has moved things along considerably. I've been called to sign a few items that will help obtain the final permissions."

She took his hand and pressed it between hers. "I'm sorry."

"The sooner it's over, the sooner it will be…" He shrugged. "Over."

"I know. And I'll be happy for you that day because it won't hang over you like this. But I'm still sorry."

His expression softened a little and lifted her hand to his lips to kiss it briefly. "You really are too good. But what will you do today without me?"

"Pine ceaselessly?" She said it to tease and hoped it wouldn't be true.

He grinned and her heart soared that she could bring him even a fraction of peace. "A terrible fate. You must have something to fill the time."

"Well, now that you mention it, I wanted to go to see my seamstress. She has some new fabrics. Then I have a new bonnet to pick up at the milliner."

"Thrilling," he said.

"It will be thrilling for you when you see me in the pretty dresses and compliment me endlessly on how fetching I look in the hat."

"True on both accounts."

"And after that my sisters have asked that I join them for tea. I was going to refuse them if you had plans for us today, but if you'll be out, I'll send an answer in the affirmative. I want to see Julia's new accommodations anyway."

He tilted his head. "Oh, that's right, she only moved out of Arabella's house recently, didn't she? Who is she paired with now? Lord Castleton, yes?"

"Yes, Viscount Laurence Castleton." She shrugged. "Honestly I keep forgetting his name entirely, so I must do better if she's going to be in any kind of lasting affiliation with him. He seems generous enough at this point." She shifted and hoped she wouldn't sound too needy when she asked, "You—you don't know anything unsavory about him, do you?"

His playful expression softened and he lifted her hand to his lips again. "No. Nothing at all that would cause me pause about her safety. I know he's been labeled as flighty, but there isn't a hint of cruelty in his behavior, at least in my circles."

"Well, if we dismissed gentlemen for flightiness, I think the courtesans would all be out of business," she said. "Thank you, Vaughn, hearing that about him is a relief."

"I'm glad I could provide it."

She touched his face. "How long until your appointment?"

Now the gentleness left his expression and a little heat entered it. "Not enough to start anything entertaining with you, unfortunately. In fact, I probably must call for my horse to be readied and head on my way. Would you like my carriage for the day? Or I can have yours sent for."

She blinked. "That would be very kind. You don't mind?"

He leaned in and cupped her face, kissing her before he answered. He was gentle at first, but then his fingers tensed and he delved a little deeper, tasting of tea and jam from his breakfast. God, she could just lose herself in that. In him. In this.

She caught her breath and pulled back. "Is that a no?"

He smiled. "I don't mind at all."

They stood together and walked to the foyer where he called for his horse and told the staff that she would be using his carriage and returning to his home afterward.

"You can poke around in my library or my study and uncover all my secrets," he teased after the butler had gone to make all the arrangements.

"Oh, that sounds very gothic," she said.

"No, I'm terribly boring, I'm sorry to say. I could try harder."

She leaned up to kiss him again. "I think I'll keep gothic to the pages of books, thank you."

The horse was brought to the door and he squeezed her hand. "I'll see you for supper."

She nodded and watched him go, waving him down the drive. Only when he was gone did she realize she'd just bade him farewell like a wife would do, not a lover. And that it had felt right and easy to do so.

"You're an idiot," she admonished herself.

"I beg your pardon, Miss Comerford?" Vaughn's butler, Langley, asked from behind her, his expression kind and open and not at all judgmental even when his master was gone.

"Oh, nothing, Langley. I think I'll take the carriage now, if it's no trouble to prepare it."

"No trouble at all, miss. Give us but a few moments."

"I'll fetch my wrap and be down shortly, please tell them to take their time. I'm in no rush and don't want to be a bother."

She went upstairs, drawing deep breaths as she did so. She truly had to get herself back under control in this situation. Because she wasn't the lady of this house and she never would be. Today she had to do everything she could to remember that.

Any calm or lightness that Vaughn had felt the last few days with Evelina was gone now that he sat in the cramped office of his solicitor, Mr. Robach, piles of papers to be signed perched in front of him. It wasn't just the inconvenience of it all, or the humiliation of it, or even the judgment he always saw on this man's face, even if he was being paid an exorbitant amount of money for his services. All those things came together in a swirl and made Vaughn question his own intelligence, his own capacity to evaluate the character of others, or even himself.

"You say this is the bulk of the paperwork," he said while he scratched his signature on the last of the teetering pile.

"Yes, my lord. The next item you sign will be the dissolution of the marriage and then it will be as if none of this ever happened." Robach gave a benign smile.

Vaughn shook his head. As if that could be true. The marriage would be over, yes, and he would be free to move on and rebuild the life that had been frozen for so long. But as if it had never happened? There were some things that couldn't be erased.

"How I wish that could be," he muttered.

"Scandal passes, my lord," Robach reassured him absently. "And you'll certainly find a new wife."

Vaughn blinked, for that concept hadn't entered his mind. What did, in that moment, was an image of Evie sitting at his breakfast table as she had been that morning. Evie in his bed. Evie in his garden.

"I suppose I will so that I may fulfill my duties," he agreed because he certainly wasn't about to debate the merits of the idea with this man. "So a couple of weeks then?"

The solicitor nodded. "Yes, sir. All the permissions will be complete by then and you'll sign the final dissolution and that will be that."

"Very good." Vaughn got up and smoothed his jacket, like he could wipe away some of the remnants of this unpleasantness. "Please send word if you require anything further until then. Good day."

"Good day, my lord. My man will see you out."

Vaughn inclined his head and then strode from the office back into the main hall. Robach's man was, indeed, waiting for him. He was a thin, nervous sort and he bowed solicitously. "My lord. Would you like to wait in the parlor while I have your horse brought?"

The stifling weight of the day was starting to settle on Vaughn's shoulders and he shook his head. "No, thank you. I think I'll wait outside and have some air."

"Very good. It shouldn't be more than a moment. Good day."

Vaughn lifted a hand in farewell as he exited the small building and drew a breath of air. All he wanted was to go home, shake off this day and spend his evening with Evie. Such a strange thought considering their beginnings, but there it was. He knew that when he was with her, she would make all this…lighter somehow. Easier. He could only hope he did the same for her.

"Blackburn."

He stiffened at his name being said. Slowly, he turned and found Florence's sister, Honora, coming toward him from down the street.

She had a maid with her, and both women looked as uncomfortable as he felt.

"Lady Simpson," he said, forgoing the intimacy of using her given name and referring to her by her title, instead. After all, they would be strangers in two weeks.

She let out her breath a little. "Good afternoon, Blackburn."

"Is it," he said, and looked off to see if his horse would be here soon to give him an escape.

She shifted. "She…she wants to see you."

He froze at that and returned his full attention to Honora. Slowly, he folded his arms. "*She* has made it painfully clear that she wants nothing of the sort," he said, and was glad his voice didn't tremble. "However, Florence is always welcome to discuss anything she has on her mind. We're married, or at least we will be for a little while longer. Until Southwater wraps it all up."

At that, Honora's face twisted with disgust. "Southwater," she repeated.

He arched a brow. "You don't approve?"

"She's destroying herself," Honora spat. "And everyone else around her."

"I'm well aware of everything she's destroying," he retorted. "But we're here now and she's made her choice. Quite publicly. I don't know what else there would be to discuss."

"I understand." She shifted. "But will you go to her? At the house he's put her in? Tomorrow at ten?"

Discomfort washed over Vaughn and he was shocked at its source. He didn't feel wrong about seeing Florence. Well, that wasn't entirely true, but it was more that the idea of calling on her in such a private way felt…wrong. Like it might be a betrayal of Evie, despite the fact that Florence was his *wife*. It was such a backward emotion that he took a moment before he responded as he grappled with it and then forced it back.

"I can call if you're certain it's what she wishes," he finally said.

Honora sighed. "Nothing is certain. But thank you for agreeing. I realize you have no obligation to do so. Goodbye."

He jolted at the finality of that farewell as she departed without waiting for his response. But of course, it *was* final, wasn't it? Paperwork would be signed shortly and then it was very unlikely he would ever interact with anyone in his former wife's family again. They would all avoid each other, try not to go to the same parties, ignore each other if they found themselves in a common room or park or museum.

It truly would be as if none of the last five years had happened. The good or the bad.

The groom appeared with his horse and Vaughn tried to gather himself as he swung up and started onto the road back home. But he felt entirely sick as he did so, and he didn't think that feeling would change for some time.

CHAPTER 17

Evelina paced the tables piled with remarkable fabrics, touching a few as she passed, trying to picture what they would look like when they had been transformed into a gorgeous gown that would draw men in and make them want.

Well, not men. Man. One singular man was all she considered as she perused. Vaughn. She hated herself for it. After all, she would likely not even still be with him by the time this fabric or that was made into a new gown for the winter. It wouldn't matter if she picked a green that matched his eyes perfectly, or chose a cut that would make him long to touch her through the silk.

"Oh, Evelina! How wonderful to see you!"

She turned from her sad little musings to find that Simone Stanhope had entered the shop. The celebrated courtesan was a good friend to Evelina and both her sisters. She and Arabella, especially, were very close. Evelina was pleased for the interruption and moved to embrace her with a smile. "Simone, it feels like it's been an age! How are you, dearest?"

"Very well. I'm just here to pick up a new gown. I was out and about and told Madame Fontaine I would come to her rather than have her deliver it."

"Ah, Miss Stanhope!" Madame Fontaine said as she came from the back as if she'd sensed the entry of a new customer. "I do have that gown. Let me fetch it."

When they were alone again, Simone linked her arm through Evelina's. "Let me guess, you are choosing some new fabrics for some gorgeous gowns that Lord Blackburn may strip off you."

Evelina laughed, even though her friend's teasing was far too close to the thoughts she'd been having. "One does like to refresh the wardrobe when it comes to a new arrangement."

"Indeed," Simone said, and there was a brightness to her gaze that Evelina found herself envying. She had no idea who Simone was currently taking to her bed, but it seemed she was enjoying herself.

"Oh, Simone, that fabric is lovely," she said, happy for the interruption as Madame Fontaine reappeared with a gorgeous rose-pink gown draped over her arm. "That's my aunt's favorite color, you know."

"Is it?" Simone said with a small smile. "Well, then I hope I'll bump into her while I'm wearing it. We do see each other from time to time out in the world."

"She always blushes when she hears your name," Evelina said with a laugh. "And often asks after you."

Simone lifted her brows. "I'm glad to hear it. I enjoy her company any time I'm in it."

"And I suppose she must be a little source of *ton* gossip for the courtesan network."

At that Simone's expression fell. "No, I would never think to use her for information." When Evelina drew back at the strength of that response, she shook her head. "I only mean that your very sweet aunt is too gentle a soul to gossip with me. But I *have* heard some gossip if you are interested."

Evelina found herself a little more interested in what kind of friendship Simone and Caroline were forming that made Simone so uncharacteristically reactive, but she nodded regardless. "You know I do love some gossip."

"Your Southwater and Lady Blackburn were turned away from an assembly last night."

Evelina gasped. "They were trying to go to a public house even before the divorce is complete?"

"Yes. They seem desperate to have Society accept them, even though they'll have plenty of time to work on that when it's all over, so I don't know why."

Evelina did, and thought again of the rumors shared by Matilda not long ago, that Lady Blackburn might be with child and that was why this last dash to the finish. Things she still hadn't discussed with Vaughn, even though a dozen opportunities had existed to do so.

"Southwater must have hated that," she said softly.

"Apparently so. They were seen having a heated argument beside his carriage afterward. They both looked angry, my source told me. Plus, in the assembly afterward, they were all the talk and not in a positive way. The tide is most certainly against them, despite their best efforts."

Evelina took it all in and then she waited for a rush of triumph to wash over her. After all, this was what she and Vaughn had been working toward, wasn't it? To tweak Harry and Lady Blackburn? To make things harder for them as some little petty revenge for all they'd been put through themselves.

But now some consequences appeared to be at hand and there was…nothing.

"You have a very strange look on your face, dearest. Was I wrong to tell you?" Simone asked and Evelina knew her concern was real. There were many who would have pressed information onto her and then pretended to care while they breathlessly marked every reaction. But not Simone.

"No, of course not," Evelina said, and took her hand to squeeze it in reassurance. "Truth be told, I am in shock that I don't feel more about it. Since Harry left, things have been so horrible."

She stopped. Was that true? Yes, at the beginning she had grieved and hurt and hated, but lately…since Vaughn, all that had felt softer. Further from her. The future seemed more interesting than the past.

She blinked. "Well, things in my life *were* horrible. But hearing that Southwater suffered or that the two of them aren't getting what they want is…it's almost as if you're telling me about two badly behaving strangers. It's interesting, but it hardly affects me."

Simone smiled at her. "I'm happy to hear it. Southwater didn't deserve you, Evie. I never thought it. If you're moving on then that is something to celebrate."

Evelina might have agreed at some point, but at present what she was focused on and concerned about was Vaughn. She would have to tell him about this if he didn't hear about it today, out and about in the world where so many were aching to give him news and see his reaction. When she did, how would he react? Because she knew he wasn't over his wife or the betrayal of his friend. No matter how many times he made love to her or eased closer to her or made her forget herself… she knew this was still a means to an end for him. *She* was that.

"Evelina," Simone said softly. "What is happening between you and Blackburn?"

She blinked because once more her friend had almost read her thoughts. "Nothing. Just an affair, you know how it is."

"It doesn't look like it. Not when I see you out with him. Not when I see you now. Are you starting to care for him?"

She pursed her lips. "That would be a mightily foolish thing to do considering I did the same with Harry. Broke the cardinal rule of courtesans. To do so twice? You and Arabella would run me out of the profession, I think."

"Arabella would go to war for you, never run you out," Simone said. "And I don't think she represents courtesans anymore, considering her happy marriage. As for me…" She trailed off and her gaze dropped. "We make the rule to protect ourselves, to put up walls so that our hearts won't be broken. But sometimes it's not possible."

"No." Evelina sighed. "Vaughn is…he is special, Simone. He's not like anyone I've ever known. But what does it say about me that I could care about, foolishly think I loved, one protector and then so swiftly transfer those affections to another? A man I'm not even really—"

She cut herself off, realizing she'd been about to reveal the pretend nature of her affiliation to someone outside of her family. Simone did her the kindness of not pressing.

"You went through a great deal before Southwater. Perhaps you mistook safety and predictability for love when he appeared, offering you lies about a future he clearly never intended to give."

She flinched, the remnants of the pain fluttering in her chest. Not as powerful though, not anymore. "I said the same thing to Vaughn. That perhaps I was blinded to any warning signs about Southwater's true nature and intentions because of what happened to me before."

Simone looked truly shocked. "You told Blackburn about your experience with Brightling?"

Evelina nodded. "Yes."

There was a heavy silence which hung between them, one that was broken when Simone said, "You deserve happiness, Evelina, if you can find it."

Evelina forced herself to smile, to be light and change the subject, but even as she did so, her heart felt heavy. Not because of Harry or Lady Blackburn or the future that had been snatched from her grasp by a cruel liar.

But because of the future she knew she shouldn't dream about with the man she longed to see now.

∼

When Vaughn saw his carriage roll up the drive late that that afternoon, his heart leapt. Evelina was back and he felt a surge of delight, which was swiftly followed by a wash of guilt over his agreement to see Florence the next day.

It was silly, of course. In this situation, Evelina was his mistress. Actually, that wasn't entirely true. Despite their passion, they weren't in a true arrangement. And even if they were, Florence was his wife. If there was guilt, it should have flowed in the other direction and yet it didn't.

She entered the parlor and there was something pinched to her expression, something dull and tired, but when she saw him, she smiled. He crossed to her and bent to kiss her, loving how her arms wound around his neck, how her lips parted on the softest, sweetest sigh.

"I didn't expect you back until closer to supper," he breathed when their lips parted, even though she stayed in his arms, looking up at him.

Now she did release him and paced away to pour herself a drink. She didn't take tea, but got herself a glass of whisky. "I ended up crying off my meeting with my sisters," she explained.

He tilted his head. "Oh? Why? I thought you were excited to snoop around Julia's new abode and determine if you needed to put on armor when it came to her new protector."

She pivoted and speared him with a glance. "I don't recall telling you about the armor."

"I guessed." He smiled, but it fell. She did look truly troubled. "Are you well?"

"Yes. I just…oh, I'll just tell you, I need to tell you."

She seemed to be talking to herself. She motioned to the settee and they took their place there together. She downed half her whisky in a gulp and then set the glass aside. Now her full attention was on him.

He took her hands. "You're starting to frighten me. What do you need to tell me that makes you so pale?"

"I bumped into Simone Stanhope at my dressmaker's shop," she began. "And she told me...she told me that Southwater and your wife were turned away, very publicly, from an assembly and they had an argument afterward, right in the street."

He felt his eyes widen at that unexpected news and the wave of righteous triumph that rolled through him. He tilted his head back and laughed. "Christ, they must have both been humiliated. What a farce."

She didn't respond, but stared at her drink. His laughter faded and he thought of Honora's unexpected approach to him at his solicitor's. "*That's* why she wants to talk to me," he murmured.

Evelina did lift her gaze then. "What? Who wants to talk to you? Your wife?"

He flinched. "She won't be my wife in a fortnight, according to the solicitor. But yes. She sent her sister as an emissary and I've agreed to see Florence tomorrow."

Evelina's expression went entirely blank at that statement. An erasing that he realized was something she rarely did with him. "I see," she said softly. "And you think it has something to do with this new societal rejection?"

"I think the timing is suspect, yes," he said, and leaned back on the settee, draping his arm along the back. "You must have felt a thrill hearing the news, knowing the two of them are sitting in their misery."

She was very quiet for what felt like a lifetime and then she met his gaze. "No," she said quietly but firmly.

He wrinkled his brow. "No? Truly?"

She shook her head. "Simone said those words and I waited for that feeling, but there was nothing. I didn't care if they were hurt or happy. And I realized I had no further interest in causing them discomfort. I just felt...I'm tired, Vaughn."

He shifted. "If you'd like we could retire early."

"Not physically tired." She got up and paced away from him and he felt every inch of that distance like it was a mile. "I'm tired of staying angry. I'm tired of tailoring my life and our time together toward how it will play to them. I just want to let it go."

He followed her to his feet as a flash of pure, powerful panic accosted him. "What does that mean?"

"You know what I mean!" Her voice elevated slightly and her fists tightened at her sides. "Following them, making sure they see us, doing whatever we can to...to tweak them. I can't do that anymore."

He tried desperately to get enough breath in his lungs as this statement crashed through him. He was shaking and he realized it wasn't because he wanted to continue to harm Southwater and Florence anymore. It was because his arrangement with Evelina had been built entirely on that. If she ended that, she ended this.

"So what does that mean for us?" he asked, wishing his voice didn't shake like his hands. "Do you not want to be with me anymore?"

The tears in her eyes were obvious for a brief moment before she blinked them away. "Am I with you, Vaughn?"

He said nothing. He couldn't. That question had erased his ability to speak. To think. To do anything but spiral into all the answers, the good and the bad. The lies and the truths that had been built in such a short, but intense time.

"I see," he said at last, trying to overcome the sense of loss that he shouldn't feel with this woman. Equally unable to cross the gulf that now seemed to stretch between them. Was that even possible given what they'd built this attachment on?

She shook her head and finished her whisky. "I think I ought to go. I think you want me to. Or need me to."

Every fiber in Vaughn's being screamed at him to stop her. To ask her to stay. To tell her...God, what would he tell her? He couldn't even sort out the cacophony in this own head, let alone put words to it that would make any sense.

So instead he inclined his head. "I'll have my carriage take you home."

Her lips pinched. "Thank you. Good day."

Then she pivoted and left him in the parlor without a caress or another word. And when she was gone, what he realized was that everything felt terrible again in a way it hadn't since her arrival in his life.

Arabella and Julia would still be at Julia's new home, Evelina was certain of it. She worried her handkerchief in her hand as Vaughn's carriage turned into the drive and kept working to remove her emotions from her face.

They would see them, of course. Both of them knew her too well. But she wasn't going to blubber and make this more than it was. It couldn't be more than it was.

She smiled at the footman who helped her down and thanked Vaughn's driver before he departed the house, back to his master. She shivered as she was welcomed into the home by Julia's new butler and taken through the bright and pretty halls into an equally lovely, if small, parlor.

Arabella and Julia were there, sitting before the fire, talking softly. When she was announced, they both looked up in surprise and then their smiles were instant as they came across the room to her.

"Gracious, I thought you weren't coming!" Julia said as she embraced her.

"My—my schedule changed," Evelina said.

Arabella also hugged her, but when she drew back there was a knowing expression. "What happened?"

That question broke through every barrier Evelina had fruitlessly tried to create and she leaned forward and rested her head on her sister's shoulder. "I don't even know."

She was guided to the settee and there she told them everything that had happened that day, from seeing Simone, to hearing about the refusal of Southwater, to the fact that Vaughn would see his wife and how she'd told him she no longer wanted to use their affair as a weapon.

"And then...then I left," she whispered. "And he didn't stop me. So I suppose it is over now. Which makes sense, as it was only ever about revenge, wasn't it?"

"Was it?" To her surprise, it was Julia who asked, not Arabella.

Evelina shrugged in response. "Sometimes it didn't feel like it."

"After you brought sex into the equation, you mean?" Arabella pressed lightly.

Evelina shifted. That would be the easy answer, wouldn't it? Passion had clouded judgment and that was the depth of it. Only it wasn't true. She knew it.

"It was the first change," she murmured. "But it was more than that. It was the times when we simply...existed together. Read books or talked or shared secrets." She shivered. "It changed when I realized how much I wanted to protect him."

She thought of Matilda's rumor about Lady Blackburn's pregnancy once more.

"Protect him?" Arabella repeated. "Oh, Evie."

"Don't say my name like that." Evelina got up and strode away from her sisters, trying to get enough breath in her lungs and feeling like it failed.

"It's obvious you have feelings, true feelings, for this man," Julia said. "It was patently clear the night we all had supper together and this only verifies that observation."

"No." Evelina clenched her fists in and out at her sides but the tingling anxiety ripping through her didn't ease. "I'm not that foolish to do such a thing twice."

"It's not the same," Arabella snapped, and got to her feet. "He isn't the same."

"Oh, you're no judge, not anymore!" Evelina said. "You fell in love and it worked for you."

"Love," Arabella repeated. "Are we comparing *love*?"

Evelina tried to open her mouth and refute that charge. Only when it was said out loud, when the question hung in the air before her, the answer felt too clear. But she didn't want to love again. She certainly didn't want to love Vaughn. He was so caught up in the betrayals that had been performed against him, there was no doubt in her mind that he still cared for his wife. Even if he didn't, he had made Evie no promises. He wouldn't want her love.

And it would only crush her in the long term, wouldn't it? Tear her apart, only on a much grander scheme than she had experienced so recently with Harry because Vaughn felt…different.

"I cannot discuss this," she finally whispered. "Please don't make me discuss this. None of it matters. He let me walk away."

Arabella's expression softened. "Very well. We'll leave it. But an argument doesn't mean an ending, you know. And we'll face whatever comes together, just as we always do."

Julia linked an arm through Evelina's. "Yes. Always."

Evelina sighed and this time there was comfort she hadn't been able to find until that moment. "Please, won't you just show me your house and tell me all about how good your new protector is in bed…oh, what is his name?"

"Laurence," Julia said with a shake of her head. "Lord Castleton, if you want to be formal about it."

"Castleton," Evelina said, and hoped it would stick this time. "Let me just be Evelina again, not the jilted former mistress of the Duke of Southwater or the unwanted co-conspirator of the Earl of Blackburn."

"We can easily do that," Arabella said, and brought her back to the settee. "First, Julia, you must tell Evie what you were saying to be before she got here. About the jewels!"

Her sister giggled, and as they put their heads together as they so often had over their years as courtesans, Evie felt a calm come over her. But it wasn't quite enough to make her forget that she had no idea where she stood with Vaughn.

And a sneaking suspicion that love was the word that fit the ache in her heart when she thought of him.

CHAPTER 18

Vaughn hadn't had a good night and this morning he felt it as he rode across town for his meeting with Florence. He hadn't slept, tossing and turning. But it hadn't been his wife and whatever they would discuss that haunted him.

No, it had been Evie. Her words about ending their plot. The way she'd looked when she walked away from his parlor and, he feared, his life. He had dreamed of the same. Of trying to catch her and having her forever out of reach instead.

So now he felt bleary-eyed and tense as he reached the home where Florence had been staying and swung down from his horse to stare up at the place. Any time he'd ridden by in the past, it had been in the night, creeping around like some obsessed schoolboy and hoping his shame wouldn't be observed and revealed.

In the light, the home was very pretty. Small, but fashionable. And it had once been Evelina's. A place she'd believed she'd live out the rest of her days, protected by the duke.

Anger stirred in Vaughn's chest and he tamped it down as he made his way to the painted blue door and knocked. A butler greeted him and he was taken down the hallway to a parlor.

He didn't think he'd ever come here during the time Evie had lived here as Southwater's mistress, but he was certain most of the sophisticated style of the place was hers. The pretty, comfortable-looking furniture, the understated paintings and wallpaper, none of that felt like an addition Florence would make to a place. No, she'd always wanted to make rooms more startling in their display of the wealth behind them. Decorating and entertaining had been the way for her to show off.

And so now she benefitted from Evie's style. Once again that anger rose up, not for himself, but for everything that had been stolen from *her*.

"Vaughn."

He started and turned to find Florence already three steps into the room. He'd been so tangled up in his thoughts about Evie that he hadn't heard her enter.

He hadn't been this close to his wife in a while and took a fraction of a moment to examine her. She was lovely, with all that perfectly arranged blonde hair and the expensively designed dress. One he'd always complimented her on, he noted.

But today he felt…nothing as he looked at her. No attraction. No frustration. No anger. Oddly, no pain.

Just *nothing*.

He inclined his head. "My lady."

"Are we so formal now, Vaughn?" she asked softly, moving even closer.

"Mustn't we be?" he asked, and meant the question. "After all, in a fortnight's time you won't be my wife. You'll be a stranger."

Her eyes fluttered shut. A little dramatically, he thought, and she lifted a hand to her chest as if that statement caused her pain. "Oh, Vaughn."

"'*Oh, Vaughn?*'" he repeated on a humorless laugh. "It was *your* request that has brought us to this outcome."

Her gaze came back open and there was annoyance in her

expression now. Apparently she had hoped for a different reaction. She shifted and folded her arms. "Well, you cannot pretend you aren't happy with it. After all, you haven't hidden *her*, have you?"

"I don't know what you mean."

He said the words and waited for some triumph to come, as it had when Evie said that Florence and Southwater had been shunned. Only it didn't. This was the culmination of all their plans, wasn't it? It was hard to recall in that moment.

"Evelina Comerford." Ice clung to every syllable Florence said. "Harry's former whore."

He didn't like the way she drew out Evelina's name or looked disgusted by having to say it. He didn't like that she had taken over Evelina's house or life. He didn't like that she used a word meant to disparage to describe her.

He moved toward her a step. "I've nothing to say to you about *her*. You lost your right at being pained by her existence long before you slept with my best friend."

She recoiled at that and at least she had the decency to blush a little at the implication of her unfaithfulness. All those other men, all those other lies, all those other humiliations. "You hate me."

He pondered those words. Not long ago, he would have had a knee-jerk reaction to them. He would have burst out yes and meant it.

"I...I did," he admitted. "For a while I did."

"And so you decided to be so public with a courtesan?" she asked. "To try to humiliate both of us by making a spectacle with Harry's leavings? To turn everyone against us?"

Ah, and there it was. Just as he'd thought, this entire interaction was inspired by the shunning. She blamed him, or at least thought that she might be able to turn him to her will so he might do...what? Protect her? Change the tide? As if he had any ability to do that.

"You turned everyone against you all by yourself and through your own shocking behavior," he said. "But perhaps that was the only way. I realize now that you were very much forced into our life together." He blinked as he thought of Evelina and her quiet acceptance and strength in the face of a far more painful lack of choices. "But this new path is the one you want, so perhaps you'll be happy now. Settled. But I don't know what else I could say or do about it now to satisfy you if I couldn't do so as your husband. Whatever happens in your future will have nothing to do with me."

She seemed utterly shocked at how he detached himself from her choices. That he didn't take the bait of offering to help her or take some blame for what had happened. He realized she'd always done that. She would blow up and pout and demand and he had always tried to give her what she wanted. What she said would make her happy at last.

Now that he no longer cared enough to do that, she was beginning to realize she had no power over him. And so was he, truth be told.

"So you don't care if I'm harmed," she said. "But do you not think I could harm you? Harm her?"

He arched a brow. "I think if you try to harm her, you'll only come out looking the fool. And you'll have to acknowledge her publicly somehow. Something you would see as a reduction. As for me..." He sighed. "What else could there possibly be to do, Florence?"

She glared at him. "We're going to have children," she snapped. "The ones I never wanted with *you!*"

He swallowed as those words hit him like a punch that was perfectly thrown. For a moment his ears rang and his chest hurt. Just as he'd told Evie, he had wanted children very much. The fact that they'd never come in the course of his marriage had been an undeniable heartbreak. Now, though, he was just as happy, for it would have further complicated an already difficult situation. It might have even kept him from allowing Florence the break in the marriage that she demanded.

It would have kept him from Evelina.

"Are you saying you are pregnant?" he asked.

She shifted and her gaze flitted down. "N-no. We thought I might be, but then it wasn't right."

He caught his breath as further understanding dawned. "And *that* was why you and Southwater went public with your affair and his intention to marry you. Why he rushed this divorce forward suddenly. So that you could claim this child as his legitimate heir rather than some remnant of me, even though we hadn't touched in months, almost a year."

She didn't answer that charge verbally, though her flaming cheeks told him everything he needed to know. Perhaps that was part of the argument between them now, too. Southwater realized there was no child. He had exposed himself to scandal for nothing. He might even have believed Florence had manipulated the situation.

God knew, she might have.

"He will have his heir," she said, voice trembling.

"Good." He nodded. "Perhaps it will settle you both. Bond you in a way we never were. Perhaps you will *finally* stop trying to find happiness everywhere but where you actually stand. I would want that for you, just as I want it for myself."

"If you truly wish to make me happy, then stop flaunting that woman all over London."

She moved closer and batted her lashes up at him. His head was spinning from these ever-changing attempts she was making to bend him to her will. As if she realized all her games were fruitless now but she still wanted to find some new way to win.

But there wasn't one.

"I won't," he said. "I will never again try to live my life in a way that will please you, my lady. Nor will I live it to harm you. You no longer matter enough to me to count you as any part of my future. I leave you to your own choices at last. And wish you as well as I can manage."

Her breath came short and harsh. "I despise you!" she screeched.

"Then it's good you won't be linked to me for much longer." He inclined his head. "If that is all—"

"Vaughn, I demand you listen!"

He backed away. "Goodbye, Florence. At last, it is goodbye."

He turned and made his way to the parlor door. Just as he reached it, a glass figurine that had been perched on the fireplace mantel flew past him and smashed against the doorjamb. He held up a hand to prevent the scattering glass from hitting his face and drew in a breath as he faced the mess in the open doorway.

Somehow this last burst of violent frustration erased what was left of his own. He said nothing, gave nothing, and left her without looking back.

In the foyer, the butler offered to have his horse brought, but he waved the man off and walked down to the stable to retrieve the animal himself. He needed to get out of this place, to leave the past behind at last. To let everything change in this moment.

And as it did, he realized the only person he wished to see was Evie. And so he rode toward her house and what he hoped might be a new start, even if he had no idea what kind of future that change might bring.

Evelina hadn't been able to concentrate all day. Her thoughts had kept turning, slowly but persistently, back over and over to Vaughn. To the fact that he would meet with his former wife at Evelina's old home. There were so many scenarios that played out in her head.

Lady Blackburn could want to threaten him, demand he give her something more than he'd already handed over in his attempt to please her. She might ask for his help, even though she didn't deserve it.

But the option that weighed heaviest in Evelina's heart was the idea that she might ask him to come back to her. That the rejection the countess had experienced a few days before might have woken her from whatever dream Harry had built up in her head. If that happened, why *wouldn't* Lady Blackburn request a return to the reality she had so squandered? After all, Vaughn was so much better than the duke she had thrown him over for. She must have loved him once and that couldn't just die, could it? Not when one's heart had once beaten for someone like Vaughn?

Even though he wasn't Evie's, the idea of him being back with his wife stung. Burned, actually. Stung wasn't a strong enough word.

There was a knock on the parlor door and she turned to watch Parsons enter the room. "Lord Blackburn for you, Miss Comerford."

Her mouth dropped open. He was here? Even after their unpleasant encounter the day before? After his meeting with Florence? Her heart leapt and she hated herself for it.

"Yes," she said. "Yes, please send him in. We'll need nothing else, no interruptions."

"Of course, miss," the butler said, and then left to collect him.

When Vaughn came in, his hair mussed from the ride over, his eyes bright and focused on her, her knees wobbled a little. She wished she didn't. Wished she wasn't fully aware of why. But there it was, an arrow to her heart that was suddenly so sharp and clear.

She'd fallen in love with him.

"Vaughn," she managed to choke out even as she shoved the horrible truth aside so it wouldn't be reflected on her face.

He closed the door behind himself and leaned back on it. He never stopped looking at her, that focused regard holding her steady even when she felt weak. "I hated the way we ended things last night."

She nodded immediately. "So did I. And all I could think about last night and today was *you*. Did you meet with Lady Blackburn?"

He flinched. "I did. It seems I was correct that the public rejection *did* affect her. She thinks I play some part in it."

Protective instinct rose in Evelina and she folded her arms.

"You? All you've ever done is try to give her what she requested. *She's* the one who caused all this turmoil, why shouldn't she have the consequences?"

A small smile tilted his lips. "So passionately protective."

She shifted. "I suppose I am. I've come to know you since we began this arrangement. And I know you never deserved any of the hell she put you through, not before Harry and not since. If that makes me your champion, I accept the role readily."

"I'd be lucky to have you fill it, thank you. And you'll be happy to know I told her I couldn't do what she ended up asking."

There was something about his expression now, even more focused and heated on her face. God, had any other man ever looked at her like this? With hunger and gentleness and fascination all at once? Many men had expression those feelings to her with empty words, but never looked like he lived every one of them.

"What did she ask?" Evelina took a shaky step toward him.

"To stop seeing you," he said softly.

Her brow wrinkled and it felt like her heart dropped all the way to her stomach. "M-Me?"

"Yes. Apparently our public connection has only magnified the problems she's experiencing."

"That was what you wanted, yes?" she asked. "Why you came up with this plan in the first place?"

"Yes," he said, and pushed off the door to pace across the room to the window. He sighed. "I suppose it was. Sometimes I look at you and I forget that. And a few weeks ago, if I had declared I would continue on just as I like and see who I wanted to see, I think it *would* have been only to make things harder for her and for Southwater." He pivoted and faced her once more. "But not now."

She couldn't breathe and struggled to find words. "Why not now?"

"Because the reason I don't want to end things with you is nothing to do with them and everything to do with *you*. I want *you*,

Evie. I'm not ready for that to end. So I wonder if you'd like to renegotiate with me yet again?"

Her eyes went wide as a wash of relief swept over her. Here she had just realized she loved this man and he offered her something real. Not love, of course. He wouldn't love her. Some part of her had to believe he still loved Florence, even if he was ready to let her go. It would, at least, take him time to get over that. And she could never again believe that a courtesan like her would have a long-term future with a man.

But that didn't change the fact that what he wanted now was a real connection. To be with each other simply because they wanted to be. And she would take that.

Slowly she crossed to him and wound her arms around his neck. She loved the solid feel of him and the comforting heat of him as their bodies molded. "Will we negotiate like we did before?"

He bent his head and brushed his lips to hers. "You'll always have the upper hand there. And I'm perfectly happy with that."

The words ended then as the kiss deepened. He cupped her closer to his body, letting her feel his desire for her, building her own for him to a fever pitch. All her fears and worries about her heart vanished in that moment, replaced by drives and desires she better understood and knew she could control. With great difficulty, she parted her mouth from his.

"Sit on the settee, my lord," she ordered.

He tilted his head as he continued to stare down at her. "I find I cannot deny you. Very well."

He brushed her lips with his again and then released her to stride across to the settee. She watched him move with a shiver and then waved her hand as he took a proper position on one side of the couch.

"Oh no," she said while she moved to the door and locked it. "Slouch. Sprawl. Give me a very nice place to perch."

His green eyes brightened with sharp desire and he slowly did as she'd asked, sliding down a little, widening his legs so that he seemed to take over the entire seat.

"Is that what you want?" he asked, tracking her while she returned to him.

She nodded and bent over. She caged him in against the back of the settee and brought her mouth back to his without taking it. "Exactly what I want. With one very small adjustment."

She dragged a hand down his body, over the muscular lines and angles of him and settled her hand against his fall front. She let out a low laugh to find him half-hard already. Perfect. She flicked the buttons open as she kissed him at last and folded the fabric down to reveal him.

"*That* is what I want," she whispered against his mouth.

He caught her hips and drew her forward, bunching her skirt so she could straddle him with greater ease. "It's yours."

She shivered at that idea, which dragged her back to the feelings she'd been trying to forget. No, there was only this. The rest she had to school, control.

She settled over him, spreading her skirts down and around them as her bare body covered him beneath. He wasn't inside yet, but he fitted very nicely between her thighs. When she rocked over him, half hard became fully hard.

"Oh, if this is mine…" she murmured, dragging her lips from his mouth to his jawline and nipping up to his ear. "Whatever shall I do with it?"

He arched a little and she gasped as he slid along her length. "You're a creative woman. I think you'll come up with something."

"Only if you do your job right."

He laughed against her neck and her heart soared. God, he made it easy. That had been part of the attraction from the beginning. Even when they were pretending the connection was all about revenge, he'd always made her smile. Always made her safe.

She reached between them, lifting a little, getting her hand under the bunched layers of her dress between them and aligned him to her body. He cupped her backside, looking up into her face and then he was sliding inside.

Both of them let out a shuddering sigh at the pleasure of his hard body sliding through her slick heat. God, it was like coming home, a pleasure unlike anything she'd felt in all her years of cultivating the response for herself and those she fucked.

He was just different. And she was going to enjoy every bloody minute of him.

CHAPTER 19

The grip of Evelina's body made the room blur and Vaughn's legs shake within the first few thrusts. That was just how much she moved him and it took every ounce of his control to not simply spend like a green boy.

He rested his head back to watch her ride him, her eyes closed, her lips parted as she moaned softly with every thrust. There was something so gorgeous about her pure abandon. Something undeniable that dragged him out to sea where he didn't care about drowning.

He would gladly drown to feel her grip around him in release.

She worked for it. Every thrust she ground against him, her sheath clenching, her breath shaking. He lifted to meet her, holding her hips through the silk of her pretty gown and watching her unravel. When she finally began to shake, her body massaging him out of control while she moaned his name in the quiet, he felt a triumph and warmth unlike anything he'd ever felt before.

She rode through the crisis, groaning and whimpering, her hands clutching his shoulders. At last she collapsed against his chest and he chuckled against her neck before he lifted up, continuing to thrust into her shivering body, this time with more purpose. The heated pleasure streaked up his cock, out of control and powerful. It was at the last moment that he pushed her back on his lap, let himself pop free of her slick heat. He caught his cock, covering the head so his release wouldn't stain her dress.

She kissed him as the pleasure faded a fraction, spread warmth through every nerve ending of his body. There was peace to what happened between them even if it was nothing peaceful. But she brought him that, centered him, somehow. Made him remember who he'd been before his world had come crashing down around him.

Made him dream of what it could be when the next fortnight was over and he was no longer a married man.

"This was a good negotiation," she laughed as she moved off his lap and cuddled up at his side. He held her, basking in the afterglow of all the passion.

"Yes. I think we should negotiate every decision this way. What to eat, where to go, when to invite your family around for supper."

Her fingers traced his chest. "It's a pretty idea. Do you really want that?"

"Yes." He kissed the crown of her head without hesitation. "We can work out the details, but this is what I need, now more than ever. Is it what you want?"

She nodded without looking up at him. "As much time as you wish to share, I'll make myself available."

He frowned at that turn of phrase. It made sense, of course. What they were negotiating, after all, were the terms of a real arrangement. He would be her protector, this time in full and happy truth. But that felt...empty somehow?

"You have a very odd expression on your face," she said, and he realized she *was* looking at him now. "Is everything well?"

"I think I'm fully feeling the effects of a very long day."

Her hands smoothed along his chest gently. "It must have been difficult. Even if you're ready for what happens next, you were married for five years. You had hopes and dreams."

He nodded. "Yes. I thought Florence and I would be together for all our lives. That we'd grow to care about each other. Love each other. That we would have children." He frowned. "Her parting salvo to me was about that."

Evie lifted her head. "About children?"

"Yes. She declared that she would give Southwater all the heirs denied to me. She even implied that she was pregnant now. Though when I asked, she admitted she wasn't. I do believe they thought she was, though, which is why he stepped up to push the divorce harder."

"So she wasn't pregnant after all," Evie breathed.

He jolted and looked down at her. He had expected she'd look as shocked as he'd felt when Florence said that. That they would commiserate on their surprise and whatever other feelings such a cruel trick created.

But Evie didn't look surprised. Relieved, yes. But not surprised.

"No, she's not pregnant," he said softly. "Evie, what did you know?"

Her lips parted and now the relief was gone and replaced by a faint expression of…panic. Not because of Florence's lie…because of what he realized now was her own.

"*Evelina*," he said.

She got up and smoothed her wrinkled skirt. Her guilt was so plain. He recognized it because he'd seen it so often on Florence's face over the years when her lies and affairs had been revealed one by one. Of course, Evie was nothing like *her*, but to see that was visceral in a way he couldn't seem to control.

He waited for her response, breathless to find out if she would try to continue whatever lie hung between them. To his relief, she said, "Matilda…she—she had overheard something like that. She told me that night we gathered with Ravenscroft, Thistlebury and Harriet."

Now he recoiled and got to his feet, shoving himself back in place so he was no longer as naked physically as he felt emotionally.

"What? That was *weeks* ago, Evie. And you never said anything to me?"

Her gaze fluttered down. "No-no. I—Matilda is very often wrong about her gossip. I didn't even know if it was true."

"And yet you still denied me the rumor, even though it might have been revealed to me in a much crueler way. It was revealed to me that way today," he snapped, and walked away from her.

When he pivoted back, she had clenched her hands before herself and she was trembling. "I know I should have told you. I'm sorry."

"I don't like lies, even those of omission. And you know why, Evie."

"I do," she said. "I do know. But I also know you—you love her." He flinched at her use of the present tense with that statement. "And yes, that you wanted children with her. And to tell you would have hurt you. And perhaps even driven you to want even more revenge. I thought until I was certain it was best to—to wait."

"I did care for her once," he admitted. "Foolishly, in the end. But understand that I never would have kept something like this from you, even if I know you also loved Southwater." He ran a hand through his hair. "I need to go."

"Oh no, please," she said, and took a step toward him.

He took an equal step back. If she touched him, he would just forgive her. He would tell himself she'd meant no real harm and it would probably be true. But he wasn't sure he could trust that voice. He'd been burned by it before. "Not forever. We will discuss this further. I just need to think."

Her hands, which she'd been holding up in a plea, fell back to her sides. She nodded slowly. "I-I understand. I do. Please take all the time you need."

"Thank you," he said, and then he moved to the door, unlocked it and exited into her foyer. His head spun as his horse was brought and then he rode off into the night, knowing that it wasn't Florence's duplicity that troubled him.

It was the idea that he had been kept in the dark by Evie. A woman he hadn't realized he'd come to have so much faith in.

Vaughn was gone in an instant and after she'd watched him ride away without so much as a glance over his shoulder, Evie sat back down on the settee where they'd made love and rested her head back to stare at the ceiling above.

Tears stung her eyes. Guilt ripped at her heart. And it hurt so damn much to know she'd let him down because she was too much of a coward to hurt him and risk the consequences. Was this what love was? Just something that felt pretty and then only hurt?

No, that couldn't be true. She saw the love between Arabella and Silas and it wasn't that. But perhaps her sister was just a lucky one in a million to find such a powerful connection. Perhaps Evelina shouldn't wish for something so rare.

Even though her heart was filled with the emotion for the man who had just strode out her door.

The door to the foyer was still open and so when there was a knock on the door a moment later, she heard it, as well as the male voices talking softly after Parsons let whomever was calling in.

Her heart leapt and she got to her feet and rushed to the foyer. "Vaughn!" she cried out, thinking she would see he'd returned because he wanted to continue the conversation.

Only it wasn't him. She came up short, her hand lifting to her lips. It was the Duke of Southwater. Harry had been talking to her butler but now he looked at her from across the expanse between them. He smiled and she drew back. That was the same soft smile he'd always given her during their relationship. The one that had faded long before he ended things between them so cruelly.

"Evelina," he said, walking past Parsons toward her.

The butler looked at her in question and she nodded to say she would accept the unexpected visitor. "Your Grace," she managed to squeak out.

Southwater tilted his head. "Your Grace?"

She didn't respond, refused to acknowledge the question in his tone or change how she addressed him. "I didn't expect you."

"I know. I simply needed to see you. May we talk?"

She sighed because the last thing she wanted to do was interact with this man when she could still feel Vaughn on her skin and in her heart. When she was still torn apart by what she'd done and hadn't done, alongside what she felt so powerfully for him.

"Please," Southwater added, and took a step toward her.

She motioned to the parlor. "Very well. I have a few moments before I must leave for my sister's."

She had no such appointment, but it left her with options, at least. He followed her back into the parlor and looked around. "Your sister's home really is fine. It's good you had it to return to."

She pursed her lips. "Yes, after you ejected me so you could give your new lover my house, I suppose it could have been *very* bad if I hadn't had this place to fall back to."

"Well, I knew you were protected," he said, and crossed to the settee where she and Vaughn had just tangled together. He fluffed up a pillow they'd crushed in their ardor and threw himself down without waiting for her to take her own seat.

She refused to respond to his statement about protection. Refused to argue with him that that was the duty he had so fully shirked. It didn't matter anymore because he didn't matter anymore.

"What do you want, Southwater?" she asked.

"Whisky," he said with a smile.

She shook her head. "That isn't what I mean."

He wrinkled his brow, seeming surprised that she wasn't warming to him. How had she ever? Now when she looked at him all she saw were his sharp edges, his selfishness, his lack of care for anyone but himself. It had always been there, hadn't it? She could see it now when she wasn't blinded by a desire for safety and calm.

"I have been thinking a great deal about you in the last few weeks," he said. "You can be proud that your behavior had the desired effect."

"My behavior?" she repeated. "What do you mean?"

He didn't remove his even stare from her face. "Come now, Evelina. You think I don't know that you turned to Blackburn as a way for you two to exact some kind of petty revenge? What other reason could you have for matching with him?"

She frowned. "His decency? His kindness? His intelligence? His attentiveness to my every need?"

His cheek twitched. "I miss you."

Those three words hit her like a punch and she staggered back. What the hell was going on? Just a few weeks before this man had stood in this very parlor after she'd asked for him to come, and told her she was unworthy of his affection. And *now* he wanted her?

"Why?" she asked. "You made your choice, you created a life-altering scandal not only for yourself and Lady Blackburn, but for Vaughn. And now you say you miss what you threw away?"

"I was caught up in something," he said. "But the cost is becoming too high, Evelina. I'll need to walk away, I think. And there's no place I'd rather be than back with you. You *must* want that, too. And when I do, it will mitigate the scandal."

"How?" she burst out. "How could you ever mitigate the damage you and the countess did?"

"Well, she'd go back to Blackburn, wouldn't she? The divorce isn't complete, it could be halted. They could play at falling back in love, Society would drool over that. And you and I could be free of this little problem in our story."

She found herself battling for breath at the utter arrogance of that statement, which dismissed every heartache, every betrayal, every cruelty that this man had performed not only in the last six weeks, but in the last year.

She would have dressed him down, would have kicked him from her home and told him never to return except for one thing: his statement about Vaughn. The fact was that he wasn't entirely wrong. If Vaughn and Lady Blackburn were to reunite, that *might* reduce the damage. Vaughn would be seen as what he was: a good and decent man who had been willing to forgive.

Her stomach turned at the idea that he would walk back into the arms of someone who didn't cherish him, but what if that was what he wanted? What if, in his heart, he did still want the future he'd had torn from him? Hadn't he mentioned his pain at its loss more than once?

"You couldn't be serious," she whispered.

He stood and stepped toward her. It took everything in her not to take an equal step back. "I am."

He moved to touch her face, and now she did step back. He frowned, the flash of annoyance in his eyes one she recognized. How many times had he looked at her like that over the years when she laughed too loudly or teased too lightly or told him she didn't feel like going to his bed because she had a headache? Had Vaughn ever looked at her like that? Like she was a bother?

No. Never. Not once.

"I understand the game," Southwater said. "That you must enact some petty punishments for what you see as a betrayal. That's fine. You take your time, think about it. I could call again tomorrow and we could discuss it further, along with my generous terms for your coming back and starting over." He caught her hand and didn't release it even when she tugged. He lifted it to his lips and pressed them to her knuckles before he backed away. "Think on it. You'd be a fool to give up a duke worth five times what an earl was worth. Good day."

He left her and she covered her face with her shaking hands. Between it all, she felt like the world was spinning and she had no idea what to think or do. And when she had those kinds of emotions there was only one place to go.

So she called for her carriage to go there.

~

Barnaby had served Arabella, and in turn Evelina and Julia, too long to find it odd when Evelina burst into the house and demanded she see Arabella without being announced. He'd simply told her which parlor and sent her on her way.

When she opened the door, Arabella was seated on the settee, a book in hand. Silas sat at the escritoire in the corner of the room, writing a letter. They both looked up as she entered.

"Evelina?" Arabella said, but didn't have the chance to rise from her seat. Evelina crossed to her, sank down on the settee next to her and settled her head into Arabella's lap. Her sister looked at Silas with concern but then rested a hand in Evelina's hair and stroked it gently.

"What is it, love?" she asked softly.

Silas got up and moved to the chair across from the settee. "Are you well, Evie?"

"No, not well at all," she whispered, and hated that tears began to sting her eyes, then slid down her cheeks. "I'm such a fool, Arabella."

"You couldn't be, you are the wisest person I know." Her sister continued to stroke her hair. "Why would you think otherwise?"

She turned her face into Arabella's knee and her voice was muffled as she said, "I love him."

She waited for the concern and the censure and the rest, but Arabella just sighed. "Oh, dearest, we established that some time ago. It's plain as the nose on your pretty face, especially when you two are in a room together."

"He cares for you, as well," Silas said.

At that, Evelina sat up and wiped her face. "Yes, he might. Sometimes he looks at me and it's unlike anything I've ever felt from any man before. But...but I ruined everything, I think. I kept something from him, I wanted to protect him, but he found out about it. He feels betrayed."

Silas leaned closer, draping his elbows over his knees. "Evie, that only proves to me that he cares. If he didn't, why would he be bothered if you lied?"

She shook her head. "Because the lie was about-about *her*. About his wife. I kept something from him about her. He walked away afterward and he claimed he just needed space to think about it, but now I wonder—I wonder if it's more than that. And if he were offered the chance to repair what they once shared…would it be better for him?"

"That is nonsense!" Arabella barked out. "Evie, that woman is a nightmare."

"I agree. But he felt so strongly about getting back at her. Pretended to hate her. But hate can be so close to love, can't it?"

"Or it can just be a justifiable response to someone breaking every rule," Silas said.

"You like breaking rules," Evelina whispered.

He shook his head and there was no teasing to his stare. "Not those. Not ever."

Arabella reached across the expanse and briefly squeezed his hand. Then she released him and put all her attention back on Evelina. "What happened next? You are keeping something from us. Tell me now."

There was no denying her when she took that tone and in truth, Evelina didn't want to. She needed help and counsel. "Harry showed up at your old house after Vaughn left me. And he…he wants me back. He wants to reset things and start over."

Arabella huffed out a breath and got up, storming across the room where she put her hands on her hips and burst out, "Please tell me you told that tosser to get bloody fucked."

"Arabella," Silas said, softly but firmly. He held Evelina's gaze. "You know this isn't real, Evie. Of course he wants to reset things. He's losing everything since he came out as Lady Blackburn's lover. His friends have turned on him, he's beginning to get bounced out of clubs and gatherings. It will take years for him to rebuild if he stays this course. But if he backs out, perhaps even finds some way to put the blame entirely on her…a man like that would always try to find an out."

Arabella nodded like her head was on a spring. "Not to mention I would wager seeing you with Blackburn, seeing you light up in a way you never did with him, must make him jealous. Not because he cared. But because he doesn't like to lose."

Evelina shivered as all those reasonable arguments sunk in. "But wouldn't I be cruel to deny Vaughn his choice? If Harry was removed from the equation, he could decide this future without the duke's interference."

Arabella's face crumpled and she looked like she was going to cry. It was shocking, for her strong sister rarely showed such emotions. She returned to Evelina and sat down, taking both her hands. "My God, you would sacrifice yourself for Blackburn?"

"Not…not forever. I don't want Harry. He took my hand and wouldn't let go and I felt like it was spiders crawling up my skin. But for Vaughn I could bear it a little while."

"You aren't being rational," Silas said.

She dropped her head. "I know. I know. But I…I love him enough to try to save him."

"I'm going to talk to him," Silas said, starting to stand.

Evelina lunged for him and caught his hand. "Oh no, Silas, don't. Please, I adore you for wanting to help, but Vaughn is the furthest thing from the villain here and he's been through so much these last few days. Just leave it be. Don't pull him into yet another drama."

Silas drew in a long breath. "Fine. If you don't wish me to interfere, I won't. But I think you're making a mistake even considering this."

She scrubbed a hand over her face. "Southwater is coming back to the house tomorrow and I suppose he'll demand an answer then. I know you're both right that in my haste to protect Vaughn, I might be considering wild and ridiculous notions."

Arabella tugged her in and hugged her. "Yes. Please don't do that.

Don't sacrifice yourself, not even for this man. If he's worth the love you declare for him, he wouldn't want it."

"I must think. I just have to think," Evie whispered.

"Then do so here," Silas suggested. "Stay with us, have supper. We can talk further about this or we can talk about anything and everything else to soothe you. Please. Stay."

Evelina stared at his man who had made her sister the center of his world and a swell of adoration for him rose. "I will, thank you. And thank you for turning even a tiny portion of the love and protection you give my sister onto me."

"She will always have my heart," Silas declared with a quick, powerfully loving glance for Arabella. "And so you will always have my sword, if you need it."

"Come," Arabella said as she moved to the sideboard. "Let me get you a drink."

Evelina nodded and sat back down on the settee. She let them fuss over her and take care of her, but even a night in their fine company didn't ease her spinning mind, the one that at that moment was willing to do anything if she could ease Vaughn's pain even a fraction.

Even if that meant multiplying her own.

CHAPTER 20

When the pounding on the door began at nearly midnight, Vaughn wasn't asleep. The rest of the household had gone to bed shortly before, but he remained in his study, staring at an untouched whisky and wishing he could make his mind stop.

But the pounding interrupted it all and he rushed to his feet to answer the door before it woke the entire house. When he threw it open he gasped in shock.

"Arabella?" he said, blinking at the sight of the petite woman on his front step.

She grunted as an answer and shoved past him into his foyer. "You arse."

He leaned back. "I beg your pardon?"

"You heard me."

He blinked at the bright anger in her eyes, the sharp judgment that she made no attempt to hide despite their disparate positions in the world. He did like her with all her fire, even if he didn't understand what was happening here.

"I'm certain I must deserve this ire, but perhaps you can tell me how. Why don't we come into my parlor?"

In reality, he *did* think he knew how. Evie must have told her sister that he left her after finding out the truth. If she'd done that, that could only mean he must have deeply hurt her and he hated himself for it. Hated this entire ghastly situation and how it tore his world to shreds and made him behave in ways he ought never have done.

Arabella huffed out a breath but followed him when he led her to the room.

"May I get you a drink?" he asked.

"No." She folded her arms.

He leaned back against the edge of the sideboard and crossed his ankles. "I assume this is about Evie."

"Of course it's about Evie, I don't give a damn about you lot unless you affect people *I* love. And you do, my lord. Oh, you most certainly do."

There was a flare of joy that worked through him at that statement, locked in amongst the anxiety and tension. He wanted to affect Evie, to know he did so was a great source of pride. But not hurt her. He never wanted to hurt her.

"I surmise she came to you after I left her this afternoon."

"Oh yes, she did, but someone came to *her* first. Do you know that Southwater showed up at her home after you stormed off in a tizzy?"

He scrambled to attention as he thought of the last time Southwater had come to her. How cruel the duke had been, how driven Vaughn had been to protect her. That had led to their first kiss. That had opened a door to all this. It felt like a lifetime ago and he'd thought it ended the matter, Southwater had spoken to her so dismissively. But now he'd returned?

"Did he hurt her?" he asked.

Arabella's breath caught. "You would fear for her safety even though you're angry."

"Of course. Evie is very important to me. Whether I'm frustrated by her lack of openness or not, I would never want to see her hurt, either emotionally or, God forbid, physically. But tell me, what did he do?"

"He didn't hurt her," Arabella said, and now her tone was a little calmer, less adversarial. Like he'd passed some test.

He let out a breath of relief, but then shook his head. "He must be as worked up as Florence at the turning of the tide against them. Did he want Evie to do something to help them overcome it?"

Arabella folded her arms. "My sister came to my home, weeping over you, torn about what to do. She made Silas promise not to bring this to you, but I never promised a damn thing, so I'm here."

"Torn about what to do?" he whispered. "What did he ask her to do?"

"Go back to him," she said, and met his eyes. "He wants her back, he wants to abandon your wife and try to return to what he had before he destroyed both your worlds."

There was a moment when it felt like an explosion had gone off in Vaughn's parlor. His ears rang and his vision blurred and he fought to maintain some composure in the face of this entirely unexpected news.

"Why—why would she even consider going back to him after what he did to her?" he asked, shaking his head. "Why would that be something she was torn over when he doesn't hold half her worth?"

"It isn't because she loves *him*," Arabella said.

He blinked, those words sinking past his shock. He opened and closed his mouth. "She is considering it to—to protect me?"

She nodded. "She knows what you lost in all this. She sees you as the victim and she isn't wrong. But she's too much like me. We learned to protect those we loved in the horrible house we grew up in, even to our own detriment."

"How would her going back to Southwater protect me?" he choked out.

"I was under the impression that she believes you must still have feelings for your wife to have held on to your hurt and betrayal so long." He turned his head as if this diminutive woman had struck him, but she didn't stop. "If she could give you back what you wanted, or at least ease the humiliation of it, she would sacrifice herself for you."

His mouth fell open. "Wh-why?"

"Why do you think, you great oaf?"

"Arabella…" he whispered, his heart beginning to pound. She was talking about something more than an affair or a friendship or a careless arrangement meant to be temporary.

She was talking about love. And once again his knees went weak at the idea that Evelina could love him this much despite all his flaws and mistakes.

"If you don't love her, if you could never love her as she deserves to be loved, you must stop this. You mustn't let her give herself away to one man who doesn't give a damn about her in order to save yourself when you care just as little." Arabella stepped closer. "But if you do love her…if what I see when you're near her is real…then you must stop her from ending any chance she has at happiness. Any chance *you* have."

The world continued to tilt. Evelina loved him. She loved him. He wanted to shout out triumph into the darkness outside. He wanted to pluck down the stars and howl at the moon with the pride that realization created.

But he didn't have her yet. He hadn't won her, he certainly hadn't come to her rescue.

"Is she at your home?" he asked.

She nodded. "She is."

"Then I'll follow you back, I'll go right now, I'll—"

"You won't," Arabella interrupted. "Because she was sleeping at last when I left and leaving her more exhausted than ever is no way to face her and have this out."

He took a shaky breath. "Very well. I won't push." He looked her up and down. "I'm surprised Windham let you go screeching out into the night to confront me."

She smirked. "Silas knows better than to stand between me and the happiness of my sisters. And I suppose he thinks you a decent man, which is high praise, indeed."

"It is," he said, and meant it. "I'm not sure I've earned it, though I'll endeavor to try. When does she meet with him?"

"Tomorrow," she said. "At ten, for it seems he cannot even give her twenty-four hours to think before he demands she answer. She has listened to our concerns and she might refuse him but—"

"I'll go to her home and speak to her," he promised. "I won't let her do anything to hurt herself. Not for me."

Arabella nodded. "Good. Good." She pivoted and started for his door. There she stopped and turned back. "What will you do? Just so I'm prepared for whether I'll have a joyful or broken-hearted sister after tomorrow."

He took in a shaky breath. "Arabella, I like you. I think once you stop hating me on her behalf that you'll like me too. But you aren't going to be the first person I say those words to."

Her expression softened and she smiled just slightly. "Good-night, Blackburn."

"Goodnight, Arabella."

She left and he moved to the window to watch her carriage depart. His heart throbbed as he stared out into the darkness. He hadn't said the words to Arabella, but they were there, sitting firmly in his heart. They defined a feeling that had begun to grow from the first moment he spoke to Evelina. From the first moment he touched her hand and felt the spark of a connection that had only grown.

He loved her.

It was shocking to know that, to feel it so strongly and without a doubt. He thought he'd felt love before. He'd tried so hard to culti-vate it with Florence over their years together, to make it fit into spaces where it most certainly didn't belong and wasn't welcome.

But there was no *trying* with Evie. He walked into a room and her warmth surrounded him. He found himself drawn to her smile and her laugh. When she hurt, he ached for her. When *he* hurt, he wanted no one but her at his side to face his demons with him. He loved to dance with her and make love to her and read with her and walk with her. There was no space in his life where he didn't picture her.

The idea that she might sacrifice herself to give him something she believed he wanted fit perfectly into the wonderful, selfless person she was. And the idea that she would do so cut through his heart like a sword wielded by an expert knight.

He couldn't allow her to do it. Even if she wouldn't be his, even if she wouldn't hear his heart or accept it he had to let her know what he wanted. Which was her. Forever.

He sucked in a shaky breath and blinked at a sting of joyful tears. He would tell her his heart.

And he couldn't wait to do that and hope that she could somehow gift him with the return of her own.

CHAPTER 21

When Evelina turned into her drive at eight-thirty the next morning, she wasn't prepared for what awaited her. She'd meant to come home after her night with Arabella and Silas, prepare herself in her best armor, force herself to eat something to settle her stomach and then wait for Southwater to call.

What she would do when that happened, she still didn't know. But she thought she'd have time to ponder as she waited for their ten o'clock appointment.

But his carriage was already there, sat in the circular drive. Her heart throbbed as she smoothed her skirt and forced a smile for the footman who assisted her down when she arrived.

Southwater got out of his carriage just as she did and gave her what looked to be a slight expression of annoyance before he wiped it away and smiled. God, had his smile always been so cold? Had she simply been blind to it and to everything negative about him?

Now that she had a point of comparison so fine as Vaughn, this man didn't live up to even a fraction.

"Your Grace," she said as she nodded at Parsons as he opened the door. "I-I didn't expect you until ten."

"I decided we needed to have this out earlier. Where have you been?" Without asking her leave, he took her arm and guided her up the stairs. When Parsons took a breath to greet them, Southwater waved his hand. "We need nothing, don't disturb us."

When he tugged her into the parlor, she yanked her arm away at last. "This is not your home, Southwater. You've no right to speak to my servants that way."

He arched a brow. "I've the right as their better to speak to them any way I desire, my dear. And this isn't *your* home, either. It's Arabella's. I wonder why she didn't sell it, why Windham didn't force her to do it to erase her sordid history, but here we are."

She folded her arms. "Silas loves my sister. He doesn't see her past as something that requires erasing. He accepts her in every way."

Southwater's brow wrinkled and it was as if he didn't speak the same language she did. He sighed. "Well, that is very good for them. I'll give them my most sincere felicitations once we have worked all this out. But I'm here now and so we should focus on us, don't you think?"

"Us," she said softly, the word tasting bitter on her tongue. She had spent so much time in the last two years thinking about them as an "us", planning for them as an "us". She'd taken great pleasure in the stability those dreams had falsely created.

But now, staring at him from across the parlor, she didn't feel anything when he said the word. Nothing except the question of what she could leverage for Vaughn with whatever happened next.

"If Windham can forget Arabella's past, certainly we can forget the recent unpleasantness, can't we? Especially if my apologies came with an increase in your pin money and a return to your home."

She tilted her head. "You would evict Lady Blackburn so easily as you did me?"

He shrugged. "She'll find her way."

"Jesus," Evelina whispered under her breath as his casual cruelty wrapped its icy tendrils around her. "You know, I think I'm glad you have been so selfish as to spring this conversation on me early. I think you must have believed that taking me off guard would make me more likely to fall into your traps, but instead it only makes me more capable of seeing through your act."

He scowled. "My act?"

"You don't want me," she whispered. "I think now that you never did. Not truly."

"Of course I did," he said, and sounded confused. "Arabella had a protector at the time and that made you the most sought-after courtesan in London. Having you on my arm was a point of great pride for me. I've always wanted you."

She blinked. Even now he was so selfish that he could only couch this declaration of desire in terms of himself. What she brought to *him*, what *he* wanted, what *he'd* looked for. Nothing was about her and her heart. Christ, he made it sound like he might have even gone for Arabella rather than her if that had been an option, because at the time her sister had been the more desirable option.

"And yet you threw me away like rubbish in the gutter," she said softly. "Even now, you only ask for me back because your cruel machinations have destroyed any semblance of respectability you had. And you see that the *ton* somehow supports Vaughn and I coming together. You think you can regain something of your reputation by returning your so-called affection to me. You'd probably blame Lady Blackburn for the whole affair and let her burn without you."

"Well, she did make convincing arguments," he said.

Evelina held up a hand. "Stop. You forget one thing, Harry. What the *ton* sees, what is real and true, is that Vaughn and I were the two injured parties in your betrayal. We came together with certain goals in mind, but we always offered each other support, solace." Her eyes filled with tears as she thought of how Vaughn looked at her. "Peace. You can't manufacture that. And even if you could, I don't think I could *ever* forget what you did. Not to me. I've come to accept that. But I would never be able to look at you and not see what you did to him."

Southwater's glare darkened further. "*Him.* You are so protective of him."

She smiled a little. "Oh yes. I would do *anything* to protect him. Well, almost anything. Not this. Not you."

"Good," a voice said from the door, and she pivoted because she knew it. Vaughn leaned against the jamb, his green eyes bright as they held hers, and he smiled. "I cannot tell you how happy I am to hear that."

~

If Vaughn had feared what he would find when he came to Evelina's house that morning, all his anxieties were washed away when she turned to find him at her door and her entire being seemed to light up. There was no denying her joy to see him, her relief at his presence and her love that seemed to turn on every light in his dark life. She was so perfect and lovely and he was shocked that he hadn't fully recognized his feelings for her sooner.

How could one be anywhere near her and not fall head over heels in love?

"Get out!" Southwater sputtered as he took a long step toward Vaughn. "This isn't about you!"

He shifted his stance, just in case his old "friend" was about to try to start a physical fight. "No. Nor is it about you. This is about *her.*"

"Vaughn," she whispered.

He put his attention back on her. "Evie, I know all this went so badly. I did it *all* badly, from the very start. But if you've even once considered returning to this man who never deserved to look at you, let alone call himself yours, in order to protect me, I must beg of you not to."

"See here," Southwater said.

"You don't have to choose me," Vaughn continued, as if Southwater wasn't even in the room. "I would fully understand if you didn't, couldn't, after how I began all this. But please don't lose yourself, not for him. Not for me. You are far too precious."

Now Southwater snorted. "Please. As if you care for her. It was always obvious that she was only a means for revenge."

Vaughn never looked away from Evie. "It started that way. My strongest emotion was anger and hatred for Florence and for you. But the longer I spent with Evie, the more she captivated me. The more I forgot about living for what I hated and started moving toward what I-I—" He took a step toward her. "I don't want to say this in front of him, but I will. I started moving toward what I love, Evie."

Her gasp cut across the short distance between them. She lifted her hands to clasp them before her chest and they trembled.

"I love you, Evelina Comerford."

The room was spinning as she stared into the eyes of this man, this glorious, wonderful, utterly perfect man who had just declared his heart was hers. For a moment all she could feel was the pure joy of knowing her feelings were returned.

"He doesn't mean that," Southwater snapped, and broke the spell. "How could he?"

She turned toward her former protector and looked him up and down. "Just because you never did?"

The truth fluttered across the duke's face. Of course he never had. He'd said the words a few times. He'd made promises like a man who did. But when it really mattered, like that horrible night her sister had been taken, he'd shown the truth of himself.

"Evelina," he began.

She motioned to the door. "Get out, Southwater. Go back to your scandal, I won't save you from it. Go live with your choices." She smiled at Vaughn. "And I thank you for them."

Southwater looked stunned and for a moment there was only

silence in the room between them. Until he erupted. "You think you have the right to try to humiliate me, you little bitch? You think you have the right to even look into my face? I'm the Duke of South-water and you're nothing but a—"

He didn't get to finish. Vaughn leapt forward, cocked his fist back and hit Southwater so hard that the duke careened backward and hit the floor, skidding backward on his arse.

"Finish the sentence," Vaughn growled as he towered over him. "And I will make certain you lose teeth with the next punch."

Evie staggered toward him, let her hand rest on his forearm. Disgust lined Southwater's face, but there was also fear and there, somewhere amongst the ugliness, regret. Not enough. But just a little.

He got up and smoothed his jacket before he pivoted and started for the door. "Good riddance to you both then. You deserve each other."

Evie sighed and went to the parlor door as he departed, shutting it so they wouldn't have to hear him shouting in the foyer.

"Should I go out and help Parsons eject him?" Vaughn asked.

She shook her head. "Arabella always hired the kind of servants who could handle themselves if need be. I think Parsons used to be in the military, he can handle one stuffy duke."

"Good, because I don't want to leave you." Vaughn stepped toward her again and took her hand.

"Did you hurt yourself?" she whispered. "When you hit him?"

He shook his head and tugged her nearer. Now they were just a breath away from each other and she shivered at the closeness. "There is no pain, not when I'm with you. What I said to him, Evie, it wasn't for show or to anger him. I really do love you."

God, those words. How could they be so beautiful and also so painful? Because when the joy of them peeled away, there were still questions and hurts beneath. A future that was cloudy and likely always would be for a woman like her.

"I love you, too," she said, reaching up to cup his cheek as he smiled like he'd just won a prize. "Foolish as it may be for a woman to fall in love with her protector."

His brow wrinkled. "Protector? No, Evelina, this negotiation will not be between a courtesan and her protector. I *love* you, Evie. You are my perfect match. To love and to be loved? I know how rare that is. I won't lose it. I want to *marry* you."

She released his hand. "Oh. Oh no, Vaughn, that isn't possible."

"Why? Many men have married their mistresses."

"Not many," she corrected.

He shook his head. "Fine, but some. Including the very recent wedding of Windham and your sister."

"Silas is the bastard son of a marquess who was always known to be wild. He lost nothing of his reputation when he married my sister. I think he might have added to it. But you are not that. You're an earl, Vaughn. And one who is already dragging a scandal behind him. And please don't tell me that it doesn't matter, because I know how it's troubled you."

"It did. But you just said the very poignant truth that I already carry the scandal from Florence's actions and my agreement to go through with a nearly unheard-of divorce. That wouldn't change if I gave you up. It would only lead to me being a very miserable pariah versus a deliriously happy one."

"But you might not always be a pariah!" she exclaimed, and drew his hands to her. "Vaughn, you cannot pretend you don't understand. The *ton* already sees you as a victim and in a few months or years there will be some other scandal big enough that will overtake this one. You could rebuild, but not if you marry not only a courtesan, but one of the most infamous courtesans in London. And not only that, but the former lover of *your* former wife's new husband."

"You think he'll marry her even after he just tried to reunite with you and declared he'd throw her over?" he asked.

She nodded. "I think he'll have little choice. This attempt to reunite with me was an option of desperation. But after everything they've done? If he can't return to what he once had and then declare he was deceived or tricked, he would have to know there's no way out."

"Florence will make sure of it," Vaughn said. "She'll do everything in her power to keep what she's surrendered so much to claim."

"And all of that will only link you to the disgrace forever if you marry me."

"It will link me to *you* forever," he said softly, and then brushed a lock of hair from her cheek.

She shut her eyes. God, he made it sound easy when she knew it wasn't. "It could destroy you."

"Look at me, please," he said. She opened her eyes again and saw how certain he appeared. How utterly beautiful and certain, like this was nothing at all. "I don't care, Evelina."

Her lips parted. "But you must—"

"No," he interrupted. "When we first commiserated over their betrayal, when we talked about the fact that Florence and Southwater intended to marry and continue on in Society, you said something to me. Do you remember what it was?"

She shook her head. "No."

"I've thought about it a great deal in the last few days. You told me that perhaps they truly loved each other and that none of this would matter to them because all they'd need was each other."

She crinkled her nose. "Well, considering what just happened, that prediction didn't age very well."

"Not for them," he agreed with a little smile. "But it ages perfectly for *us*. That is *our* story, if we let it be. I only need you, Evie. If you're right and I'm fully shunned from every club, drawing room and ballroom in this nation, I will choose our parlor and our garden and our bedroom with you every time."

Her breath was almost nonexistent at that declaration. "Vaughn—"

He cupped her cheeks. "Every bloody time, Evelina."

"Oh, you are so convincing," she murmured, and lifted her hands to cover his.

"Does that mean you're convinced?" he asked with a nervous laugh.

"You're spinning such beautiful fairy tales and I want to believe them so deeply. I want to think we could ride off into some romantic sunset and never be touched by reality again."

"Then believe it," he said. "Believe me because I do. I do, Evelina. Will you? *Will* you?"

"Will I?" she repeated, her knees shaking.

"Marry me. Will you marry me, Evelina Comerford? Be mine every day and night until the world stops spinning. Please."

It was the first time she saw a waver in his certainty. Not because he didn't want this. Every part of him shone with the power of how deeply he loved her. *Her*!

No, his uncertainty came from the fact that he wasn't sure of her answer. And why would he be? She had resisted thus far, finding all the problems that might circumvent the love they'd both declared. And yet now, as she stared up into the eyes of the man she loved, she realized he was right. What they felt would always triumph over those problems.

"Yes," she whispered, and lifted up on her tiptoes to kiss him at last. "Yes, yes, yes."

His arms came tight around her, hugging her like he never wanted to let her go. And she realized that now that she'd agreed, she would never have to let him go, either. The joy overcame, the love won and she had never been so happy in all her days.

EPILOGUE

One Month Later

They decided on a very long engagement. Vaughn was most definitely in a rush to call Evelina his countess, but he also wanted to make sure she had the wedding of her dreams. Watching her and her sisters giggle over trousseau and try to hide the plans for her gown was a delight unlike any he'd ever known.

And it wasn't as if he didn't still get to be with her. She technically still lived in Arabella's old home, but in reality they went back and forth between his estate and her house, sleeping in each other's beds and arms and planning out every detail of their future life together with even more focus than she planned the wedding.

It was impossible not to fall more and more in love with her every day and so he just let himself, reveling in every new detail he learned about her. Surrendering every secret he'd ever kept about himself.

He scribbled a few more notes in his ledger, trying to get his attention back to matters at hand so he might finish this bit of estate work before Evie returned from an afternoon of shopping with her sisters. He hadn't done more than a few lines when there was a light knock at his door.

"Come in," he called out as he put a few more numbers into the column.

When he lifted his head, he found Evelina there watching him. He drew in a sharp breath at how lovely she was. She'd had an entirely new wardrobe designed in the last few weeks. It had all been a great secret and he loved seeing her unveil each new gown. This one was a sunny yellow, finely detailed damask silk, and it suited her perfectly. What he loved most, though, was that she no longer wore gowns with the easy hooks so she could dress herself. When he'd pointed that out after he saw the first new gown, she'd said she no longer needed to escape.

God, how his chest had swelled with pride that he'd created safety for her. It was all he ever wanted.

"That is a beautiful new dress," he said. "It's good I was busy when you left because you wouldn't have made it out the door looking like such a treat to unwrap."

She laughed as she entered the study fully and closed and locked the door behind her. He had started to rise, but she waved him back and came around his desk to settle herself into his lap. She smoothed her fingers through his hair, then leaned in to kiss him.

"I'm yours to unwrap now," she said. "But I see you're busy."

"Not very," he said. "Just managing a few estate items. Moving some money around so that if you wish to do any redesign once you're countess, everything will be in place. We'll go out to the estate next month, I think. We can invite Arabella and Silas and Julia and Aunt Caroline, as well, so they can all see it. I cannot wait, Evie, you'll love it."

"I will. Because you do," she said.

There was something about the way she looked at him that brought him up short in his musings on the happy future. "What is it? Did something happen?"

It wouldn't have been the first time. They'd been public with their plans to wed and the reaction had been as mixed as they'd both expected. Some froze Evie out, froze him out. But they also retained all the friends who mattered. None of it had seemed to trouble her as long as it didn't bother him, not until this moment.

She shook her head. "Nothing like that. But when we out at the shops, I was approached by a lady. God, I don't even know her name. I'm going to have to work harder to learn them—that wasn't how I used my *Debrett's*, I admit. I think she was a marchioness, perhaps? Anyway, she very clearly wanted to be the first to let me know the news."

"The news?"

"It is as we suspected. Once they had no other means of escape, Florence and Southwater were married over the anvil in Gretna Green last week."

He smoothed a hand over her back and waited to feel something about that. "And what did you say to her?"

"That I wished them joy. Though I've heard they have little of it. In the end, they both know each other's heart and neither is of a particularly true bent. I do wonder how you feel. After all, you were her husband for a good many years."

He sighed. "I think I only pity them. They made some very ugly choices, but they must have wanted to love each other, hoped that there would be happiness for them. That neither of them is fully capable of that is truly sad."

Her smile softened her expression. "You are too good, Vaughn. No wonder I love you so."

"And as for hearts—" He touched her cheek with a fingertip. "The only one I care about is yours."

"Well, it belongs to you," she said, and rested her head on his shoulder. "For the rest of our lives." She smiled. "I also have to tell you something else."

He wrinkled his brow. "About them?"

"No. About us. I've been keeping a secret. Just a little one, and not for long, but I think it's safe to tell you now after discussing the details with my sisters today."

He searched her face, tension gripping him, but when she smiled and looked so filled with joy the worry was replaced by excitement. "And what is your secret?"

"It seems we may have to rush our wedding, my lord. Move it up by at least a few weeks because we wouldn't want anyone to have any questions about…about the baby."

He heard the words and stepped back, his backside hitting the edge of his desk as he stared at her. "Baby. Whose baby?"

She laughed. "Ours, Vaughn. I'm—I'm pregnant. I was almost entirely certain, but when I missed a second month of courses and have been feeling sick in the morning, my sisters have convinced me it isn't all in my mind."

There was a joy unlike anything he'd ever felt that rose up in him, flooding him with hope and happiness and tears that welled in his eyes as he stared at her.

"Are you—are you happy?"

He caught her hand and drew her even closer in his arms. "Happy isn't a descriptive enough adjective, Evie. Happy doesn't even begin to describe it."

She cupped his cheeks for a kiss and he held her against him, loving how her warmth filled him. She was everything to him, and now she would give him everything he'd ever hoped or dreamed for. And *that* was a very happy end to what had started as a sad tale, indeed.

EXCERPT OF THE TROUBLE WITH SEDUCTION

THE COMERFORD COURTESANS BOOK 3 (APRIL 7, 2026)

Julia Comerford had always known people whispered about her. As one of the infamous Comerford Courtesans, three sisters all making their way in the world through their connections with lovers, she'd grown accustomed to it. What she wasn't accustomed to was the fact that since her eldest sister, Arabella, and her middle sister, Evelina, had both married in the last year, that the topic of the whispers about Julia had changed.

The Last Comerford Courtesan.

Poor girl.

She must be desperate.

They even spoke, in whispers loud enough that Julia couldn't pretend not to hear, that certainly she would *never* have the luck of love that her sisters had found. And she smiled and pretended and put on the show her sisters and their good friend, fellow courtesan Simone Stanford, had taught her.

Inside though? There was no denying Julia feared the gossips might be right. The worst part was that all her life she had been only one of the sisters who had believed in love. She'd dreamed of princes and castles and the happily ever afters written about in fairytales. She fantasized about the stories of courtesans who had been swept away by besotted protectors who gave them a ring, a name, a home and children. Society be damned!

One would have thought that once she saw her sisters each live out that joyful story, she would have had even more faith that it might exist for her. But she didn't. Whatever she read in books, whatever she fantasized about from operas or romantic plays, she had never felt even a flutter of the abiding passion and adoration she saw shared between Arabella and her husband Silas or Evelina and her husband Vaughn.

No man had ever looked at her like she was everything. And she'd never ached for someone so deeply that it was as if she were being denied some kind of lifeblood by being parted from him. The truth of romance and love seemed to cut deep. And so she was becoming, just as the whispers said, *desperate*.

"I say, Julia!"

She blinked as the reality of the room and the company she shared it in came back into focus. Her current protector Viscount Laurence Castleton had brought her to a Cyprian Ball that night and the room spun around them with brightness and laughter and sensual tension.

He held out a drink for her, an expression of annoyance on his otherwise handsome face.

"My apologies, Laurence," she said, pushing away troubled thoughts and taking the offered madeira. "I somehow went miles away in my mind."

He harrumphed and took a place beside her as he sipped his drink. "I'd say so. I was forced to say your name three times before you acknowledged me."

She pursed her lips. Castleton was a good protector. He had provided a small home, a generous purse and he wasn't the worst lover she'd ever gone to bed with. He was even interesting, at least sometimes. And no one could deny how handsome he was with dark blue eyes, dark hair, broad shoulders and a jaw that could cut glass. He seemed like something from a book.

Two dimensional, her wicked mind whispered and she forced the thought away. She took his arm and leaned against him so her breast pressed against him.

"I admit I *was* distracted and that is unconscionable. Would it make you feel better to discover I was thinking of you?" A lie, of course. But women had been telling pretty lies to men to stay out of trouble for millennia. What did one more matter?

There was a slight softening to his expression. "Perhaps. Some wicked little thought, was it?"

She forced slight smile, hoped it seemed playfully shy. "Always, dearest."

He laughed and she relaxed a fraction. At least he wouldn't be angry and sulk all night. Laurence was king of the silent treatment and when it went on for too long, Julia felt like she was going mad.

She drew in a breath to talk to him about anything that would pull his attention from her distraction when someone said, "Laurence!"

There were few enough people aside from herself who called the viscount by his first name. She drew a short breath before she turned with her protector to find the one who did it most often. It was his cousin, Alexander Castleton, a tall man, equally handsome to his cousin, though Alexander had a wiry strength and darker, brown eyes. The two men always called each other by their first names since they shared the last.

"Ah, Alexander, I didn't know you'd be here." Laurence pulled away from her to shake his cousin's hand with great gusto. "You remember Miss Comerford."

As Laurence indicated her vaguely, Julia inclined her head. "Mr. Castleton. A pleasure."

Castleton's gaze flitted over her, a brief perusal that was always followed by a quick dismissal. "Miss Comerford."

She drew in a little breath. Laurence's cousin had never liked her, she didn't think. Actually, she didn't know *what* he felt about her. He watched her sometimes from across rooms or when he was speaking to his cousin. It wasn't a leer like some men did, it wasn't a disgusted dismissal as some others showed. It was simply… unreadable.

Why he might have negative feelings toward her, she wasn't certain. After all, men had mistresses, it was the way of the world. She tried very hard not to act a fool or ever embarrass those she shared time with. She had the reputation of her name, but of the three sisters she had worked hard to be the most respectable.

And yet Alexander Castleton was chilly as a winter's day when he was near her. Even now he looked away and refocused on his cousin. Laurence was still talking, it seemed.

 "Managed to pull yourself away from all those dreary family duties, did you?" Laurence asked.

There was a slight tightening to the other man's jaw, a barest hint of annoyance at the question or the circumstances, she wasn't certain.

"I never find spending time with my mother dreary," Alexander said. "But yes, grandfather is in a snit."

"I imagine I know about what," Laurence chuckled.

Julia bent her head. She knew of the parties the men discussed, of course, but there was nothing she could add to the conversation. Courtesans didn't involve themselves in family discussions. She'd been taught that lesson by her sisters and other courtesans.

"I'm sure you do." Alexander shook his head. "Laurence, must you tweak him endlessly with your…your behavior?"

Julia felt him glance at her rather than saw it and fisted her hands at her sides lightly. If Alexander Castleton disliked her, she thought the Earl of Heathfield, the grandfather of the men, might just despise her. He'd given her the absolute cut direct at an opera once. Practically spit on her. She'd been humiliated and yet

Laurence had seemed thrilled by it. He'd never been so passionate as he had been that night and never had been again.

"My behavior is none of his concern nor yours," Laurence said. "I do nothing more or less than any other man in my station."

The light sigh Castleton gave in response sounded like it was threaded with deep exhaustion. But he remained calm as he shrugged. "I suppose you don't."

There was an uncomfortable silence that stretched between the two men and Julia squeezed Laurence's inner elbow to encourage him to try a little harder. As she did so, she gave her best courtesan smile to Alexander.

"Mr. Castleton, I hear you're part of the collective invested in Mr. Grayson Danford's steam engine."

Alexander's eyes widened as if he were astonished at this topic, but he tilted his head. "Er, yes. You've heard correctly, but I don't know how."

Her smile became more genuine. "Oh, we have our ways, sir."

"The whisper network of women," Laurence muttered with a dismissive shake of his head.

Julia ignored him. "I must admit, I'm fascinated. I saw the steam engine that pulled that train to Wales when it was toured around afterward and it was so complex and fascinating. To be a part of that, even on some small level would be thrilling."

To her surprise, Alexander Castleton was now just staring at her, lips slightly parted, eyes wide like she was speaking some foreign language rather than discussing a topic he should have, in theory, had interest in.

"Yes," he said at last. "The potential for the engine and all its uses is thrilling, indeed." He turned away from her and focused his attention back to his cousin. "I wanted to say good evening to you before I departed, so I'll bid you goodnight now. And…and a good evening to you, Miss Comerford."

He didn't wait for a response, but pivoted away from the two of them without a backward glance as he moved through the busy ballroom with as much precision as a jungle cat.

Pre-Order The Trouble With Seduction at retailers everywhere now! Available for download on January 6, 2026!

Her Favorite Duke

The Broken Duke

The Silent Duke

The Duke of Nothing

The Undercover Duke

The Duke of Hearts

The Duke Who Lied

The Duke of Desire

The Last Duke

To see a complete listing of Jess Michaels' titles, please visit:

http://www.authorjessmichaels.com/books

ABOUT THE AUTHOR

USA Today Bestselling author Jess Michaels likes geeky stuff, Vanilla Coke Zero, anything coconut, cheese and her dog, Elton. She is lucky enough to be married to her favorite person in the world and lives in Oregon settled between the ocean and the mountains.

When she's not out birding or rewatching Bob's Burgers over and over and over (she's a Tina), she writes historical romances with smoking hot characters and emotional stories. She has written for numerous publishers and is now fully indie.

Jess loves to hear from fans! So please feel free to contact her at Jess@AuthorJessMichaels.com.

Jess Michaels offers a free book to members of her newsletter, so sign up on her website:
http://www.AuthorJessMichaels.com/

facebook.com/JessMichaelsBks
instagram.com/JessMichaelsBks
bookbub.com/authors/jess-michaels